DATE DUE

FEB 2 4 2005			

SNAP *HOOK*

OTHER BOOKS BY JOHN R. CORRIGAN

Cut Shot (Sleeping Bear Press, 2001)

HARDSCRABBLE BOOKS—FICTION OF NEW ENGLAND

Laurie Alberts, *Lost Daughters*
Laurie Alberts, *The Price of Land in Shelby*
Thomas Bailey Aldrich, *The Story of a Bad Boy*
Robert J. Begiebing, *The Adventures of Allegra Fullerton: Or, A Memoir of Startling and Amusing Episodes from Itinerant Life*
Robert J. Begiebing, *Rebecca Wentworth's Distraction*
Anne Bernays, *Professor Romeo*
Chris Bohjalian, *Water Witches*
Dona Brown, ed., *A Tourist's New England: Travel Fiction, 1820–1920*
Joseph Bruchac, *The Waters Between: A Novel of the Dawn Land*
Joseph A. Citro, *The Gore*
Joseph A. Citro, *Guardian Angels*
Joseph A. Citro, *Lake Monsters*
Joseph A. Citro, *Shadow Child*
Sean Connolly, *A Great Place to Die*
John R. Corrigan, *Snap Hook*
J. E. Fender, *The Frost Saga*
The Private Revolution of Geoffrey Frost: Being an Account of the Life and Times of Geoffrey Frost, Mariner, of Portsmouth, in New Hampshire, as Faithfully Translated from the Ming Tsun Chronicles, and Diligently Compared with Other Contemporary Histories
Audacity, *Privateer Out of Portsmouth: Continuing the Account of the Life and Times of Geoffrey Frost, Mariner, of Portsmouth, in New Hampshire, as Faithfully Translated from the Ming Tsun Chronicles, and Diligently Compared with Other Contemporary Histories*
Dorothy Canfield Fisher (Mark J. Madigan, ed.), *Seasoned Timber*
Dorothy Canfield Fisher, *Understood Betsy*
Joseph Freda, *Suburban Guerrillas*
Castle Freeman, Jr., *Judgment Hill*
Frank Gaspar, *Leaving Pico*
Robert Harnum, *Exile in the Kingdom*

Ernest Hebert, *The Dogs of March*
Ernest Hebert, *Live Free or Die*
Ernest Hebert, *The Old American*
Sarah Orne Jewett (Sarah Way Sherman, ed.), *The Country of the Pointed Firs and Other Stories*
Raymond Kennedy, *The Romance of Eleanor Gray*
Lisa MacFarlane, ed., *This World Is Not Conclusion: Faith in Nineteenth-Century New England Fiction*
G. F. Michelsen, *Hard Bottom*
Anne Whitney Pierce, *Rain Line*
Kit Reed, *J. Eden*
Rowland E. Robinson (David Budbill, ed.), *Danvis Tales: Selected Stories*
Roxana Robinson, *Summer Light*
Rebecca Rule, *The Best Revenge: Short Stories*
Catharine Maria Sedgwick (Maria Karafilis, ed.), *The Linwoods; or, "Sixty Years Since" in America*
R. D. Skillings, *How Many Die*
R. D. Skillings, *Where the Time Goes*
Lynn Stegner, *Pipers at the Gates of Dawn: A Triptych*
Theodore Weesner, *Novemberfest*
W. D. Wetherell, *The Wisest Man in America*
Edith Wharton (Barbara A. White, ed.), *Wharton's New England: Seven Stories and* Ethan Frome
Thomas Williams, *The Hair of Harold Roux*
Suzi Wizowaty, *The Round Barn*

SNAP HOOK

JOHN R. CORRIGAN

University Press of New England
HANOVER AND LONDON

Published by University Press of New England,
One Court Street., Lebanon, NH 03766
www.upne.com

Printed in the United States of America
5 4 3 2 1

Library of Congress Cataloging-in-Publication Data
Corrigan, J. R. (John R.)
Snap hook : a Jack Austin mystery / John R. Corrigan.
p. cm. — (Hardscrabble books)
ISBN 1–58465–332–9 (cloth : alk. paper)
1. Golfers—Fiction. I. Title. II. Series.
PS3603.O773S65 2004
813'.6—dc22 2003027193

This novel is set in the world of the PGA Tour, and while the Tour and the PGA Tour Charities Office are real, and while a number of real players are mentioned, the characters and incidents in this book are solely the product of the author's imagination. Any resemblance to actual persons or events is purely coincidental.

For my mother, Connie Corrigan

There's never any knowing which of our actions, which of our idlenesses won't have things hanging on it forever.

—E. M. Forster, *Where Angels Fear to Tread*

. . . Have you ever
had a vision? Have you ever shaken
your head to pieces and jerked back
at the image of your young son
falling through open space, not
from the stern of a ship bound
from Vera Cruz to New York but from
the roof of the building he works on?

—Philip Levine, from "On the meeting of García Lorca and Hart Crane"

ACKNOWLEDGMENTS

My father says smart people don't have all the answers. Smart people just know where to find them. In writing this novel, I certainly attempted to follow that adage. Many people gave freely and generously of their time, knowledge, and expertise. I wish to thank the following:

First and foremost, my mother, who years ago was my Joan Lerman.

Thanks to Lisa, always the first editor, for offering honest feedback and supporting me throughout this project; to my father, who stayed up one July night as I rocked a teething baby, to discuss the plot; Keith McBurnie, my father-in-law, for taking a research trip; Matt McHatten, of Presque Isle, Maine, for answering corporate banking questions; my cousin and former Secret Service agent, Jon MacDonald, who returned phone calls, e-mails, and critiqued parts of the manuscript; FBI agent Jim Osterrieder, who gave up a Monday afternoon to take my call and answer questions regarding money laundering and fraudulent transactions and later read parts of the manuscript; and Andy Pazdee and Allison McClow, of the PGA Tour Offices, for providing PGA Tour stats and various facts.

Thanks also, to my sister, Kelli, for your never-ending support.

As always, many thanks to J. P. and Laura Hayes, who answered questions and took time from their two-month (if that) off-season to read the manuscript and offer insights into life on the Tour that no one else possibly could.

These people made the book better. Any mistakes are entirely the author's.

A heartfelt thanks to John Landrigan at the UPNE for believing in the series and for the attention to detail, precision, insight, and care with which he edited. John, you're everything an author could ask for. I appreciate your efforts. And thanks also to others at UPNE—Mary Crittendon, Melinda Ferriot, Rochelle Bourgault, Barbara Briggs—and to John Lyman.

Also, to my agent and friend Giles Anderson, thanks for making it happen.

AUTHOR'S NOTE

In May, 1993, ten men died when a Lithuanian crime group attempted to extort money from a fellow crime syndicate. Shortly thereafter, FBI and Russian police received an anonymous call that led to the discovery of twenty-seven wooden crates in the basement of the Lithuanian Joint-Stock Innovation Bank. What was inside those crates—and others found in various locations—was 4.4 tons of beryllium destined for Switzerland and sale on the open market at nearly ten times the market value. One media outlet deemed the effort "capitalism, Wild East style."

SNAP *HOOK*

I first heard of the PGA Tour's plan to bring golf to the former Soviet Union from Brian Taylor.

It was 9 A.M. on a bright morning in early January and we were in his office at the PGA Tour headquarters in Ponte Vedra Beach, Florida. He was leaning back in a high-backed leather chair with his hands clasped behind his head, smiling. It was a corner office with lots of windows. What little wall space there was held photos of him with golf's royalty.

I didn't know him well, but figured he had reason to smile. He held a powerful position among the Tour's brass at a young enough age to be rumored the next commissioner. He had neatly trimmed blond hair, clear blue eyes, and the deep tan of one who spent nearly as much time outdoors as I do. His cologne smelled husky, its aroma reminding me of my home state—Maine—and wood smoke in the fall.

As director of PGA Tour Charities, Brian Taylor was the man responsible for getting and giving more than $50 million annually. He was charged with raising millions each year to help people, a job almost as nice as my own.

"I bet you smile a lot," I said.

"It's good to smile, Jack. What makes you say that?"

"I bet business is good."

He leaned forward and set his hands—palms down, fingers spread wide—on the desk blotter. "And, Mr. Austin, I'm in the best business of all: the business of giving. The Tour has raised $475 million for charity since 1968."

"Impressive."

"Which brings us to Nash Henley. Would you like coffee?"

I said I would and he went to get it.

I had come from Orlando, where I was staying with my better half, Lisa Trembley. We had spent most of the off-season in my beloved Maine, but had gone to Florida a couple weeks ago, where I could prepare for the upcoming Tour season. Lisa is head golf analyst for CBS, a former NCAA women's golf champion, and past reporter for the *Washington Post.* At one point, we'd set a date to marry. We had, however, dropped that date after a stroke-throwing scandal erupted into a potential story she had tried to blow open, and I, in a futile attempt to protect the game's reputation, had tried to hide the scandal from her—resulting in a symbolic clash of our careers. Now we remained together, but had no plans to wed.

For over a decade, I've made my living playing the PGA Tour. The Tour was officially formed in 1968. Since then, and due in large part to Tiger Woods, the Tour's popularity has exploded to the point where a player of my stature (no wins but thirty-four top-ten finishes) can afford to help others. I had come to Taylor's office to discuss donations I was making to the First Tee program and another Tour charity, and to discuss Nash Henley.

Taylor returned with two mugs that had PGA TOUR stenciled on them. The air was peppered with hazelnut. At Tour headquarters, they don't skimp. When Arnold or Jack dropped by, they probably had Juan Valdez brew it himself.

"Hope you like cream, Jack."

He was dressed for business: white button-down shirt, starched and creased; tan suspenders; red silk tie with blue diamonds; and tan slacks. A gold Rolex jangled loosely from his wrist. I felt underdressed in my white shirt with MAXFLI on the breast and khaki pants. At least I had on Brooks Brothers loafers.

"We like to help the less fortunate." He sipped some coffee. "Kids like Nash Henley."

His voice carried an elitist affectation that bothered me. In reality, that was what we were doing, since Nash needed money for college, but I wasn't just giving it to him. I was offering summer employment. To me, there was a difference. Whether Nash or Brian Taylor knew it, I didn't know and didn't care.

"Got some tax forms." He set his mug down and shuffled some papers.

Next to his leather desk blotter, a plastic cube held photos of him, a thin woman with short blond hair, whom I assumed to be his wife, and a small baby with his near-jade-colored eyes and the smattering of a blond mane. The baby wore pink.

"Have kids?"

I shook my head. "Single."

"I thought you and Lisa were married."

"Not technically."

"I used to fear commitment, too."

That wasn't it. It's like a midcareer swing change. I'd seen guys waste a decade trying to recover from tinkering with the form that had gotten them this far. I was in love, I was happy, and I was loyal. Why change anything?

"Nothing like parenthood, Jack," he was saying. "Anyway, what you're doing—this scholarship—is great. A lot of guys wouldn't let a ghetto kid carry their bag all summer. Does it worry you?"

"What are you asking? His experience level worries me, sure. Where he comes from doesn't."

"I didn't mean it like that."

I drank some coffee.

He sighed. "I think what you're doing is great. That's all I meant."

"Look, I know about the two British Open fiascoes—Jean Van de Velde's eighteenth hole and Ian Woosnam's penalty for having fifteen clubs. Some say those are caddying errors. A couple players even told me it's crazy to go with an inexperienced caddy."

I sipped some coffee, which was excellent.

"And . . . ?" he said.

"And a caddy can help, but the player is always responsible for his final score."

He shrugged and nodded.

"Besides, there's more to this."

He waited.

"Kid wrote me a letter."

"Must've been some letter."

The letter had been marred with spelling and punctuation errors. In fact, after meeting Nash—and speaking with him—I couldn't get over the contrast between his speaking abilities and his written skills. He articulated himself verbally with great ease and thoughtfulness; yet, writing seemed to pose a real challenge. Intrigued—because I wanted to learn more about Nash, but for more personal reasons, too—I had done some research, quickly learning Nash's predicament was one way dyslexia manifests itself.

"Said he'd caddied in the summer, that he had read an article about me having dyslexia."

"I see where this is heading. Are you an exempt player?"

"No. I haven't won."

"Then I respect this even more."

"I'm not a fool, Brian. This is my career. I'm not going to jeopardize it. I've interviewed him and had dinner with him twice. He knows the ropes and he's going to follow my regular caddy, Tim Silver, for two weeks. But I've got dyslexia, too. I know what the kid has gone through."

The letter, for all its mechanical problems, had been heartfelt and sincere. From it, I believed the kid was willing to work and truly needed the job. Also, Silver had decided to put his master's in journalism to work. He'd gotten the necessary material to write the book he'd always spoken of—about life on Tour—and was leaving me. I needed someone. Then Nash's letter arrived. I told him I'd give him a shot. That remained my only promise.

"His employment will probably still qualify as a charitable donation. Why not just write a check for his college and get a pro caddy?"

I'd been asked that before and once again shook my head.

"The guidance counselor at Nash's prep school told me if he went back to the city he might not make it out again."

Brian raised his eyebrows. When he lifted the cup to sip, the Rolex made a tiny tinkling sound.

"Besides, he asked for a job, not money. I respect that. He wants to work. I told him I'd give him a chance. If it works out, fine; if not, I'll let him go."

"So he needs money *and* a place to go?" He took his coffee cup in both hands, leaned back in his chair, and thought about that.

So did I. Having grown up middle-class in rural Maine, I knew I had no real concept of this kid's life, only that abstract understanding of the inner city and the violence poverty can breed that is possessed by anyone with a means to have escaped it.

After Nash's letter, I read an article in the *New York Times* about Nash's prep school, the Horizons School, in western Massachusetts, which specialized in helping learning-disabled youths. Although the tuition was over $30,000 a year, the article made me think that if such a school had existed when I'd been younger it might have saved me a lot of painful experiences. It was a cause I wished to support. I had called the school and guidance counselor Joan Lerman told me more about Nash Henley—that he'd received an Arthur Ashe Scholarship to attend, that his SATs were so low he'd not been able to receive a football scholarship to college. He would, of course, qualify for a large financial aid package, but the college he was to attend cost even more than Horizons and was asking him to contribute almost seven grand a year. She had assured me he'd do well working as my caddy. Her assurance, however, meant little. She knew nothing of the Tour. I made it clear that he would have to do well, that caddying on the PGA Tour was not a job to be taken lightly. I was to pay him $700 a week, 10 percent of my earnings, and cover travel expenses—and expected Nash Henley to earn it.

"Kid's a hell of a running back, I'm told," Taylor said.

"Job requires more than that. It requires chemistry between player and caddy. When I flew to Massachusetts to meet him and had dinner with him, kid thanked me for the opportunity four times."

Taylor shrugged, "He's a rugged kid."

I nodded. As a professional athlete, who religiously ran and lifted weights, I, too, had been immediately struck by the physical condition of Nash. He was a big kid, maybe six-one, as thick as I was, and, although I didn't like to admit it, much more muscular, probably weighing 220 with a very low body-fat percentage.

"While I've got you here," Taylor said, "I wanted to ask you about something else."

"Shoot."

"Peter and I are working with a philanthropist on a deal to build a championship golf club in the former Soviet Union. I'm organizing the venture."

He enjoyed saying that last line. His intense eyes narrowed and his voice was passionate.

I knew Brian Taylor was diligent, tireless, a driving force behind the Tour's noble reputation for philanthropic contributions—but bringing golf to Russia? This move might very well land him in the commissioner's seat. Brian had been a solid collegiate player. Yet, when his brother—two-time U.S. Open champion Pete Taylor—had headed to the Tour, Brian had turned in his clubs and earned an MBA from Columbia University. I knew Pete had a charitable foundation, although I'd never heard of this venture.

"Golf's version of ending of the Cold War?" I smiled.

He didn't seem amused—a common reaction to my jokes.

"I'd like to have a few pros go over, give some clinics, promote the game. What do you say?"

"A Tournament Players Club in Russia?"

He nodded fervently. "Not an official TPC, but maybe, eventually, the same caliber. A start-up project."

"Are we playing a tournament there?"

"Hopefully, at some point in the future. We're building the facility to promote golf, first. You don't think it's a good idea?"

"Everyone should be exposed to golf. I just didn't expect it, with the economy there and everything. Don't they already have golf?"

"There's an executive course in Moscow. No par-fives and two-hundred-dollar green fees. Peter and I want to take golf to the Russian people."

That last sentence rolled off his tongue, as if rehearsed.

"I've never been to Russia," I said. "I'm in. Who's designing the course?"

"We're not there yet. I want to get some players on board early. Make it easier to get corporate sponsors in the future."

He offered more coffee. I accepted and he went for refills.

When he returned, I was looking at the photo on the wall of Payne Stewart with the 1999 U.S. Open trophy.

"A shame," he said, "isn't it?"

There was nothing more to add. "Yeah," I said. "Terrible."

The phone on his desk buzzed. Brian hit the intercom button.

"A Dr. Silco is here to see you," a female voice said.

Brian stared at the phone, thinking. Slowly, he pushed the button. "Send him in." He turned to me with what seemed a forced smile and clapped his palms together enthusiastically. "This is the guy working with Peter and me on the Moscow project, Jack. Be great for you to meet him."

Silco emerged through the large office door and shook Brian Taylor's hand. I began to feel old. The benefactor was Brian's age, maybe even younger, with rich, black hair. Silco wore a gray suit. His pale face was terribly rutted, the remnants of what must have been severe teenaged acne. The room was filled with the scent of Silco's cologne, which overpowered the hazelnut and Taylor's fragrance.

As they shook hands, Silco glanced at me. "I can come back at a more convenient time."

His diction hinted of a European accent. I couldn't help but notice his teeth—yellowed, jagged—and one on the top right was missing. He was short and squat and his bearing made me recall the Russian farm peasants I'd seen in textbooks; he stooped and looked down often.

"Nothing is wrong, is it, Victor?" Taylor's eyes searched as he stared at Silco.

"Not"—Silco stole a quick glance at me, then looked at Brian—"on my end."

"These things take time, of course," Brian said.

Silco made no reply and there was a pause.

I could feel tension between them.

"Professor Silco," Taylor said, shifting gears, "this is Jack Austin."

No recognition whatsoever.

"It's okay," I said. "Only my mother recognizes the name."

Silco didn't get it.

"He's a Tour player, Victor. He'd like to help out with the golf course."

"Ah, I see. How wonderful."

"Jack," Taylor said, "this is Dr. Victor Silco, a professor at the University of Miami."

I shook Victor Silco's hand. "What do you teach?"

"I'm working on a research grant. Nuclear medicine."

I'd hoped he'd say literature, so I could utilize my hobby—reading drama and poetry—to wow him.

"So, you're promoting golf in Russia?" I said.

"It's good to make contributions," Silco said, pronouncing *contributions* as if the first "i" were a long "e."

"Do you have a moment, Brian?" Silco said and glanced at me again.

Silco wanted privacy and this was Brian's ticket to the largest accomplishment of his career.

"I can wait outside," I said, and did.

. . .

Twenty minutes later, Victor Silco moved quietly past me, departing to the sun-splashed parking lot.

The door to Taylor's office had been left open, so I walked in. He seemed not to notice me. Deep in concentration, he sat very still behind the desk, his chin resting on steepled fingertips. He stared blankly out the picture window, his face pale. There was a line of perspiration on his forehead.

"You all right?" I said.

He turned to me, startled.

"Sorry."

"It's fine. Good luck this season, Jack."

"Good luck with your venture," I said.

His face went rigid. As I left, I wondered why.

I would deeply regret learning the answer.

Nikoli Silcandrov had gained two hours driving west, crossing over to Mountain Standard Time and now sat in a booth with two others and the baby in an El Paso diner.

The air smelled of grease and spices from the enchiladas, which men in suits and others wearing workboots and jeans ate at the counter. Across the Rio Grande, he had seen Juárez, Mexico—a desolate place, one of poverty, of sun-beaten earth, a place where houses appeared to be built of cardboard. What he had noticed most was the sand, the fine granules the wind seemed to blow everywhere.

No one in the booth spoke. Nik lifted a heavy ceramic coffee cup and sipped. The coffee tasted old, bitter, as if the pot had sat on the burner all morning. Silently, he looked at the infant sleeping in the car seat next to him.

At least it had been done, he thought.

Now they would wait on Brian Taylor.

The diner was quiet. Downtown construction tore up the sidewalks. If Brian Taylor had just made the transaction, he thought. Hadn't he sent Victor back to Taylor's office in January? Hadn't Victor returned after that meeting and said it was set? Then again, what did Victor know about business? Through the window, the Texas sun shimmered off the pavement. He could not remember the last time he had misjudged someone, but he had never met Taylor. It was his own brother, Victor, who had misjudged the man.

. . .

It had begun nearly six months earlier.

Nik had gone unnoticed in the quiet park. The Florida sun was hot, the winter grass a shade of tan. He sat on the bench, legs crossed, leaning back casually, a folded newspaper in his lap. To a passerby, he may have been there to feed pigeons.

Nik hated pigeons. He was there to watch Victor make Brian Taylor the offer. A fortune—Nik's own fortune—weighed heavily on his mind. Behind dark glasses, his eyes never left the men.

That morning, he had gone to the gym for a two-hour workout. To take his mind off his fatigue—as he strained through three sets of ten with 285 pounds on the bench press—he thought of the puzzle. Others might call it a twenty-year journey to riches, to a life of which, as a boy in the Soviet Union, he had only dreamed.

The journey had been constructed in pieces. As he sat on the park bench, under the Florida sun, he watched those pieces come together: brother Victor and his education (his grant and subsequent specialty had been luck); the shipment of beryllium (it took money to make money, he knew); and Brian Taylor and the PGA Tour.

That day, he looked on as brother Victor and Brian Taylor acted out parts to a script Nik had written. He had made great sacrifices for Victor and had given him the responsibility of finalizing the deal. He did not want his younger brother to know he doubted him. However, as Victor and Taylor stood in the shade provided by an ancient oak, Nik stared contemplatively, noting Victor's dress and movements were businesslike, lacking the bravado he himself worked so hard to display. *Navy blue.* Nik shook his head. Victor wore a navy blue suit, as if the deal were being struck on Wall Street.

Bravado and balls, he had thought. Those were needed here. Not navy blue suits.

Taylor, a blond man, dressed in a red Polo shirt and wearing a gold bracelet, stood across from Victor, shifting back and forth. Nik could see he was uncomfortable listening to Victor. Moments later, Taylor stopped swaying. He froze and stared.

Victor nodded once.

Taylor spoke, his face animated. From the park bench, past a swing set and jungle gym, nearly thirty yards away, Nik saw

Taylor's forehead crease then saw Taylor lean closer as if he'd not heard correctly.

Victor, hands motionless at his sides, nodded once more and made a second short reply.

When Brian Taylor took a step back, Nik knew Victor had correctly relayed the threat. It was Nik's threat. Yet he knew Taylor thought the transaction was between only Taylor and Victor. That was fine with Nik. He had learned long ago it never hurt to have a fall guy—even if it's your brother.

Then Brian Taylor spoke again.

A sly grin creased Nik's mouth as he saw Taylor shake Victor's hand. The deal had been struck.

Taylor turned and walked away, smiling. A positive sign, but, Nik thought, wouldn't $2 million make most people smile?

That day, six months earlier, the puzzle had been complete. It had led Nik from the former Soviet Union to Miami, to a Florida park and the world of golf, a rich man's sport.

From dirt floors, to golf. Not just golf, but the PGA Tour.

Nik didn't laugh often. At that, however, he had chuckled, albeit softly.

. . .

Now, Nik leaned back in the booth in the El Paso diner and stretched. Outside, wind blew sand across the pavement. The sand changed patterns at random, at one point rolling like a snake before scattering into dustlike particles. He turned quickly away from the sand; it was too much like the dirt of his youth.

Nik hadn't been to the gym in two days. Later, he thought, he'd make time to do push-ups and sit-ups, maybe squat-thrusts, something. He sipped the burned decaffeinated coffee, glancing at the two people seated across from him. Each had complained upon seeing the no-smoking sign. Both looked like they needed a cigarette, Nik thought.

Each had made it to America, as Nik had. Unlike Nik, neither found what he or she had hoped. The man, Oleg, sat drinking coffee. His fingernails were long and yellowed from smoking. He was shorter than Nik. His face was gray and fleshy, his neck spilling over his shirt collar. A long scar ran under his right eye to the middle of his cheek. His brown hair hung in greasy strands along his forehead. He rarely spoke. People in his business, Nik thought, eyeing the slight bulge in Oleg's leather jacket, never talk much. In fact, Nik knew he himself didn't say much either. Maybe men of action rarely speak.

Next to the man, sat Katrina, a pale-faced woman Nik brought to care for the baby. She drank Coke. He noticed her unsteady hands as she raised the soda. She was nineteen and already had the blank stare he'd seen on streets during his youth, and again when he arrived in Miami. It was the look of so many who could not or would not *take.* Beneath her V-necked cotton shirt, Nik could see chest bones that ran like sticks beneath her flesh.

Heroin? He had no use for a junkie.

In any case, he knew Katrina would lose at life's game. She was a whore with four children. Yet she could care for the baby. Besides, when he got tense, who better to have around than a whore?

Next to Nik, the baby slept. With the baby, they were positioned on the U.S.–Mexico border. Waiting. If newspapers or television had too much on the kidnapping, they could drop down to Juárez. He'd never liked Mexico—hot and dirty—but, if need be, he could stay there. Yes, he was now Americanized, but remembered with clarity how it had been and from where he had come. He could never forget the town, which, looking back on his childhood, seemed made of dirt—dirt floors, dirt yards, dirt beneath his fingernails, on his own flesh, on his brother's. Worse still, dirt on the clothes and face of his father. He'd never forget seeing his father knocked to the dirt, nor the look of shame that enveloped his father's face, became his father's persona, for years that followed. Nor would he forget the loss that was so visible in his father's eyes when he looked at young Nikoli.

Why hadn't his father learned what was so obvious—that one had to *take* a different life?

The door to the diner opened. An olive-skinned police officer entered, carrying a newspaper. He removed his hat politely. His black shirt stretched over his stomach, the buttonholes pulling tight. He walked slowly past Nik's booth and sat along the far wall, facing them.

The scar-faced man across from Nik glanced uneasily toward the cop, then back to Nik.

Nik shook his head.

No need. Taylor would not go to the cops; he had been warned. Nik glanced at the baby. Despite his inability to judge character, even Victor could not have failed to correctly transmit the second threat.

Taylor was not the type to jeopardize his child's well being. They had only to wait, and check the account. The money would eventually appear.

The only real problem could be media attention. Taylor could not control that. Nik knew children were abducted every day in this country, but Taylor was part of the PGA Tour, which would guarantee publicity. Even so, the attention would die down. The money would eventually arrive. The question would then be: Would Nik return the baby?

The baby, Catherine, began to cry. Nik glanced at the cop, who appeared not to have heard. Gently, Nik reached down and stroked the baby's pale hand. It was the length of his index finger.

Nik glanced at the cop again. The cop was still reading the paper.

Juárez, Mexico. If push came to shove, if things got too hot, he could return to that type of third-world existence, but not forever. People said money would change him. It had. He loved his new life. Even his new name: Nik. Sometimes, mostly when he was tired, he slipped, pronouncing it the old way, emphasizing the "i," almost rolling it into a long "e" sound. That didn't happen often.

Nik looked down at Catherine. The fair baby lay in the car seat purchased at Wal-Mart when they'd gotten baby formula. Her pale blue eyes stared up at him. He took his thick hand and stroked the girl's golden hair, his touch nearly sensual.

"We are almost there, *malenkaya devochka,*" he said. "*Baby girl,* almost there."

Outside, the wind blew the sand against the window.

The shadows were long on the eighteenth green at The Country Club in Brookline, Massachusetts. It was late afternoon on a Thursday in June, the opening day of the Greater Boston Open. It was the tourney's inaugural event and held at the venue of the 1999 Ryder Cup.

Shadows, however, would have little effect on my day. I had a birdie putt—from a dangerous sidehill lie—for a seventy-four. The score was even worse than it might sound, since the championship layout at the nation's oldest country club plays to a par of seventy-one. Not the start I had hoped for, although even Tiger had not broken par this day. The wind was blowing, the greens were putting like ice, and I had a new and eager caddy, a rookie with no big-league experience whatsoever.

I bent to fix my ball mark, using a tee to push up the indentation.

Garbed in a white caddy's poncho that tied on the sides and had AUSTIN on the back, Nash stood leaning against my golf bag. He yawned as if the pace of the round bored him. Sleek, narrow sunglasses dangled from a cord around his neck. His large deltoid muscles were clearly visible as if his shoulders ran to his nape like no neck existed. Veins protruded from his coffee-colored biceps and forearms.

He was a quiet kid, yet thanked me for even the slightest deed. In fact, on the ride from the Horizons School to the Boston suburb where we now stood, he had not spoken, only sat in back with thick leather headphones on, listening to music that had been clearly audible to Lisa and me in the front seat.

I marked my ball with a dime and tossed it to him.

Startled, Nash caught it. He remembered what I wanted, wiped the Maxfli clean with a towel, and flipped it back. We were waiting for my playing partner, Pete Taylor, to putt. He was leading the tourney at four under par. I was eight strokes behind. Pete was a slow player and examined the break from all angles.

I walked to Nash. "How are you doing?"

"Fine," he said, then shrugged as if giving up. "Is this it, Jack?"

"The epitome of athletic challenge, isn't it?" I eyed the slope of the green. If I made my sidehill slider, I could make up a shot on Pete and finish at three over.

"Going for it on fourth and nine from the ten," he said, "that's the epitome of athletic challenge."

To my left, beyond the gallery Pete had drawn, I could see the vacant first tee, where the day had begun five-and-a-half hours earlier.

"You know what we tell baseball players?"

He looked like he was humoring me, but managed, "What?"

"In golf, you've got to play your foul balls."

It was a line I'd read somewhere and many people chuckled at it. Nash, however, did not.

"I mean, this it for me? Lugging your bag around all summer, washing your ball? Can I give yardage or read greens? I saw Tim Silver do that."

"Tim's got a lot of experience," I said. "I appreciate your competitiveness, how you see this as a team. You'll get more responsibility as we go."

I made several practice strokes, rolling my shoulders back and through.

"I just don't want to be your *boy* all summer."

Slowly, I straightened and we made eye contact. "I don't need a *boy,* Nash. I need a caddy."

Across the green, Pete Taylor was crouched behind his six-footer. His caddy, Stump Jones, stood behind him, gesturing at the direction in which the putt would break.

In customary fashion, caddies and players meet at the course an hour or so before the round to hit balls and putt, preparing in whatever fashion the current state of the player's game dictates.

Earlier that morning, on the driving range, Nash watched closely as Pete and Stump prepared for the round. I had believed he realized the weighty responsibility he'd been given, that even toting the bag was a big deal. After all, this was my livelihood. The assumption had been my error.

"I just want to do more. I'm bored."

I had a putt to hit. I didn't have time for this.

"I don't care if you're bored," I said. "If you're staying . . ."

His eyes darted to me, then to the ground. It wasn't much, but reminded me that he was still a kid, albeit in a man's body. He wore a tough outer shell—silent, distant, and independent—but he was still very much a kid. Given Joan Lerman's remarks about his academics, and what I knew of their effects on teenage self-esteem, he probably needed to be wanted.

But this was my career.

"If you're staying," I repeated, "and you get a chance tonight, Nash, pick Stump's brain. He's been caddying out here for thirty years."

"What's he going to tell me?"

I exhaled slowly. "For one thing, he'll probably suggest you don't piss off your player just before he putts."

His eyes went to me, then away. He wiped his open palm on his pant leg. We both were quiet as Pete attempted his six-footer to save par.

Stump's advice paid off. Pete made it, center cut, and finished the opening round with a sixty-seven.

"Nice putt, Pete," I said, moving to my marker.

"Let's see you wake that putter up," he said.

I read the putt again. I try to think only positive thoughts before any shot. For an American, positive thoughts are not difficult to come by at The Country Club. If the 1999 Ryder Cup win doesn't get you going, the club's history should. In 1913, a twenty-year-old Brookline native, Francis Ouimet, who caddied at the club, beat one of the all-time greats at this site to win the U.S. Open. Ouimet sent Harry Vardon, who would go on to win six Open Championships and one U.S. Open, back to Britain, head hanging.

But I had to be careful with this sidehill bender. Tournaments are never won on Thursday; but they can be lost on any given Thursday. If I missed, at least I'd be left with an uphill comeback attempt. If I stroked it too firmly, however, I might leave myself a longer putt than the one I now faced.

No one in the business reads greens like Stump Jones. He could probably stand on a green blindfolded and barefoot and tell you what type of grass it was, judge the speed, and decipher which way the grain went. By contrast, I was completely on my own and couldn't afford to lose more ground because, as amiable as he was, Pete was tough as rock salt with a lead.

Crouched behind the ball, I judged the left-to-right putt to break two feet. I stood and gently nestled the putter's blade behind the ball. I exhaled, letting my shoulders go slack. In my mind's eye, I envisioned the ball taking the break and finding the bottom of the cup.

When my putt slid four feet past, I wished Stump had offered a little insight.

. . .

"Do you think the situation with Nash is going to work?" Lisa said. We were in the bedroom of our hotel suite at the Courtyard by Marriott, four miles from The Country Club. She had been blow-drying her hair and paused to ask the question, the rumble of the hairdryer halting.

She stood looking at me in the wall mirror and waited.

I waited, too. She wore only a bathrobe. The longer she waited, the longer it would take her to dress. Why rush?

We were off to a dinner reception to celebrate the Taylor brothers' venture into the former Soviet Union. I was already dressed and seated on our bed, reading. Her question was one I was avoiding. Absently, I ran a hand over my five o'clock shadow.

"Well?" she said. She had the eyes of a fawn—large, oval, the color of almonds.

"Yes—yeah—I hope so."

Her hands, holding the dryer and brush, fell to her sides. "What kind of answer is that?"

"Yes," I said, definitively.

She shook her head and the rumble of the blow-dryer began again. I stood and looked out onto Beacon Street. Brookline was founded in 1705 and a walk around town put the history textbooks I'd read in high school into context. The S. S. Pierce Building was there and one could walk to Coolidge Corner. I hadn't been a history major, though, and went back to the bed and my copy of Philip Levine's *The Simple Truth.*

The book won the 1995 Pulitzer Prize for poetry. I know putts more than I know poetry; however, I agreed with the Pulitzer voters. This book was fantastic—even to a guy who was probably missing a lot of the subtleties. If I was, it didn't bother me. It was calming to read poetry after the day's frustrating seventy-five. Being dyslexic, I am a slow reader. Maybe that had been my original attraction to poetry: The shorter form allows you to receive something immediately.

A section from the poem "On the Meeting of García Lorca and Hart Crane" stopped me cold:

> . . . Have you ever
> had a vision? Have you ever shaken
> your head to pieces and jerked back
> at the image of your young son
> falling through open space . . .

I imagined a child falling through dark space and my mind ran to Nash and to Roxbury, his home. I thought of the opportunity he'd requested, the one I was trying to provide. But golf was my career. He needed to become a quality caddy.

The dryer paused again and Lisa tilted her head to one side and brushed her thick black hair. "Couldn't have been easy for him at that school."

"You see the cars with bows on them at graduation?" I said.

Lisa used some type of body lotion and the room smelled gently of strawberry.

"Nash was going to a school that costs thirty thousand dollars a year. At graduation his friends had cars waiting for them. What's Nash get? To go to work for you."

I grinned. "That's not the thrill of a lifetime?"

"Jack . . ."

"I know what you're saying."

"And we took him clothes shopping tonight." She set the dryer and brush on the vanity and went to the closet to select a dress.

The suite had a living room with a television, a sofa and loveseat combination, a bar, and a desk. When I'd been a rookie, I lived out of my car. Thus, everything since had been an improvement. Before we'd begun traveling together, I had stayed at midrange hotels, by Tour standards. Now it was suites.

The night's reception was to be held within walking distance. I was glad. The day had been long and the last thing I wanted to do was drive the courtesy car around the streets of Boston, or, worse, get on the I-95 or Route 128 racetracks and battle traffic.

"I gave Nash his first week's pay," I said. "He *did* spend his own money on the clothes."

She glanced from the closet to me. "Sure, but he needed us to tell him what to buy. This is a complex situation, Jack."

I knew that. We were quiet and I looked down at the book again. Then I shook my head. "It's better for him to be here with us. They told me as much at his school."

"What's his home life like?"

The phone rang on the nightstand. I recognized Tom Schilling's voice immediately. He was in charge of Tour security. Once he had been with the FBI and I'd always wondered how. Divorced three times, he dressed like a golfer, had perfect teeth, gelled hair, and used the galleries as a personal dating venue.

"Jack," he said, "I need a number where I can reach Perkins. Right now."

That was typical Schilling-speak. I felt like hanging up, but heard something in his voice. Perkins and I had grown up next door to one another and had roomed at UMaine. He'd been an NFL lineman, was a former homicide detective, and now owned a private investigations business in Boston. When the stroke-throwing scandal had erupted and a skinny kid named Hutch Gainer had appeared at my door begging for help, I called Perkins. Where local cops left off, he had picked up. That was how he'd met Schilling, and Perkins had about as much use for the guy as a pit bull does for a kitten. I knew he'd rather have me post his number on a neo-Nazi Website than give it to the Tour's version of Maxwell Smart.

"It's unlisted."

"This is official, Jack. I got his answering service. I need to speak to him. Just tell me where I can reach him."

"Official? This isn't the FBI."

"Jack, goddamn it, this is life-and-death. I need his home number."

I knew he'd never track him down; Perkins had just bought a house in New Hampshire, but the urgency in Shilling's voice went up another octave. "What is it?"

He paused, then: "You know Pete Taylor's kid brother?"

"Sure. Brian."

His words were very deliberate. "He's got a four-month-old daughter, named Catherine. Somebody took her."

"Kidnapped?"

"Yeah. I want to hire Perkins to help find the baby. He's as annoying as you, but I can't argue with his results."

I swallowed razor blades and thought of Brian Taylor. Then I recited Perkins's New Hampshire number.

. . .

At 7 P.M., all 156 entrants, plus members of the media and a few caddies, were in a huge conference room for the Taylor brothers' and Dr. Victor Silco's dinner reception, introducing the proposed golf venture near Moscow. Only Pete Taylor and Victor Silco were there and word of Brian's tragedy spread quickly. On the phone, Schilling had gone on to mention there had been no contact from anyone yet. It had struck me that the *best*-case scenario was someone would call with a ransom demand.

I watched Nash stare at the chandelier and look around the dining room as if memorizing his surroundings. He sat wide-eyed, his mouth slightly open. The reaction made me appreciate the life the Tour provided.

The room looked like it had been set for an award ceremony or an expensive wedding reception. The theme was royal blue—carpet, wall hangings, and wallpaper. Roughly fifty circular tables had been robed in white linen, silver flatware, china, wineglasses, and centerpieces.

Nash and I were alone at our table and I sipped ice water and worked on a dinner roll. Our date, Lisa, was near the bar speaking solemnly to Pete Taylor and his wife, Sharon, whom I'd met only one time before. She was a striking blonde in a scoop-necked white evening gown that fit tightly, hugging her hips and displaying smooth thighs. I assumed the conversation was about Brian. Lisa rarely had trouble getting players (read: men) to talk. Tonight, dressed in a short black cocktail dress, she probably could have gotten O. J. Simpson talking. Yet she was not asking questions, just listening. When a young guy I recognized from *USA Today* approached aggressively, she walked away. The kid said something.

I watched Pete shake his head and wave him off. Sharon looked bored and finished what looked like a rum and Coke.

Minutes later, Tour Commissioner Peter Barrett stood at the lectern and prepared to address the masses. Lisa and Sharon approached the table to sit with Nash and me. Nash got up and pulled Lisa's chair out for her. She smiled and thanked him.

Sharon was drunk. That was obvious. Even more obvious, however, was that she was looking at Nash the way a window-shopper eyes a display.

The room went silent as we waited for Barrett to speak. His address was brief. He introduced, first, Dr. Victor Silco—who said only that he was glad to be able to help his native land and thanked Peter and Brian Taylor. Barrett then introduced Pete—who asked us to pray for Brian, his wife, Cindy, and their daughter, Catherine—and said the Moscow venture would go on.

That was it. The reception room was the size of a basketball court and, before the addresses, had been nearly as loud as a Lakers game. Following Pete's request for prayer, however, the room fell silent for several moments. The realization that this had happened to one of our own, a member of our family, hit home.

When Pete joined our table, Sharon continued to look at Nash, the eighteen-year-old caddy for whom I was responsible. Nash sat idle, glancing at the floor, hands in his lap.

"Let's get a soda," I said.

He nodded vigorously and followed me to the crowded bar. I had no intention of discussing the birds and the bees with this kid, and Sharon's behavior obviously made him uncomfortable. So I let it pass and ordered a Heineken and a Coke for Nash. It was not a cash bar. When I reached for my wallet to leave the tip, Nash shook his head and threw down $5.

"I got it," he said. "You tipped last time."

As Lisa had said, we'd taken him clothes shopping that afternoon. Yet he did not wear any of the outfits Lisa helped him choose. Rather, he wore the one formal outfit he'd brought: a navy blue sports jacket, gray slacks, and a shirt that looked like it had traveled at the bottom of his suitcase. His current attire, I knew, had been a very conscious decision. He had bought the new clothes with the money I'd paid him. I looked at his money on the bar. He was supposed to be saving money for school. At that moment, however, the issue was larger than a tuition bill. I let him get the tip.

Stump Jones, Pete Taylor's caddy, appeared next to us and asked for another "goddamned light beer" because he was "on another of his wife's goddamned diets." His dark eyes looked red and unfocused, telling me he'd had several previous "goddamned light beers." His shaved head was the color of an old penny and his camel-hair sports coat tugged at the shoulders. The nickname was appropriate—he was built like a bulldog. He was drinking beer and swearing—probably not the adult example to which the Horizons School brass wanted me exposing Nash. On the other hand, Sharon Taylor was the alternative. Besides, Stump was the best caddy in the business. When I heard him engage Nash in conversation, I hoped, for my own sake, he could teach his craft. I listened optimistically.

"Nice playing, Jack," Stump said. "It was windy." He looked at Nash. "Got to tell you, kid, if you're going to loop out here, you better loosen up."

"What?" Nash said.

"Kid, you didn't say goddamned boo all day."

"He's just starting out," I said. "Don't take it personally, Stump. Nash is concentrating, learning the ropes."

"I wondered why you never tended the flag all day. Why didn't you ask for help?"

Nash looked at his feet and shrugged.

Stump forced his way past a few people to the end of the bar and made room for Nash and me to lean against it as well.

"I was about your age when I first come out—nineteen or twenty," he said. "I looped in Houston from the time I was a kid."

"When you first started, you ever get bored?" Nash said and drank from his Coke.

"You mean Jack, here, don't keep you entertained?"

"Hard to imagine." I took a pull from my Heineken bottle.

"It's *you* that's got to entertain *him*, my boy." Stump set the beer bottle atop the bar. His hands were thick and veined, the palms callused. There were scars like pink worms in the dark flesh.

"Entertain him?"

Stump shook his head and grinned at me. "This boy's green, Jack. Where'd you get him?"

"He's got potential," I said.

Stump took a pull on his beer. "You got it all backward, kid. What's your name?"

Nash told him.

"These guys just the horses, Nash Henley. We're the jockeys."

I thought that was an overstatement, but kept my mouth shut. Nash said nothing, clearly considering the remark.

"You think about that. Class'll continue tomorrow on the course." Stump winked at me. "And I like to talk. Come ready to talk, Nash." He walked away.

When they put the food on the table, Nash and I returned. Lisa glanced at me with a look that said she was not enjoying herself. There were two empty glasses before Sharon Taylor.

It was after 8 P.M. and I figured the kitchen staff had come within minutes of me passing out when the food arrived. It was chicken breast in a white cream sauce, steamed vegetables, and baked potato. Nash asked the waiter about the contents of the white marinade. The waiter's reply led him to scrape as much sauce off the meat as he could. He ate the chicken breast, plain. Lisa had done the same and smiled at Nash.

"Traveling with you two all summer," I said and frowned, "I'll end up weighing less than my golf bag."

"Or at least feeling really guilty," Lisa said.

Nash smiled. It was nice to see. I hoped he was settling into his new surroundings.

"It's not good to be too thin, Nash," I said.

"I think he looks great," Sharon said. She sat across from Nash, her elbows at the sides of her plate, hands folded together, her chin resting atop them. She batted her eyelashes like a shy high-school girl. It didn't work. She didn't look shy; it made her seem desperate.

Nash lowered his head and ate, ignoring her.

Pete Taylor chewed silently and stared straight ahead. I wondered if he was thinking of his brother or the drunken condition of his wife, who was absolutely gassed now. Giggling, she turned from Nash to take a tiny bite.

The comfortable surroundings I had hoped for had quickly deteriorated. It wasn't an easy meal and was a hell of a way for Nash to be introduced to life on the Tour.

I tried to loosen things up. "Watching your cholesterol?" I said to him and smiled.

"Trying to lower my body fat."

"What is it now?" Sharon asked, trying to casually dab her mouth with the cloth napkin. Except it's hard to appear casual when folding the napkin poses a real challenge.

"Seven percent." His eyes darted back to his food.

"Looks even less than that." The two *th* sounds so close together gave Sharon difficulty. Alliteration wasn't her forte.

And the pass, however slurred, had been obvious. Lisa's narrowed eyes affirmed as much. I felt the back of my neck get warm.

Sharon flagged the waiter and got a refill. Pete continued to ignore her and seemed comfortable doing it, which made me wonder if he was accustomed to this. He spoke to me about the tournament. As I listened to him, I watched Sharon carefully.

Her eyes stayed on Nash. When we finished dinner, she ordered another drink.

"Honey," Pete said, "we should head out. I want to get up early and practice."

"You're leading the damned tournament. You don't need more practice. All you ever do is practice."

"Sweetie, I'm leading because I practice."

The waiter returned with Sharon's drink and coffee for the rest of us. Sharon took half the rum and Coke in one gulp.

Pete shook his head. "That's your fifth drink, sweetie. Let's call it a night."

When she looked at him, her gaze seemed distant and her eyes were wet. Not tears; it was the alcohol.

"You think you know everything, Peter," she said and drank the remainder. Then she refocused on Nash. "You lift weights, don't you?"

Nash nodded politely and rubbed his palms with his linen napkin, removing perspiration.

"It shows," she said.

"That's enough, Sharon," Pete said. The room was very loud with conversation and the echo of clattering silverware. I was glad.

Pete stood. "We're going now."

"I'm not," Sharon said; then to Nash, "How old are you?"

"All right," I said. "You're drunk, Sharon."

"And you're in last place, Jack."

"We're not in last place," Nash said, his voice suddenly defensive.

Then Lisa was on her feet.

"Gentlemen," she said. "Shall we?"

. . .

In the elevator, Lisa was looking at Nash with what I thought was parental concern. The elevator moved slowly. The cables made a low whirring sound. The air felt thick.

Then Nash chuckled. Amid the tension, it seemed loud, a startling sound in fact.

Lisa and I looked at each other. Nash continued and Lisa began to laugh with him.

I didn't know what was going on. "What's funny?"

"Sorry," he said and shook his head.

"What?" Lisa said.

"Nothing."

"Something," I said.

"Don't be mad. But the more white people I meet, the more I think y'all crazy."

We all laughed at that.

The dirt yard of Nik's youth appeared often—occasionally in dreams (he would wake on sweat-soaked sheets), but usually his past rushed at him like an unruly river. And waters that thick do not flow only in dreams.

He could be anywhere and waves crashed down. Often the exchange of money (purchasing a ticket to see a movie, even) caused ghosts to grab his throat, squeezing until he saw his own father handing money to men who appeared each Friday night like dark shadows. On those evenings, years before, a hush fell over the house soon after supper. In winter, only the sounds of wind cutting the open fields surrounding their desolate home or snow scraping windowpanes like sandpaper was heard as the family tensely went about its nightly chores. Younger brother Victor, their mother, and their father knew the men would soon arrive and the air around the wood stove was still, breathless.

When the men did come, his father, like a defeated schoolboy, handed money to them—money they needed for groceries, to heat the water they bathed in, money to repair holes in their shoes. It was the money needed to buy their mother the medication she was so desperate for.

Each time, the money was turned over without a fight. Young Nikoli would see his father's face—the look so wounded it surpassed shame, a look that ran to a complete and total loss of dignity. It was an expression Nik vowed never to wear.

When his mother died, the expression became permanent on his father's face.

That was the life Nik had known. The economic collapse of the Soviet Union only reinforced what his father's experiences taught him: That taking what was needed, getting what you wanted, anyway you could—*that* was how life worked. Seeing his father wear that look, like a tattoo on a Russian criminal, made Nik vow to be stronger than his father, and as he began to enjoy the fruits of crime-ridden Eastern capitalism, he sought to become the *strongest.*

Which he had done, he thought, setting the suitcases on the wheat-colored living room carpet.

It was a furnished apartment, the Wayne Inn, on North Mesa, a main street running north-south the length of El Paso. The woman carried in the car seat with the sleeping baby. The man with the jagged scar followed, shut the door, set his bag down, and quickly withdrew a nine millimeter pistol. He slid a round into the chamber.

The apartment could be rented weekly, a motel converted to rental units. It wasn't the best alternative—only one exit, the front door, and they were on the third floor, thus forced to enter via cement stairs leading from the parking lot to the wraparound veranda. However, the tenants were not the types to ask questions, which had been a prerequisite.

The interior did not approach what Nik had grown accustomed to in Miami. He had lived in Miami only several months. The journey, however, had taken so long, so much energy, that living in the beach house and dining in Miami now fit him so well it was as if he'd been raised in that atmosphere. Certainly that had not been the case. In fact, he'd sent Victor to the United States many years before moving there himself. But Victor was his younger brother who, Nik thought, scanning the interior of the apartment, much like their father, would never *take*. So the expense of Victor's education—even at the delay of Nik's own journey—was a sacrifice he had been willing to make.

His plan had always been in place—not the details (the North Korean deal seemed to have fallen into his lap)—but his goals, his constant effort to rise from dirt floors had remained constant. Now, as he looked at the filthy windows, he thought back to the plan. It was nearly complete.

That knowledge alone would allow him to live this way.

The apartment's front door opened into the living room. Beyond, was the dining room, with the kitchenette. A hall led to two separate bedrooms and a bath. The ceiling was vaulted and lined with skylights, which might yield to easy surveillance, he thought.

He had said nothing when Katrina entered and called the apartment beautiful. Rather, he noticed the cigarette burn on the carpet and thought it would be nearly impossible to return to this lifestyle for good. He'd worked too hard, had overcome poverty once already. It had taken money to make money. Now it would take big money to keep big money. He was one step away, the pieces were in place and needed only to be connected. No more dirt floors. They were behind him.

Brian Taylor would keep his word. Eventually.

Nik glanced behind him at baby Catherine.

Brian Taylor *would* keep his word; the baby assured that. When it happened, Nik knew he'd never have to do something like this again. He'd live out his days enjoying the lifestyle he'd earned, the life he had taken.

He sat on the dusty sofa. He couldn't simply kill Brian Taylor. It wasn't the physical act he feared. In truth, he had left a rose-colored trail from Russia to his new existence.

Across the room, the baby began to cry.

No, killing Brain Taylor wasn't the problem. It was that Taylor still had all that money.

Friday morning at 6:30, I entered the hotel lobby and found Nash bright-eyed and waiting. He held a paper coffee cup out to me. He wore his CD player on his belt, a wire running up his side to the headphones. We had gone off late Thursday, so my Friday tee time was 8:22 A.M. I took the coffee, gladly. It smelled rich and was hot on my throat.

"You drank coffee yesterday," he said. "And you weren't in the workout room this morning, so I figured it would help you wake up."

"Thanks very much. You worked out this morning?"

He was clean-shaven and wore a pair of the khaki pants Lisa had picked out, Nike running shoes, and a Polo shirt. He nodded.

We left the lobby and headed to my courtesy car. Nash bobbed and weaved to the music as we walked.

"Every morning," he said, speaking loudly.

"The bag weighs fifty-five pounds and you're going to carry it five miles."

He shrugged. "I did chest, then three six-minute miles on the treadmill."

"Not bad," I said. "Personally, I like to run four five-minute miles, but I overslept today."

He grinned as we got in the car.

. . .

At the course, as promised, Stump Jones helped Nash. They emerged together from the clubhouse, each carrying a golf bag. Stump said something and Nash laughed.

We hit next to Pete Taylor and Stump on the range. Nash stood next to my bag as I lobbed sixty-degree wedge shots to the center of the fairway. I used the club face to gently pick balls off the pyramid in which they had been arranged, positioning each in the center of my stance. I concentrated on keeping my forearms in a tight V and watching the club face sweep through the ball, not looking up until, in my peripheral vision, I saw the divot dance in an end-over-end airborne tumble.

The range was lined with players in various stages of preround preparation—some hitting shots, some talking to equipment reps, others casually chatting, *How's the family? How are you hitting it? Trying a new ball this week.* Even chatting about hometown Major League teams.

Over the cacophony of clubs *clack*ing as they struck balls, and the chatter, I heard Stump talking to Nash.

"Nash," Stump said, "you check his back out? It gave him trouble last year."

"Huh?"

"Ask Jack how his back feels. If it's stiff, and he wants to hit driver, tee the ball for him."

"Tee it?"

Stump nodded. "You don't want him bending over any more than he has to, if his back is acting up again. Remember, both your paychecks depend on his back."

Nash glanced from Stump to me, then back to Stump.

"Also, tell him he's hitting it good," Stump said.

I had just hit a high lob shot.

"That looks pretty good, don't it?" Stump said.

"I guess."

"You don't know," Stump said. "Do you?"

Nash didn't respond. I knew he had caddied at a country club outside Boston, that it had taken him an hour to get out there, and that he'd done little more than carry the bag.

"Even better," Stump laughed. "So they all look good. Means you don't got to lie."

Nash laughed at that. So did I.

Like the previous night, I didn't say much. Stump Jones had

been a guru to several current Tour caddies. I would let Nash soak it up. We were fortunate to have been paired with them. Pete had won two major championships. We were playing together only due to the stripped-down field, he and Tiger being the only "name" players to come. The Greater Boston Open was a new event. I usually played a heavy schedule anyway—thirty or more tourneys—but had viewed this as a chance to play against a weaker field and capture my first title.

After the sixty-degree wedge, I moved to my seven-iron. I brought the club back in a wide arc, keeping my left arm stiff and dragging the clubhead back low for the first two or three feet of the take-away. As the club face rose, my front knee flexed, my back leg stiffened, and my hips cleared out. At the top, the club finished just short of parallel. I began the descent: my left hand pulled downward, my hips swiveled back to my left side, and, as my hands reached my belt, my hips were back to square. My bottom hand rolled over the top one, snapping the ball airborne. I finished with my belt buckle pointing down my target line.

I had caught it flush and held the follow-through. The seven-iron carried 165 yards, bounced once, and stopped.

As I loosened up, Stump walked Nash through my golf bag, showing him various routine items: my standard two-dozen Maxfli balls, two Magic Markers (with which I scribbled identification dots on the balls), a hundred tees, two new gloves, a towel, some Power Bars, suntan lotion, extra socks, Oakley sunglasses (which I never wore), a rain cover, a rain suit, a sweater, thin winter golf gloves, and my hand-held tape recorder (which I used to record various swing thoughts).

Although Nash didn't have yardage this week, Stump explained the yardage book as well. I was hitting my three-wood and preparing, mentally, for the round. An opening-round seventy-four was a bad score regardless of the conditions, although not many guys had gone low Thursday. Therefore, I still had a shot at making the cut. The course fit my game; it was short and could be had. The fairways were tight, but the greens, although windblown and fast, were not difficult to read. On top of everything, I was hitting the ball well. Thus, I could go mid-sixties and pull into contention.

But only if I could relocate my putting stroke.

. . .

After the warm-up, Nash and I headed back to the locker room for breakfast. A hearty buffet had been set up and Nash, the only caddy in the room, had a nutritious breakfast: loads of fresh fruit and bran flakes. I drank orange juice. I had yet to work out all the details of our routine. Caddies were not allowed in the locker room. But I had larger problems. As I poured Wheaties into a bowl, I noticed Tiger's face smiling at me from the box's cover. I shook my head. The last thing I needed was Tiger smirking at me when I was battling my putter.

Brian "Padre" Tarbuck walked by and groaned about the pin sheet, a paper players and caddies receive prior to each round illustrating where all eighteen holes are cut. Padre had once been a priest. Now he had two Tour wins, exempt status this season and next, and was one of my closest friends. He had a short beard and was the closest thing golf had to a sex symbol. The previous summer someone had found a magazine article naming him one of the most eligible bachelors. We'd had a field day with it—taping the article to his locker and making I LOVE YOU, PADRE T-shirts that three of us wore in the fitness trailer one afternoon. Someone had taken a photo of us and I'd made a Christmas card and sent one to Padre in December. He had never given me the satisfaction of mentioning the card.

This morning he was in no mood for jokes and asked if I'd seen the pin placement on the 335-yard, par-four fourth hole. I had not, but knew the fourth was drivable, if you hit a high tee ball with a lot of carry. You need carry because six bunkers surround the front of the green. The safe shot, of course, is a layup to your most comfortable wedge yardage. For me, that's 115 yards out, a distance that allows me to use a fifty-six–degree wedge, which I can hit high and spin.

"Got to hole it on four to get it even close," Padre said. "Five paces from the front edge, about eight from the bunker."

During a practice round, I had hit three tee shots and reached the green with two. On Thursday, however, that approach had not paid off. I'd made double-bogey, dropping two of my three shots on that hole. Today, I needed to make up shots and the fourth might be a place where, if I drove the green, I could do it.

I was still thinking of the fourth hole as Nash and I headed to the first tee.

. . .

Pete Taylor and Stump Jones were waiting. No one had caught Pete. He was still leading the tournament at four under. I knew, because the wind had died down and people would shoot low scores, I'd have to get my three-over-par total to at least even, if I wanted to make the cut. Which meant a sixty-eight.

Both Pete and I parred the first three holes. We stood on the fourth tee silently. I heard a distant roar and knew someone had done something—canned a long putt, or stuck an approach shot stiff. It was that kind of roar, one after a decade on the Tour, I knew was positive. It made me think I needed to get going.

Pete turned back from the sound and shook his head. "This hole is reachable and playing even shorter with a breeze at our backs, so they put the pin where no one can go for it—even from the fairway."

"A layup might not make any difference," Stump said. "God-damned tough to stick a wedge between the hole and that front bunker."

Stump wasn't talking to me, although I agreed. From 115 yards out, I can hit seven of ten within eight feet, but that's only 70 percent—not much better than the odds on me driving the hole. I decided to go for it.

"They Tiger-proofed it," Stump said.

"What's that mean?" Nash said, genuinely interested.

"'Cause Tiger can drive this green every time," Stump said, "they put the pin in a place where he can't knock it close."

"A term people came up with," I said, "after Tiger won his first Masters. The next year, Augusta had new trees on some holes."

I could tell he wasn't following me.

"People hit the ball farther now than they ever have, so things are done to take the driver out of our hands."

"People don't like Tiger?" Nash said.

"I can't speak for everyone," I said. "But I love the guy. He's made us all a lot of money."

Pete pulled a long-iron from his bag, nodding in agreement. "Five years ago, first place usually paid a hundred and twenty thousand dollars. This week it's seven hundred and forty thousand dollars."

With the lead, Pete played conservatively, hitting the iron to the center of the fairway. Needing birdies, I didn't have that option. Although it was only the fourth hole, I pulled my driver.

I brought the club back slowly and made a good pass, down and through the ball. It came to rest thirty feet from the hole. I couldn't see the lie, but hoped I'd be putting.

"If that's my player," Stump said, to Nash, "I don't let him hit that club. He blows that drive and neither of y'all make a paycheck this week."

Nash's eyes went from Stump to me.

He was saying I'd been greedy. Maybe—but I'd pulled off the shot. It hadn't been Stump's business. Nevertheless, he had long been a guru out here and he was taking Nash under his wing, so I walked quietly to Pete's ball.

Pete was 125 yards from the hole and selected what looked like a standard, fifty-six–degree wedge, made a smooth swing, and took a large divot. The shot landed in the front fringe. Both he and Stump called to the ball, ordering it to halt. It did not, as if taunting before tumbling into the bunker. Neither man could do anything except avert his eyes. This time the roar was for our group—and it wasn't positive. It was the long *Ooohh* the gallery makes when offering condolences.

Pete blasted his sand shot to within four feet and tossed the club to Stump in disgust.

Nash and I stood at my ball, observing the lie.

"That drive looks pretty good now, huh?" Nash whispered.

I liked the fact that he was competitive—and viewed us as a team—but didn't want him to offend Stump.

"Stump knows what he's doing," I said.

"Except he was wrong."

"There's a lot of different ways to play this hole. I played it several different ways during practice rounds. *For me* this was the best choice."

I had hoped I'd be putting. That wasn't an option. The ball had scooted off the fringe and nestled in the rough between a bunker and the green. I was pin-high, but thirty feet from the hole. The chip would require care—the rough was ankle-deep. I had to hit down on the ball—firmly—to get it out, but I didn't want to overcook it and watch it run by the hole.

I took my sand wedge, flexed my knees, and positioned the ball off my back foot. It was a shot I'd made thousands of times, a shot one can never feel completely confident over. The grass between the ball and club face can cause many things to happen.

"Slow down," Nash said. He was behind me, calling to the ball.

I didn't bother to yell commands. I'd known it had come out "hot" the moment I'd hit it. It would wave to me on its way past the cup.

I had an uphill five-footer for birdie.

"Pays to be a long hitter," Pete said. "You've got that for birdie and I'm just getting started."

"Maybe it ain't Tiger-proofed after all," Stump said.

Pete missed his six-foot par putt and tapped in for bogey.

I stood behind my ball and eyed the five feet of green between it and the cup. Making birdie on what was sure to be a make-or-break hole for a lot of guys would be a great way to leap from my putting slump.

I lined up the ball—it was dead straight—and stroked the putt. It stopped a foot short. I hunched over, squeezed the bridge of my nose, and swore before tapping in for par. Neither Stump nor Pete said a thing. They both knew the stroke had been horrible. *Never leave a birdie putt short.* Not when you're fighting to make the cut. Not when it's an uphill putt, for God's sake.

The whole thing made Victor Silco sick: his role in it; the threat he'd been asked to make—and had made—and now—and this was the worst part—a baby girl named Catherine was missing.

Nikoli had done it.

It had seemed so inconceivable to Victor. Even upon relaying the threat to Brian Taylor, he had not believed it would happen. It wasn't that he thought Nikoli could not do it or feared doing it. His brother was, after all, still Nikoli Silcandrov. In fact, following his father's death, Victor had always known his brother, at eighteen, had saved the family from a life of utter poverty by "going to work." Victor had long heard the talk, first of Nikoli's neighborhood "protection" service, and later of the neighborhood "sales" where the items Nikoli confiscated were offered back to neighbors at extortion prices.

Now Victor had taken part in that way of life. When he had come to this country, he had changed his surname. The effort had been symbolic, a distancing of his present self from his past. Also, it had been a conscious attempt to lessen the connection others would make between himself and his academic career, and his brother and Nikoli's way of life. Victor had told Nikoli the name change had been simply to make it easier for Americans to pronounce his name. Yet Victor had always wondered if Nikoli had accepted that explanation.

Now, sitting in his small office, its walls seeming to squeeze inward on him, the name change hadn't mattered or worked. Victor had entered Nikoli's world.

The fluorescent ceiling lights buzzed; their glow pulsated down on him. The air in the office was still and seemed thick, almost difficult to breathe. Absently, he reached across the gray metal desk to a pile of cluttered papers containing data for his research. It was for a paper that was to be the climax of the grant he had received, a grant to return to the University of Miami and the Jackson Memorial Medical Center for research on computed tomography, or CT scans, which allowed for a detailed scan and study of internal organs. He was to present his findings at the Frederik Philips Magnetic Resonance Research Center at Emory University.

Now he doubted he could bring himself to finish the project. What was the point?

How had he been drawn into Nikoli's world? The answer to that, he knew, consisted of one word: fear.

They had grown into different men. Brothers, yes, but their relationship was now based on Victor's debt. Since Nikoli had moved to Miami, he had called Victor several times to dine. They had been evenings that all followed the same script: Nikoli boisterously ordering the most expensive champagne the restaurant offered; Victor, sitting embarrassed, stealing glances at his watch. Indeed, Nikoli was his brother, but more importantly, Nikoli had sent him to the United States nearly fifteen years earlier and helped him through college and a physics degree, then had paid entirely for medical school.

Yet, now faced with what he had taken part in, Victor realized just how much he feared Nikoli. Above all, it was the fear Nikoli seemed able to project—even onto his brother—his face, his eyes, his voice all coming together to produce an unspeakable effect, a quiet irrational vibe, like a whisper in the night that told anyone, *I can kill you.*

Even his own brother. It was the reason Victor had agreed to help Nikoli. To insult the man who was his own flesh and blood, to say the way Nikoli chose to make his living—the living that had put Victor through school—and to call Nikoli's way of life inappropriate, would go beyond insult.

Victor had no desire to see how Nikoli handled supreme insults.

Victor shuffled the papers into a neat pile and stacked them on the corner of the desk. Years of school and teaching and research couldn't be for naught. Nikoli would return the girl and Brian Taylor would make the transaction, keep his share of the money, and keep his mouth shut. Then all would go on as before.

He leaned back in his chair and slowly exhaled. He remembered his first reaction to the call from Nikoli saying he had moved to Miami permanently. Victor, although he would never admit it, feared that people would discover Nikoli's past, that his own reputation in the field of nuclear medicine would be tarnished. To Victor's knowledge, Nikoli had never been arrested. Although he knew his brother's career had surely escalated beyond theft and extortion, no one questioned where the money to attend the university, where he was now conducting his research, had originated. Likewise, Victor had refused to ask Nikoli how he had given him an education for which others spent a lifetime in debt. Some questions are better unasked. Many others are better unanswered.

Things had become clear the first time Nikoli sought a favor.

Victor stood now and paced across the office, thinking, recalling events. His hands were clenched at his sides. He had been asked to attend the Korean Society of Nuclear Medicine Conference in Seoul, South Korea. The request had not come from superiors at the University of Miami. Rather, Nikoli had appeared one afternoon, plane tickets in hand, a child's grin on his face.

Even then, Nikoli's world had never entered their conversations. During the long flight, they spoke, instead, of times past, remembering how their mother managed to smile every day, how she had once chased young Nikoli with a broom for bringing chickens into the house and hiding them beneath his bed. All that was said, regarding how each man's life had differed, was how, at eighteen, Nikoli had "gone to work." Then, four years later, Victor had reached eighteen and left for America and school, courtesy of Nikoli's generosity.

What of Victor's work? What of his papers published in the *Journal of American Medicine?* All his research had been to *help* people, to *save* lives. Now a little girl named Catherine was in the hands of a man Victor himself feared.

The room was spinning. Brian Taylor only knew Victor's face

in connection with the crime. Why hadn't Nikoli called? Where had he taken the girl? What if Brian Taylor told the police? He wouldn't—he had 2 million reasons not to—but this was his daughter, Victor thought. What if he did? Victor didn't even have information to bargain with. Did Nikoli know that? Was that why he had not called? Why had he not said where he was taking her?

Victor stopped pacing and returned to his chair. Elbows on his desk, his head rested in his palms. Only days before—maybe only hours before—this paper, this data had meant more than anything. The CT research had been to save lives, not ruin them. That was the reason he had entered nuclear medicine: to take the world's greatest power and use it to better mankind. That time, that person—it all seemed far away. He wondered if any of it had been real.

Behind him, degrees hung on the white wall. He had never asked Nikoli why he had attended the conference in Korea or what he had done while Victor had been in workshops. The conference had been two years earlier. Eighteen months ago, Nikoli settled into a lifestyle neither had dreamed of while growing up in a world that, Victor thought, as he stared at his degrees, had seemed made of snow, of ice, of windswept farm fields—and of dirt.

The second round had been completed. Nash and I stood on the practice green surrounded by Maxfli balls. There were only a handful of spectators watching. I was glad. I was working on my stroke—if you could call it a putting stroke. A more accurate description for the roundhouse motion that had produced a thirty-eight–putt outing was surely a hook. Or a flat-out pull. For some reason, I was bringing the putter back outside the line, then in, across my body, yanking the ball left.

I had missed the cut.

The Tour has its own travel office in Ponte Vedra Beach, Florida, and a person, Eric Hilcoff, stationed in the locker room during tournaments to help players, wives or girlfriends, coaches, and caddies arrange travel schedules. Usually, upon missing the cut, one cleans out his locker, has Eric arrange a flight, and gets out of Dodge—and away from memories of missed putts and poorly struck shots—as quickly as possible. Lisa, however, was working; I would stay the weekend and practice.

Now it was approaching dinnertime. Nash was quiet and had been since the thirteenth hole. I knew what was bothering him. I remained silent and hit putts. I had vowed to give him a chance. I had done that. Given the day's thirteenth hole, Nash had failed, but had tried damned hard. I knew he felt responsible for my having missed the cut. Indeed, he'd been competitive to a fault, causing me to receive a two-stroke penalty. Yet, I had needed thirty-eight putts in eighteen holes, a total that was far from respectable. Even two-putting every hole—thirty-six putts—would have been enough to make the cut.

Nash didn't see it that way. I sensed he was waiting for me to fire him.

As we stood silently, I considered what had happened and Nash's options, if he were let go. I recalled Joan Lerman's remarks. Mostly I thought of my career. I was a pro golfer. Not a social worker.

All in all, Nash had done a fine job. No yardage, no reading greens, but he'd raked traps and stayed next to me. He'd done little things—complimented shots I didn't like (apparently heeding Stump's advice). He was a polite kid. Also, the rule he'd broken was vague. He'd quoted the rulebook to me afterward, confused as to how he'd broken it. His reciting the text of the rulebook illustrated that he'd read it thoroughly, as I'd asked of him.

The bottom line was: The kid was trying like hell. I considered that, as I putted.

All golfers have something they fight, some part of their game that, when things head south, is usually at the forefront. Tiger Woods occasionally fights short putts; some guys fight a double-cross, a snap hook, under pressure. My personal antagonist has always been taking the putter back outside the line and pulling it across my body, missing left. To counter this, I've developed what I called my "three-second stroke." It's not a cure *Golf Magazine* would feature, but for whatever reason, if I take the putter back slowly (and I got this by watching Loren Roberts putt), I always bring it back straight. The result of a straight take-away, of course, is a straight follow-through, producing a putt that rolls at the intended target.

Two other players were at the far end of the practice green, working in silence. Many of the fans had left. Lisa and her media colleagues were gathered in the pressroom with the leaders. Some players were at the fitness trailer. Nash and I stood on the practice green. I asked Nash to count off, as I made my stroke. He did.

"One . . . two . . . three . . ."

To a passerby, it would appear we were working on a dance routine. Then Nash interrupted my rhythm.

"Jack."

I was bent over, and looked up. The sun was an orange flame above the tree line beyond him.

"Sorry about the penalty. I'll go."

I straightened and looked at him for maybe five seconds. His eyes held a sincere sorrow, his manner shamed.

"Ian Woosnam even gave his caddy a second chance."

He knew nothing of Woosnam's caddy's blunder—fifteen clubs in the bag at the 2001 British Open. Yet it didn't matter. His face registered relief. It did not register joy nor contentment, which made me wonder what awaited him at home. It also reaffirmed my decision. He was *relieved* that he didn't have to return home.

On the thirteenth hole, he had cost me two strokes by breaking Rule 16–1(d)—"testing the surface." Before handing me the putter, he had taken the blade and scraped it across the green, then said, "Jack, this seems slower than the last green."

Most golfers of experience make similar observations. Even beginners know a burned green will run fast and wet greens to be slow. Likewise, Tour players have a more complex understanding of which type of grass they are playing on—Bermuda (in the southern states), for example, has a lot of break and grain that always grows toward the setting sun; bent grass (mostly in the northeast states) has a soft grain, meaning the grain will follow the slope, which can lead to lightening-quick greens. I had made the same observation Nash had made with my feet and eyes, but his action and comments were clearly in violation of the "scraping the surface" test, a two-stroke infringement. Thus, I had told Pete and called the penalty on myself.

The upshot of that—but more so the result of my thirty-eight putts—was that I had missed the cut by a stroke.

During the winter, I had sent Nash a copy of the USGA's *Official Rules.* Yet, golf is a complex game. I'd known such things could happen this summer, but had not thought they would. Although he had caddied, Nash had never played even one round.

I would soon change that.

I stroked a ten-footer. The ball missed left and ran three feet by. Exasperated, I handed him the putter.

"What?"

"I'm tired. You hit some."

"Putt?"

"Yeah, might as well learn the game this summer."

He held the putter like a bat—split-handed—and made a terribly wrist-ey stroke, knocking the ball past the cup, off the green. I kicked a second ball to him.

The second attempt came up short.

"Mind if I give you a tip?" I positioned his hands in an overlapping grip—left index finger resting gently atop his right pinky. Then I put my hands on his shoulders and rocked them back and forth.

"Your hands and wrists shouldn't be involved," I said. "Move the big muscles."

He nodded.

The next ball stopped two inches short of the cup.

"Maybe we'll have *you* putt next week," I said.

As we walked off the green, he smiled proudly. When he realized I was watching, he turned away, apparently still ashamed of the failure.

It had been a quick flash on the screen, but Nik knew Brian Taylor's face, the unmistakable blue eyes.

He stopped channel surfing.

The golden locks, the white teeth, those eyes like gas flames. Taylor was on television. The shock of seeing him was overtaken by despair (had he gone to the police?), then by anger.

Nik pounded the recliner's armrest. He pointed the clicker at the twenty-five–inch set and hit the volume. The central air-conditioning cycled on, fighting to keep the apartment at seventy-five while it was over one hundred outside. So he turned up the volume even louder and waved Katrina to take the crying baby to another room. The apartment smelled of smoke and cooking grease.

It was CNN's *Headline News*. Before Nik arrived in this country, he imagined all Americans looked like the ones on television. Recalling the day in the park, when he had watched the meeting, he thought Brian Taylor *did* in fact look like those TV people.

Now Taylor *was* on television, his blue eyes bloodshot, his tanned face pale.

Nik leaned forward. The television zoomed in. The wall behind Taylor was white with PGA TOUR script in blue and repeated like wallpaper. There was a microphone.

Oleg looked from the television to Nik. "Is that—?"

Nik waved him off and adjusted the volume again.

". . . I just want my little girl back," Taylor was saying. "We don't know who has her, but I will do whatever I have to in order to get her back. My wife and I are making a public plea to whomever has Catherine. Please don't hurt our baby." Taylor began to cry.

The television flashed a head shot of Catherine, the tiny four month old with a round, pink face.

Then a man in a suit was speaking about the search for the child. The screen said Captain Steven Miller, Florida State Police. An overfed American cop, Nik thought. The cop spoke of what Nik read in the newspapers: Authorities were awaiting a ransom demand, that the longer this went on, without any contact from the kidnapper, the less hope there was of a ransom demand forthcoming. At that statement, Nik heard a woman sob. Then the camera was on a blonde next to Taylor.

A reporter asked what other scenarios were being considered.

The cop said that of course there was the possibility the girl had been taken—he glanced uncomfortably at the Taylors—with no intention of being returned. Taylor groaned. Nik heard the woman's loud sobs again. The camera went back to Taylor's sobbing wife. Nik thought she *should* be Taylor's wife—blond hair, blue eyes. The cop said that scenario would not be considered fully until all others had been exhausted.

Next, the commissioner of the PGA Tour spoke, pleading for anyone with information about the missing girl to "*please* come forth."

Nik turned off the television and went to the window.

Nothing outside looked out of place. He had developed a sense of what should be there from constantly looking out—the parking lot with old cars, several low-riders, small Hispanic children playing shirtless on the pavement.

Taylor, he thought. The liar. *We don't know who has her.*

The other thing he said—*I will do whatever I have to in order to get her back*—had caught Nik's attention.

Did he mean it? Was he finally ready to make the transfer?

Perkins had arrived. The message button on my hotel phone was lit. When I called the desk, I was told to meet him in the restaurant at 7 P.M. That was when Nash and I were to meet Lisa for dinner anyway. Nash had gone for a run; Lisa was interviewing those players still employed; and I was sitting in my hotel room with the Philip Levine book, trying to get golf out of my mind for a while. The poem "Blue" began:

> Dawn. I saw just awkling.

I squinted and refocused.

Dyslexia is an affliction, not a disease, because there is no cure. After years of struggling, I know to stop when something makes no sense.

I paused and re-read:

> Dawn. I was just walking
> back across the tracks
> toward the loading docks
> when I saw a kid climb
> out of a boxcar, his blue
> jacket trailing like a skirt,
> and make for the fence.

It made me think of Nash. I picked up the phone—and called a number I had been calling after golf rounds for years—and planned a surprise for Nash to take place the following day. Given my occupation, the gifts would be easy enough to arrange.

We had not discussed it, but I was pretty sure I knew some of what he had gone through in school. When I had grown up, no one had known what dyslexia was. A teacher had once told my parents, "Face it. Some kids are just slow." I had received a scholarship to a Catholic school, where I struggled daily with academics, which led to struggles daily with self-esteem; for, to an adolescent, the two are always linked. For me, an "A" on an assignment never felt earned; rather, it felt like I had fooled someone. That's the outlook one has when one *knows* one isn't smart. It had been a terrible way to experience education. Even now, a quick self-analysis told me I read a lot because, as if by doing so, I could disprove the laughter that had thundered each time I had been called upon to read aloud. On top of the experiences I could relate to, Nash Henley had grown up in a place I could only imagine. He deserved a surprise.

. . .

Nash and I entered the hotel's dining room and found Lisa sitting across from Perkins. Nash was dressed in jacket and tie. I had on khaki pants and a golf shirt. He had been embarrassed when I'd appeared at his door dressed casually. We had taken him to dinner at the Taylor brothers' reception and that had been a dress-up affair. He hadn't said so, although I assumed he thought that was how we dressed for dinner every night. On this night, he asked if he should change. I felt bad about his embarrassment and said he looked great. I was glad to find many people in the dining room dressed in suits—business people, agents, and the like.

"Look who walked over strutting like John Wayne and joined me," Lisa said to me and motioned at Perkins.

Perkins stood and I shook his hand. He squeezed, trying to bring me to my knees.

Lisa looked at Nash. "That about defines their relationship. A twelve-year-old mentality, but both are gentlemen around me."

Nash shook Perkins's hand and stood looking up at him the way most people do—a steady gawk. Perkins's hair was more white than blond. His eyes were blue and he had a jaw you could split wood on. He was six-foot-five, 275 pounds, with the same size waist as I have, thirty-six inches. Garbed in jeans and a navy blue sports jacket over a white T-shirt, he looked imposing. Before he took off the sports jacket, I saw him pause and reach inside, beneath his armpit. Carefully, he shrugged off the jacket, folding it in half, and setting it on a chair beside him.

"Didn't want everyone staring at the gun?" I said, sitting down across from him. "You undid the shoulder holster and pulled it off with the jacket."

"You're wearing your gun?" Lisa said.

He shrugged. "I'm working."

"You got a gun?" Nash said. "What kind?"

"A nine millimeter."

Nash nodded. "So you're a cop."

"Private," Perkins said. "You know guns?"

"See a lot where I'm from. Cops have nine-millimeter semiautomatics; drug dealers have the big stuff."

"Where are you from?"

"Roxbury."

Perkins smiled. "Just there last week."

I explained that Nash was caddying for me to earn money for college and that he had played prep football.

A waiter took our drink orders: Lisa had a chardonnay; Perkins and I had Heinekens; Nash ordered a Coke.

"Nash," I said, "Perkins used to play ball."

"Where?"

"UMaine, then for the Patriots for two seasons," Perkins said.

"You played in the Show, man?"

Perkins nodded. He did not nod modestly.

Nash was poised to ask more questions, but the waiter reappeared. For dinner, Nash ordered the chef's salad, I ordered chicken Parmesan, and Lisa had fajitas. Perkins ordered a twenty-ounce steak, a baked potato, a side salad, another beer, and asked the waiter to make sure they served warm dinner rolls. Watching Perkins eat can be a form of entertainment, or it can serve as motivation (if you're not hungry and need something to spur you on), or sickening (if you're feeling under the weather and can't stand the sight of food). Personally, I just try to stay out of his way.

"You going to eat all that?" Nash said, shaking his head.

Perkins ignored him and looked at me. "I'm here on business."

"I figured as much. How're Linda and Jackie?"

"Great. Jackie points to your picture and waves. Linda taught him that. She won't let me teach him how to point and give you the finger."

"I wish she'd work on that with you."

Nash followed us back and forth and momentarily smiled.

"Your pal Tom Schilling hired me. Got a twenty-eight handicap, but I'm officially employed by the Tour. I met with Brian Taylor and his wife this morning."

"Brian's a good guy," I said. "I thought the cops were on that."

"They are." Perkins looked at Lisa. "It's easier when I can talk in front of you. The Hutch Gainer thing bothered me."

"It bothered me, too," she said. "I was on the outside looking in."

"This time," I said, "everyone is on the outside, huh?"

"Maybe," Perkins said.

"What's that mean?" Lisa said. She never stopped being a reporter, which meant she could smell a story anytime, anywhere.

Nash was drinking his soda, his eyes following the conversation.

"I don't know," Perkins said. "Taylor broke into tears every five minutes. Even his wife looked at him like she was trying to figure out what in the hell was wrong with the guy."

I recalled the day Perkins's wife, Linda, had given birth, and the look on his own face, standing behind glass, holding the tiny baby for Lisa and me to see. In his eyes, as they dipped to gaze proudly at young Jackie, then back to us, there had been an emotion I had not seen from him, a pride so intense it ran to love and maybe to something beyond, something I'd never experienced.

I shook my head. "I can't even imagine what he's going through."

"I can," he said. "I don't like it. He's not mad. He's not scared.

He just cries. Guy running the show is a Trooper named Miller. I told him I didn't like Taylor's reaction."

"What are you saying?" I said.

"I'm saying he's too emotional. Miller agrees."

"How should he act?" Lisa said. "The man's daughter was kidnapped."

"No. I'm not explaining it right."

"Not everyone reacts to things in the same way," she said.

"I know that." Perkins sighed and shook his head. "Let's talk football, Nash."

They did.

Nash said, "What position did you play?"

"I used to play line."

"How come you quit the Show?"

"The Show quit me, Nash." Perkins drank from his beer.

Nash narrowed his gaze, contemplating that.

"What do you play?" Perkins said.

"Tailback."

I said, "Nash is playing college ball next year."

It took two members of the waitstaff to bring Perkins's meal. I asked if I should sit alone so they could make room at the table. Perkins did not hesitate with his response. Nash grinned. Lisa just shook her head.

"After the Hutch Gainer thing"—Perkins cut into the slab of meat—"I got a hand-written thank-you note from Tour Commissioner Peter Barrett."

I had never received a hand-written note from our commissioner, but saw no need for Perkins to know that. I had, however, read recent newspaper articles where Barrett urged the Tour family to come together. Many players had made donations to raise a $250,000 reward for any information that led to the whereabouts of young Catherine Taylor.

"Where are you playing next season?" Perkins said to Nash.

"I got recruited by Clemson but"—his eyes fell to his salad—"I'm going to Curry College instead."

"In Milton, Mass.," Perkins said. "I've heard of it. Did you play in Boston before prep school?"

Nash nodded.

"I thought the name was familiar," Perkins said. "I read some articles about you. Jack, your caddy, here, holds the state rushing record. Broke Ricky Thompson's records."

"He plays for the Forty-niners now," Nash said.

"I know who Ricky Thompson is," I said.

"Why'd you turn down Clemson?" Perkins said.

I could see Nash squirm. He glanced at Lisa, running his tongue along his upper teeth. His eyes went to me, then over Perkins's shoulder, staring blankly into the distance. "They turned me down. SAT scores." He chuckled softly. "I'm not real smart is what it comes down to."

"That isn't what Joan Lerman tells me," I said.

"She's a nice woman," Nash said.

"You wouldn't have graduated from Horizons if you weren't smart," Lisa said.

"It's a school for people who aren't smart."

"No," I said. "It's a school for people who need help. Dyslexics usually have above-average IQs, Nash."

He shrugged. "Maybe if I can make all-American three times, or set some rushing records, an NFL team will take a chance on me."

"I didn't play big-time college ball," Perkins said. "I made it. It can be done."

. . .

That night in bed, Lisa looked solemnly at me. We had both been reading.

"I'm very disturbed by what Nash said tonight at dinner."

"Yeah," I said.

"You haven't said much since."

"I know."

"Jack, what is it?"

"More and more the kid reminds me of myself."

"You don't think you're dumb."

"I'm thirty-five years old now."

"Did you when you were Nash's age?"

"Yes."

She didn't speak, only sat staring at me. The room was lit by the lamps on each side of the bed.

"You never told me that before," she said.

"Not much to tell. It's the past."

"Nash is bringing back your past."

He was. When he doubted his own intellect, I instantly flashed to days when I would count heads in my third-grade classroom to see which paragraph I would be asked to read. I tried to memorize it in time. Every day was *the day* I would show them all how well I could read.

I knew why I read a lot now. I would never be a fast reader, but now I was a good reader. Seeing Nash's face tighten when he'd made the remark about being "not real smart" showed me what I had overcome.

It also brought back ghosts I didn't want to see.

Lisa touched my face. "I never knew anything about learning disabilities before I met you. Even now you switch letters and numbers occasionally, although it doesn't seem to bother you."

"I'm old enough to realize I've made it despite everything."

She sighed. "All I know is it's awful for anyone to feel dumb."

I didn't say anything. I kissed her, set my book on the nightstand, and clicked my light off. As I closed my eyes, I felt her hand lightly pat my chest.

. . .

Later, I was standing in front of the window, looking out at the night, when she called my name.

"What's wrong?" she said.

"Nothing."

"Come back to bed."

I did. We lay on our sides, staring through darkness at one another. I had been with other women. Indeed, I'd thought I loved others. Upon meeting Lisa, however, I quickly discovered my reasoning had been skewed. She had always possessed the ability to convey emotion without words: the touch of her hand as we strolled to dinner; a reassuring smile in the press tent; a glance as we rushed through an airport lunch.

On this night, she held my face in her hands, her fingertips and palms soft against my cheeks. I closed my eyes as if warm waters were washing over me. Then I said I loved her. She kissed me. Kisses grew to lovemaking.

When we finished, she fell asleep, her head upon my chest. I lay in the darkness, appreciating the strawberry scent of her hair, and gently stroked the smooth skin of her bare back.

I had told Nash to meet me in the hotel lobby at 6 A.M. I was little early, waiting, with a cup of coffee and my thoughts.

For most players, endorsement contracts cover travel expenses. It costs between $75,000 and $100,000 to spend a year on Tour—living in hotel rooms, eating out, and flying from event to event. For others, endorsement contracts make you an instant millionaire. My deal with Maxfli was to carry a bag with the company's name on the side, play the irons, use the ball, and wear a logoed shirt and cap for $2,000 a week, roughly $70,000 annually. That didn't leave much take-home money. However, the company had always treated me as if I were Tiger Woods, and when I'd asked for clubs for my caddy, someone left them for me. Shiny steel irons, metal woods, and a putter, in a lightweight stand-up bag awaited me at the front desk. Nash wore the same size shoes as I did, so I set a box of Footjoy "Dryjoys" next to the clubs. Now I sat on the sofa, waiting for him to appear.

As I drank coffee and scanned the complimentary newspaper, I was reminded that I'd missed the cut by the steady stream of players leaving the lobby for early morning tee times. We acknowledged each other with awkward waves and nods, the way people do when both sides are aware of one's embarrassment. Everyone misses cuts. Yet we are not salaried; every player knows you must "play to stay," that if you're not playing the weekends, you'll soon find yourself in danger of losing your card. However, earning enough money to keep one's card is only the statistical—and the most easily understood—side of my awkward exchanges with colleagues passing me in the lobby. There was another and more personal aspect to what made me uncomfortable: I thrived on pride—pride as a professional, pride as a man who firmly believes he is a world-class golfer and will forever refuse to think otherwise.

It all made staying in cities with Lisa, after missing a cut, difficult, and probably explained why I had made twenty-four of thirty cuts the previous season and thirteen of sixteen so far this year. Most players leave immediately. We call it "trunk-slamming." Staying around to watch when everyone—including your significant other—is still involved is awful. Therefore, Nash and I would spend the day in Maine playing a municipal course. It was about three hours away, but the home course of a man dear to me.

Nash approached, dressed in navy blue shorts, a polo shirt, and sunglasses dangling from his neck.

"What's this?" he said, motioning to the bag and shoes.

"It's a surprise." I set my coffee down. "We're playing a round in Maine."

"Maine? I thought you were practicing here all day."

"Nope."

"Did you say 'we'?"

"You and I—and a friend."

"I can't play golf, Jack."

"You're a good athlete. You can learn. These are for you."

He pulled the three-iron from the bag, held it up, and examined it. "It's new?"

I nodded.

"I can't—"

"Yes, you can. Consider it a graduation present."

"That's what Lisa said when she got me the shirt."

"Come on. We'll miss our tee time."

. . .

We were heading north on I-95. There was a lot of commuter traffic, but on I-95 in Massachusetts, commuter traffic goes nearly eighty. We were making good time.

"Jack, I saw clubs in the pro shop. They cost too much. I can't accept them."

I told him they were given to me by the company and that I am sent numerous pairs of shoes before each season, and upon request, any time.

"Besides, golf is a game for life. When your football days are over, you'll still be playing golf, and if you take care of them, using those same clubs."

As we drove, Nash controlled the radio. I consider myself pretty hip; however, the speakers were screaming something I couldn't and didn't wish to decipher.

"Who is this?"

"Snoop Dog."

"That's a band?"

"No, man. You've got to get with it."

"What happened to Bruce Springsteen?"

"People found out he couldn't sing."

"This guy isn't even trying—he's just talking."

"He's rapping, Jack." He chuckled and looked at the scenery roll by.

"Nash," I said, "Joan Lerman told me Curry College has a good learning disability program."

"It's not Clemson football."

I thought about saying, *life isn't only about football,* then thought of myself at eighteen. The Maine State Golf Championship had meant everything.

"You know, I use a calculator to add my score after each round."

"That a dyslexia thing?"

"Yeah. I can add, but when my paycheck depends on it, I don't want to take the risk. UMaine isn't a golf school. In the winter, I had to shovel a patch off the football field to hit wedge shots. I made it. Don't be so down on Curry."

"You had a hard time in school?"

"Yeah. Didn't have a Horizons School when I was a kid. I went to Catholic school and dealt with some old-fashioned nuns who thought I was lazy. One could swing a ruler like John Daly."

He didn't get it.

"Eventually I was tested and diagnosed as learning disabled—it was a broad definition back then."

He went back to his window. "Who are we playing with? I'm not going to do very good."

"That's the last surprise of the day. You miss your folks, Nash?"

It got his attention. He looked at me for several moments, then shook his head and said simply, "No." He turned back to the window and glanced out again.

I knew the conversation was over, and that he didn't want to discuss his home life further. When I'd taken him to dinner, upon visiting him the first time at the Horizons School, I'd mentioned his parents and home life. He'd become instantly tight-lipped.

It all made me wonder about many things, but I didn't know him well and had all summer to get the answers I sought.

. . .

The Meadows Golf Club, in Litchfield, Maine, may be only a three-hour drive from The Country Club in Brookline, Massachusetts. They are, however, separated by much more.

The first time I'd played golf, my father had taken me to a local municipal course, Cobbossee Colony, a $10 venue outside Augusta, Maine. Afterward, we'd sat in the one-room clubhouse/pro shop and ate hotdogs with onions. Images of that day never left me—the *clack* of Dad's cracked persimmon driver striking the ball; me bouncing on the front seat of the pickup as we pulled into the dirt parking lot; my tee shot fouling into pine trees. I remember running into the woods—smiling all the way—searching for my ball, and I remember sinking one putt, a five-footer, then leaping into the air. It might have been for a nine, but that didn't matter.

I have always loved those types of courses—T-shirt–and–jeans golf, where kids and first-timers are welcome.

The Meadows is that type of club. Built in 1998, $22 gets you eighteen holes. The parking lot is dirt. Par is sixty-eight. From the blue tees, the track plays to only 5,814 yards—obviously a pitch-and-putt compared to longer-is-better-approach of the Tour. The greens, however, are small and you have to maneuver the ball. More than anything, though, I like the company I always find at the Meadows. For me, playing the Meadows means going home.

Nash and I were on the first tee when a silver-haired and bearded man appeared. He wore khaki hiking shorts with a black nylon belt and a blue Maxfli golf shirt. He was a half-foot shorter than me, wore the same Maxfli hat as I had on, and carried the same Maxfli clubs and bag setup Nash had received. His eyes were slate-gray and lively, the eyes of a man with a joke to tell. My father had the thick hands of a carpenter, an easy smile, which Nash quickly responded to, and shoulders that explained why I'd learned to do push-ups each and every night. I'd learned more than a push-up routine from watching this man. I thought Nash could benefit from meeting him as well.

They shook hands. The sun was overhead. My father extended his hand to me. He was a Mainer, born and bred, and had worked there his entire life. Maine is a place where a man is judged by the character of his handshake. My father's was strong and dry.

"So he's got you playing golf?" he said to Nash. Then to me: "I watched the second round on television. You're bringing the putter back too fast."

"I figured."

"Old geezers get the honors." He bent and teed his ball.

The first hole at the Meadows is downhill, 387 yards. The fairway is tree-lined and, with a breeze at my back, I might have given the green a run from the tee. This round wasn't about driving greens, though, nor was it about score.

Nash drank Coke. I could smell the suntan lotion my fair-skinned father wore.

Dad slashed a low fade to the center of the fairway, leaving 150 yards to the hole. No warm-ups, no practice swings. He loved to compete and quickly got the game going. "Short but straight, Nash. Accuracy, accuracy, accuracy. I get two shots a hole playing with him. You get four today. Rip it, kid."

Nash addressed the ball, tentatively. I adjusted his grip, laying his right pinky over his left forefinger.

"Take a practice swing," I said.

He did. It was a long, loose, flowing swing. Bobby Jones said one's golf swing never deviates tremendously from that very first swing; you can tighten and tweak, but that original motion is more or less what you're left with. The take-away and delivery illustrated that Nash was obviously a natural athlete.

"Just keep your head down," Dad said.

Nash hit a low—but straight—shot that rolled and stopped short of Dad's ball.

I hit last and put my five-wood wedge-distance from the pin. As we moved down the fairway, my father asked about Lisa, my position on the money list, and my mental state.

"Tough missing the cut," I said. "But it's not the first time and won't be the last."

"One-twenty doesn't leave much room for error."

"I've made thirteen of sixteen cuts, but haven't finished high. I'll probably be one hundred and thirtieth after Sunday."

Nash asked what we were talking about. I explained the top 125 on the money list retain their playing privileges the following season.

"Mainers are workers," Dad said. "Everyone goes through hard times. Just work through it."

We paused at Nash's ball. He set the can down.

Dad surveyed the shot. The rough guarding the front right side of the green reminds me of a Scottish links course. The course designers left the land's natural terrain—tree roots, even rocks.

"You've got purgatory short and right, Nash," Dad said. "Left is good and long isn't that bad. At least you can chip on from behind the green."

We all paused at the sound of men cheering. No one was in sight. This was Saturday morning golf, and someone had done something memorable.

"So I should aim left and long?"

"Exactly," Dad said.

Dad knew Nash had never played before. That didn't matter. He was teaching Nash the game. It brought back my own childhood—that day at Cobbossee, that five-footer. My father had taken the game up relatively late, around his thirtieth birthday, and had loved it immediately. It allowed him to be outdoors, although so did bird hunting. Golf, however, offered something more. It was an honest game where he could judge his performance solely against himself. He had seen the game as a tool as well, I think. He'd used it to stress honesty ("Did you take a penalty stroke, Jackie? You took a preferred lie in the rough, didn't you?") and perseverance ("You can accomplish anything you set your mind to, son.").

Dad handed Nash the seven-iron and he and I watched Nash swing. This time, Nash looked up. The ball nudged forward only several yards.

"Try it again," Dad said. "Keep your head down. This is a game of trust."

"Trust?"

"You've got to trust your swing. In football you trust your offensive line, right? Here, you trust yourself."

Nash contemplated that briefly. So did I. Wonderful analogy.

Nash hit the ball again. This time he pushed it right. Like all golfers, Nash leaned to his left—as if his body language could move the ball—and exhaled deeply when it rolled into the thick grass and rocks. He sighed. I slapped his back.

Dad hit his shot. He twirled the club like Paul Azinger as he watched his ball land just short of the green.

"A chip and a putt, Nash," Dad said and motioned to me. "We'll see if Goliath can handle the heat."

He tried to stare me down.

I chuckled and they moved to the undergrowth where Nash's ball lay.

Dad began explaining the unplayable-ball rule to Nash.

"You mean rule twenty-eight?" Nash said, and rattled off a passage from the rulebook. Dad and I paused to listen.

My father smiled broadly. "Pays to have a smart caddy."

"I know," I said.

Nash looked at his feet.

I went to my ball and hit a high shot with my sixty-degree wedge. It landed and spun back about four feet, stopping eight feet to the right of the pin. Not great, but the day wasn't about golf. Across the fairway, Dad helped Nash set up to hit his fifth shot, which accounted for his unplayable-lie drop.

They spent the morning walking side by side. Dad made Nash laugh often and loudly. I thoroughly enjoyed watching them. It was Saturday morning, but the small eighteen-hole public course wasn't busy. A group of college kids riding carts, toting coolers of beer played through us, as did a pair of old-timers. No one pushed us or held us up.

During an interview with Lisa, Tiger Woods had said an ideal day was spent golfing with his father. I'd always felt that way. Golf is a game upon which father-son relationships can be built, a game that teaches lessons in humility and integrity. My father used the game to teach me many things as a boy. Yet more than that, we had *shared* the sport. Our late-afternoon rounds had been spent laughing or taunting each other, slapping each other's back or reacting in agony when one of us made a putt to win a hole. Those afternoons had also been where we had discussed greater issues, like college and sex and love.

We played only nine holes. Nash broke sixty, Dad shot forty-four, and I finished with a thirty-one. The day had not been about golf.

It seemed rounds with my father never were.

Nik sat staring at the baby. Katrina was at the opposite end of the sofa holding Catherine. Nik noticed the baby's fair skin. The baby's tiny hand—he could fit both of hers in his own—rested on Katrina's shoulder. Katrina leaned the baby forward and held a bottle to her mouth. As the baby drank, Nik saw the tiny infant look at him, blue eyes wide open, a crinkle at the corner of her mouth.

"We're lucky she took to the bottle," Katrina said.

Nik didn't know what she meant, but it wasn't important. He had checked the account. On television, Brian Taylor had said he would do *anything* to get his little girl back. Then where the hell was the money? How long did Taylor think he would sit in this shit-hole apartment?

Not for months, or even weeks.

Nik stood and went to the window. He had *earned* the right to live a different life. That life did not include a fleabag apartment in El Paso, Texas. It was in Miami. It was his, one he worked so hard to take, one he could live forever—with the money Taylor was to transfer.

So many years, he thought. He'd worked for so many years. Started off a skinny teen, stealing and selling. Then respect earned contacts and opportunities smuggling and trading cigarettes, vodka, and blue jeans. Those opportunities led to larger ones. Two years earlier, one particular opportunity brought him face-to-face with a Korean gentleman looking for someone to broker a deal, someone who could speak Russian to an outfit in Lithuania that promised to smuggle beryllium to the North Koreans for ten times the legal market value. Nik had stepped to the forefront, offering to do more than broker, to undercut the Lithuanians—by going directly to their seller, which he had done, quickly and stealthily, before fleeing to south Florida.

Beryllium, Victor told him, was a reflector of neutrons and used to build missile-guidance systems, high-performance planes, and nuclear warheads. Nik did not understand how neutrons were reflected and nearly grinned recalling the conversation. He knew the Koreans did not intend to make planes with the stuff, but did not care about their purposes. Beryllium had proven to be a grand commodity.

He went to his bedroom and closed the door, stripped to his boxers, then began doing sets of thirty push-ups, rolling onto his back, then thirty crunches.

Following Brian Taylor's transfer, he knew the money the Koreans had paid would be clean, spotless in fact, having come from the PGA Tour Charities Office. Still, to be certain, Nik would then move it once more, to Canada, into a legitimate business.

It had taken money to make money. Beryllium sold legally for $600 a kilo. To undercut the Lithuanians, Nik had been forced to purchase the crates of strangely shaped silver-colored parts for nearly $3 million. It had been money he did not have. Therefore, he had acquired a partner, someone to fund two-thirds of the venture, while he did the dangerous legwork.

The air conditioner cycled on, bringing Nik out of his trance momentarily. Then he regained his concentration on the past. Vladimir Remeikus was a white-haired man Nik had once looked up to. Remeikus had seen Russia's economic collapse as an opportunity and, Nik knew, had made several fortunes. When Nik had approached him about the Korean opportunity, Remeikus seemed eager to get involved. He had told Nik in detail how there were many research labs in the former Soviet Union still staffed with well-trained scientists who had little work and no money and how that combination—with beryllium left over from the Cold War tempting them—was a potential gold mine. However, Remeikus had not tapped it. Thus, he had given Nik $2 million in return for half of the $24 million following the sale.

Then Nik had put forth his own $1 million life's savings and met with the dealers.

After the transaction had been completed, and $24 million had been tucked safely "offshore," as they called it, under the guise of a fictitious corporation, he had fled to south Florida—with Remeikus and the Lithuanians wondering what had happened.

Then a stunning blonde from the gym mentioned Brian Taylor's plan.

Nik had learned wire transactions entering the United States for $10,000 or more are subject to a reporting requirement forcing the bank receiving the funds to declare their origins. He had heard stories of others' failed attempts to structure those wire transactions into a continuous flow of amounts less that $10,000. Moreover, he had no desire to arrange his life around constant $9,000 increments. The life he had fought so hard for, worked so hard for, was not one that hinged on *increments.* Therefore, his so-called corporation made two deposits—the first, for $6 million to the PGA Tour; then the second, for an additional $18 million, had gone to the PGA Tour's Charities Office and Brian Taylor was to chalk up those additional monies as "cost overruns." Then Taylor was to dump the $18 million into a different charity, which, for Nik, was the pot of gold at the end of the journey. From there, Nik would move the money—thoroughly cleansed—to western Canada.

He rolled slowly onto his back and began doing crunches. He knew that, for the blonde, it had been nothing more than pillow talk—"My husband," she had said, "is helping the PGA build a golf course where you're from." It was strange, he thought, how things can fall into place. Originally, *she* had even approached *him,* explaining that her husband traveled often, and asking if Nik would be interested in a drink. He recalled their first date and how she nearly passed out at the bar.

That was how it had begun, how Nik heard about the Tour's plans for golf in Moscow. Next, he had called on Victor to repay the educational debt.

Through the door, Nik heard Catherine crying. In his mind, he replayed the public details: Officially, the Tour received two matching $6 million donations, one from U.S. Open Champion

Pete Taylor, one from Dr. Victor Silco, a Russian immigrant trying to do something for his native land. The Tour would fund the rest of the project.

Nik recalled his personal plan: The Tour would keep the original $6 million, never learning of the second donation—$18 million—from which Taylor had been instructed to keep his $2 million cut, leaving $16 million. Nik would then buy into a legitimate business venture, a chain of seven Canadian restaurants that did $5 to $7 million in annual sales at each establishment.

It was flawless. The money would be laundered *before* being deposited into the Canadian restaurant chain. Once in restaurant chain's cash flow, it would be spotless, in effect, laundered twice. Nik, vice president of the chain, could receive extra-large dividend payments each year. Everything was set. Everyone was waiting on Taylor's transaction.

His torso drenched with sweat, his breath coming in short gasps, Nik continued the push-up–sit-up regimen, his mind considering not the pain his body felt, but rather the current predicament: The longer Taylor waited—even in the PGA Tour's $475-million charity operation—the riskier the entire scheme became.

What if the money had already been discovered? It was a lot of money. A chill rocked him. The pace of his push-ups quickened. Why had Taylor not made the move?

Victor. Nik knew Victor was Taylor's fall guy. To Taylor, it was Victor's money. Nik would call Victor, listen to the inflection of his voice, see if he had been contacted by police.

All the maneuvers had been made of necessity. Nik knew the IRS would not stand pat as he built a Miami beachfront estate. Questions would be asked, but he had no mortgage. He had known he would have to give up some money. Yet doing so allowed him to keep nearly two-thirds—much better than the U.S. tax rate—and relax for a while, step back from the action entirely, if he chose. There were times, however, when he thought of Remeikus and the Lithuanians, of the money they had lost, and wondered if they planned to procure revenge.

. . .

Sweat streaking his face, Nik emerged from his room. It had been only two days; however, the two-bedroom flat smelled of stale smoke. A leather coat lay in a corner, a heap of clothes on the floor next to it. Nik had claimed the queen-size bed in the largest bedroom; Katrina slept with the baby in the other bedroom and got up with her at night. Oleg slept in the living room on the couch.

Nik went to the kitchen, poured water from the faucet into a cup, and drank. Katrina never took her eyes off the baby. Her refusal to acknowledge his glistening torso bothered him.

He showered, his nine-millimeter an easy reach on the toilet seat. There had been only one knock at the door in two days. It had turned out to be a flower delivery to the wrong apartment. At least Nik now knew they were prepared: Oleg had moved quickly, reaching behind the sofa, clutching a double-barreled shotgun, taking his place behind a chair. Nik had answered the knock, his nine-millimeter held out of sight behind the door. Katrina had the baby hidden in a padded footlocker behind a trap opening Nik had cut in the closet wall. The padding dulled the crying; for, even if arrested, Nik had told them, if the baby was hidden, she could still be used. Also, if left in a footlocker inside the closet wall, she would never be found and used as evidence against them. He had seen Katrina shiver when he'd said it.

Nik felt the dynamics of the three-person group changing. He had noticed Oleg's eyes on the young whore, Katrina, more often since they arrived. It was a fact that troubled him, although the woman was not, by Nik's standards, attractive. She was thin and plain: straight sandy hair; pale, drawn-in face; and bone-skinny beneath her clothing. She was Nik's; that had been established. Yet, could he lend her for a night? Pleasing Oleg, whom he might need for protection, could prove wise.

. . .

Nik was dressing when Katrina appeared at his bedroom door.

"Nikoli," she said, "it's the baby."

He pulled a World Gym T-shirt over his head. "What is it?"

"A fever."

Nik went to the couch, where the baby lay motionless, and took the tiny child in his hands. "She's not crying."

"She's sick, Nikoli."

Katrina had dressed the baby in a pink jumper they had gotten at Wal-Mart. She had done so proudly, as if the baby were her own. It had bothered Nik at first, her possessiveness of the child. Then he had decided it was for the best. Someone had to care for the baby, and she would certainly do that.

"My name is Nik," he said. "Not Nikoli. What is wrong with her?"

"Her eyes do not look right. She is very hot. We should take her to a doctor."

"No." He shook his head firmly. "No."

He handed the child to her. It felt hot. The baby was his only means of getting the money. Now Catherine was sick. Even he could see that. Her face was red, her mouth slightly open, her eyes glazed.

"What happened?" Nik knew Katrina heard the accusation in his voice.

"What do you mean?"

Oleg was behind her now.

"You are here to care for the child," Nik said.

"I am, Nikoli. I am."

"It is sick. Is it not?"

"A cold. Just a cold."

"You said a doctor."

"No. Only a cold."

"You are certain?"

When she did not answer, he began to pace, thinking. He needed to call Victor, but compared to this, even that could wait.

"No," Nik said. "No."

He went to his room to think. He emerged one hour later and said, "You keep the baby here. Inside. Go to a pharmacist, ask what to give her. But she remains inside."

Katrina nodded vigorously.

"I must go today," Nik said. "I will call. Keep the baby inside."

"Where are you going?" Oleg asked.

"To get what I have worked for."

The Tour, in trailer after trailer, had moved to the Greater Hartford Open, rolling like a circus to another venue. The Tour has two forty-eight–foot fitness trailers for players—only—to work out in. Nash and I were in a World Gym in Cromwell, Connecticut. It was Monday morning and the place was nearly empty. The sound of distant barbells clanged. I was on my back, doing dumbbell bench presses, getting tips from my caddy.

"If you twist your wrists inward at the top," he said, "and squeeze, you get more chest definition."

Nash was on the bench next to mine and shaming me by using sixty-five–pound dumbbells, to my fifties. I told myself I was doing more reps than he, but my ego still stung. Two guys big enough to be members of the World Wrestling Entertainment were near us, grunting. Also near us were two Tour players, who apparently took lifting serious enough to need more than the fitness trailer. One was Grant Ashley, a diminutive southerner, who'd said he was trying to gain twenty yards off the tee. The other guy was a rookie I didn't know.

I was taking Nash's advice and thinking about putting as I worked. Between sets of fifteen, I hit the floor to do thirty crunches. My routine was to work one muscle group each day—chest, legs, shoulders, biceps/triceps. I did a back exercise every day, alternating between dead lifts and a twisting side stretch, for which I would stand, arms outstretched, and pull a thick rubber band away from a wall, twisting my torso to do so.

"How're you doing with the yardage book?" I moved from the floor to the bench.

"Talked to Stump a little about it," Nash said. "He said maybe we could play a practice round with them."

"Sounds good," I said. "Today?"

He pushed the sixty-five–pound weights up slowly, his eyes fixated on a spot on the ceiling. Finishing his set, he let down the weights, his arms opening into a wide arc like a reverse butterfly, and dropped them the final foot. The weights clanged on the floor. He never spoke during sets. He was focused, making sure to gain the maximum from each repetition. His dedication and work ethic were traits I admired.

He stood and waved his arms in big circles. Across the gym, in a room separated by glass, women in spandex jumped around. Some moved clumsily. I heard the steady beat of aerobic music.

"I don't know when they're teeing off," Nash said. "You want me to call Stump and check?"

I shook my head. "Get in shape for football season."

"You know"—he grinned—"you're not too bad a boss."

"Give it time. I haven't thrown a club in the pond and made you fish it out yet."

It was the first time we had really joked. It was nice and, I thought, the result of our golf outing. Nash learned a lot about me that day—who I was, where I had come from. Maine wasn't Roxbury, but he had liked Dad and seemed to trust me more.

I went back to my workout, concentrating on my breathing—exhaling as I pushed the weight up, inhaling on the way down—when Perkins suddenly leaned over me. He put his hands atop mine on the dumbbells.

And pushed down.

His grin was evil.

"Asshole," I squeezed out, struggling to push the weights up.

He chuckled lightly and took them from me. "Got to talk to you, buddy." He turned and set them down on the floor, as he might a couple of his son's picture books. I had worked out with him; fifty pounds was a warm-up.

I sat up on the bench, grabbed my towel off the floor, and wiped my face.

Perkins looked around. "That Grant Ashley?"

"And you tell me it's a sissy sport," I said. "You do follow golf."

"Can't talk here."

I raised my brows. "Serious?"

"Yeah. It can wait. I've got to make some calls, anyway. I'll meet you at the course."

"An hour," I said.

. . .

"Brian Taylor knows something about his daughter's disappearance," Perkins said. "I'm sure of it."

We had met near the clubhouse and walked to a secluded area beneath a tent where concessions would be sold. Perkins wore jeans, a navy blue sports jacket over a white T-shirt, and loafers. His white hair looked golden in the sunlight. His expression contrasted greatly with the light's affect. His mouth was set rigidly, his eyes direct, and his hands motionless at this sides. He looked as if he dreaded coming to the conclusion.

"How do you know that?"

"I mentioned some of it before—the crying jags."

"Uh-huh."

"Today, Taylor was run off the road. He's in a hospital."

"Jesus." I stepped back.

It was maybe eighty-five degrees, but the air was dense with New England's midsummer humidity. My golf shirt was sticking to my sides.

"You said 'run off the road.' Did Taylor say that?"

Perkins leaned forward and spit casually, the way tobacco chewers do. "He wouldn't say shit if he had a mouthful. Told the police captain, Miller, he can't remember. Miller said they can tell by the car. And Taylor called nine-one-one right before the crash, said someone was chasing him."

"There's a clue."

"I've known something was fishy. Now he says he can't remember what happened? He called for help. Miller played the nine-one-one tape to him. Taylor says it doesn't jog his memory."

"What about the car?"

"No skid marks until very close to the crash site, like a car chase. Someone left a dent and red paint on the driver's-side rear of Taylor's car, like he was angling him toward the shoulder. Skid marks would indicate Taylor tried to brake after losing control of the car."

We were quiet, watching venders set up beneath other tents.

"Getting ready to pounce on the yuppies, huh?" Perkins said, motioning to them.

"Just pouncing on their wallets."

I thought back to my one interaction with Brian Taylor, to his odd meeting with Dr. Victor Silco. "What's the latest on the Russian golf venture?"

"Just started on that," Perkins said. "Why?"

"I met Victor Silco in Brian's office in January. He was there to speak to Brian. The meeting must've gone all right—the venture is still a go—but it was odd."

Perkins glanced around and absently shrugged his shoulders as if to free something inside his sports jacket. Then his eyes returned to mine. "What do you mean by 'odd'?"

"I don't know. They wanted privacy—it's a big-money deal, I assume—so I sat in the lobby for a while. When Silco left, I went back in. Brian seemed upset."

"Describe 'upset,'" Perkins said.

"I don't know. Jesus, it was six months ago. He told me to have a good season. When I said the same to him, he looked upset."

"Great help," he said.

I tried to rebound. "He looked like he was thinking."

Perkins's face told me it was useless.

"I've got a phone call in to Dr. Silco," he said. "When he returns it, I'll set up a meeting. I'll ask him about your vivid description of the encounter."

. . .

I was on my way to the locker room when I saw Nash standing outside one of the fitness trailers—with Sharon Taylor. Nash had his back to me and I heard the hum of Sharon's voice, though I could not make out what was being said. When she saw me, Sharon's expression turned guilty. What bothered me was that when Nash turned around, his did too.

"You find Stump?" I said to Nash.

"Not yet," he said.

"How are you, Sharon?" I said.

She didn't answer. Instead, she looked at Nash and said, "Remember what I told you." Then she turned and walked off.

"What's that all about, Nash?"

"Nothing," he said. "I'll get the clubs and meet you at the practice green."

We were silent as I putted. There were nearly fifteen players on the green with us. I wasn't about to bring up Sharon Taylor to Nash in that company. As I hit sixty-foot lag putts, my mind rushed back and forth from Brain Taylor's suspicious car crash to my caddy's mysterious talk with Sharon Taylor.

I was his boss, not his father. Yet I was responsible for Nash—maybe not legally, but certainly ethically. I knew Sharon Taylor was bad news. What I didn't know was what she had said to him, or how to broach the subject.

Nik had made eye contact with Brian Taylor before the gray Mercedes hit the shoulder and went off the road. Of that, Nik had made certain. He had followed Taylor, while making sure no one else was, and had carefully selected a secluded section of A1A. Of course, Brian Taylor did not recognize him. They had never met.

But Nik had followed him far enough, passing twice (waving both times) for Taylor to realize what was happening—and to make the mental connection to Catherine's disappearance.

Nik had seen it in his eyes.

After the first pass, nearly touching Taylor's rear bumper, when Nik pulled even with Taylor again, he had seen the recognition in the frightened man's eyes. To be sure, on the second pass, Nik had held up a sign.

Brian Taylor knew why someone sent his car skidding across the pavement, down the embankment, and into a field of tall grass. Of that, Nik was certain.

It had made him smile as he had driven away.

Now, he sat on the bed in his Ponte Vedra Beach motel room awaiting the evening news. His newly acquired—blue—rental car was parked in the space in front of his room, as he ate a hearty dinner consisting of two skinless chicken breasts, a plain baked potato, and green beans. He had gotten the meal at a place that advertised "home-cooked take-out." After his workout—300 push-ups and sit-ups—and the events of the day, it tasted well deserved.

The first car had been easy enough to discard. He had driven to a chop shop run by a Russian immigrant, whom Nik knew respected him greatly, and had sold the red Ford Taurus SHO—with the gray paint smear near the damaged, right front bumper—for very little. The owner of the auto-repair establishment, appropriately named the Body Shop, had smiled at the $500 price.

Nik got off the bed and went to the window. The motel lot was empty. As it should be, he thought. It was a step below even the El Paso apartment.

How badly was Brian Taylor hurt? He had seen the airbag deploy in Taylor's Mercedes, and the field posed no real threat to a car of that quality. However, there was always the possibility that Taylor had landed wrong and broken his neck, or something else had gone wrong. Any accident posed those threats. With so much money at stake, Nik considered them all. Yet he had been forced to act. Catherine was ill.

He picked the phone off the nightstand and dialed the 915 El Paso area code and spoke briefly to Katrina. The baby, she said, was sleeping nearly all the time now and had not eaten.

"Nikoli," she said, "we must take her to a doctor."

"No. I will be back tomorrow."

He hung up.

Next, he dialed Victor's number. The phone was grabbed on the first ring. That was typical. Victor had always been nervous.

"How are you, partner?" Nik said.

"Where are you? What have you done?"

Nik heard fear in his brother's voice.

"Don't you mean what have *we* done?"

"Nikoli, you've got to return the girl."

"In time. How have you been?"

"How have I been? I'm part of this." Victor's breath and words came in a frantic rush.

"It is business, brother. What is wrong with business?"

"Nikoli, I helped you, as you asked. I want to be out of this now."

Nik knew what that meant: Victor was scared. However, if he fled, the golf venture was over, his money potentially gone.

"Listen to me," Nik said. "Has anyone questioned you?"

"They called today. I can't do it, Nikoli."

"Yes, you will. You will do it and you will be calm." The money depended on it.

They had said too much already. Nik hung up. If Victor's phone was tapped they had said way too much.

Victor was frightened. What if Taylor had gone to the police or the PGA Tour? No, he had not. Victor would have been questioned immediately, had that been the case. Taylor would not do that. Little Catherine guaranteed that; however, following the crash, someone had called Victor and now he was terrified.

. . .

Nik finished a protein shake after dinner, then twisted the top off a bottle of Michelob Light, and sat again on the hotel bed. He wore only boxer shorts and a World Gym T-shirt. The outfit exposed his thighs, which seemed to jet out bulkily. His shirt stretched across his chest.

Could he trust Victor to keep his mouth shut? How frightened was Victor? How long would it take Taylor to make the transfer now? Would he do it before Victor met with authorities?

Finally, the news anchor appeared on the TV screen and said matter-of-factly that earlier that day there had been a hit-and-run accident on A1A. The anchor reported a brief history of the Taylor girl's kidnapping, and said authorities were "looking into the accident further." Taylor's condition was listed as stable.

Nik leaned back against the headboard. Three days, he thought. That was how long—at most—it would take for Taylor to get out of the hospital, get home, and make the transfer.

Catherine was a small baby, young and fragile. What if she turned gravely ill? Nik considered that. Would he return her even if Taylor made the transfer? He could take the money and flee.

Only Victor could implicate him.

"What do you mean 'talking with Sharon Taylor'?" Lisa said to me.

We were having dinner in the hotel restaurant at the Marriott in Rocky Hill, Connecticut, which was only a couple miles from Cromwell where the Tournament Players Club at River Highlands is located. I was having a Heineken. I felt like having six.

The restaurant was spacious, and due to lots of plants, gave the feeling of privacy. The carpet was immaculate and slate-colored. The maitre d' was a crisp-looking guy who moved gracefully and stood with a posture that made Stone Phillips appear to slouch.

"They were standing there," I said. "I heard Sharon's voice. I don't know what she said. Ironically, we played a practice round with Pete Taylor later. Nash had arranged it, to work with Stump Jones. He couldn't even make eye contact with Pete."

"He felt guilty?"

"At the very least uncomfortable, for whatever reason."

"Is it safe to assume"—she sipped some chardonnay—"Sharon approached Nash and not the other way around?"

I didn't say anything.

"Jack . . . ?"

"I asked about it on the drive home. He was tight-lipped about what they talked about or how long they talked. I don't like that. At all."

The waiter returned and took orders: spinach salad with sliced chicken and low-fat Italian dressing on the side for Lisa; filet mignon, salad, and garlic bread for me. Nash was eating room service.

"So you think Nash is hiding something," she said the moment the waiter turned to leave.

It took me a while to respond. He was a kid, eighteen years old. She was—as obnoxious as I found her—a stunning blonde. He lacked self-esteem. On one hand, I could see how her looks and her compliments could draw him in. On the other hand, he was a bright kid, a good kid, who knew right from wrong.

"Someone I know called this a complex situation," I said.

"Complex or not, it can't get out of hand, Jack."

"I know that. I think Nash needs to hear someone tell him he's good. Sharon does that."

"She's married."

"Yes."

"And he's not stupid."

"No," I said, "he isn't. I'm saying he's coming from a background we don't know much about, except that he hung out with a lot of very wealthy kids last year."

"What did the people at Horizons tell you about his home life?"

"Not much. I asked and they said he was poor. Apparently somebody at Nash's public high school called Horizons, got the ball rolling."

"Meaning someone asked for help?"

I shrugged and drank some beer. "I don't know. I'll find out very soon, though."

The waiter brought dinner rolls and my salad. I felt guilty eating in front of Lisa, who had to wait for her salad to arrive with my main course. She was one of those people who could *forget* a meal, simply work through it. For me, they were sacred, so I didn't feel so guilty that I couldn't eat. After all, there were rolls she could munch on.

"Sorry to eat in front you."

"I've grown to know that food is a crucial part of your life."

I smiled.

"Besides," she said, "I'm not feeling that hot."

"Headache?" I followed a bite of salad with half a roll.

"No. My stomach is turning."

"Nash?"

She waived that off. "I guess."

"You're never sick. Eat something funny today?"

"Fruit for breakfast, a portabello mushroom sandwich for lunch."

"What do you expect? Probably had Brussels sprouts for snacks. That healthy stuff will do it to you every time."

"Not funny." Her face suddenly drained of color. It was like watching a shade being pulled down. She stood and covered her mouth. "Oh, my God," she said and dashed from the table.

I followed her to the ladies' room and stood outside, waiting.

She appeared minutes later, looking no better. "I have to go back to the room."

I explained the situation and the maitre d' said my meal would be sent up to our room.

"Food poisoning," I said to Lisa in the elevator.

. . .

Lisa lay on the bed as I drew a bath for her. Minutes later, as she eased into the hot water, she said, "I need to speak to Perkins. Can you get him on my cell phone? After dinner, I was going to ask him some things about Brian Taylor's accident."

"You're off duty tonight," I said.

"Jack, it's *the* story. I have an inside source and I'm going to use it."

It's hard to believe how much power someone five-foot-five and 120 pounds has when she looks like Lisa and lies before you, in a tub of steaming water, her glistening body naked. I managed a weak: "But Lisa, you're sick."

"Just find him, please."

I sighed. "He's coming here at eight, but you need rest. We'll go to the bar to talk."

"No way."

"Lisa—"

"I'll be out of this tub at quarter of eight."

"You're white as a ghost."

"I only have a couple questions, but they're the ones no one else has found answers to." She produced a sly grin.

"You're a warrior," I said.

"You'd better be if you're a woman in sports journalism."

. . .

When you travel more than thirty weeks a year, hotels become your home. When hotels become your home, you obviously want something spacious. Now that I was traveling with Lisa, we stayed in suites. Her guaranteed income more than tripled my Maxfli contract. Nevertheless, I was too proud to mooch off CBS, so we went dutch, splitting expenses.

This suite had a bedroom, a large bathroom, and a living room with a television, a sofa-loveseat combination, and a fridge. The carpets were off-white, colorful generic artwork all hotel rooms have hung on various walls, and the bathroom was tiled and spacious.

Perkins entered the way he usually did, like he was footing the bill. He plopped onto the sofa, put his feet on the coffee table, and said: "What are you doing tomorrow?"

My eyes narrowed. "Practicing. Why?"

"Got anything cold to drink?"

I had Heineken and Gatorade in the fridge; Lisa stocked Evian and Diet Coke. I knew what he wanted, but he was too easy to annoy. I went to the fridge and held up the Gatorade. He quickly shook his head. I held up the Diet Coke. He gave me the finger. I got his beer and sat down on the loveseat across the coffee table from him. He seemed to take up two-thirds of the sofa.

The door to the adjoining bedroom opened and Lisa walked out, looking pale and wearing a one of my white Maxfli golf shirts, that hung to her midthigh, and baggy gray sweatpants.

As he raised his beer, Perkins eyed the pad of paper and pen she held.

"Need to talk to you," she said to him.

"How're you feeling?" I said.

"Better. Do they have a suspect in the hit-and-run?"

Perkins had just set the beer down, but lifted it again and took a long pull. He had dealt with Journalist Lisa previously and knew that, even at six-foot-five and 275 pounds, he was a guppy being circled by a shark. He set his beer bottle on the coffee table. "Nice to see you, too. How am I doing? Nice of you to ask. I'm pretty good. And you?"

"Sorry," she said. "I'm not feeling too well and wanted to cut to the chase."

"Don't know much about the chase," Perkins said. "That's why I came here to see your knight in shining armor."

Lisa looked at me. "What do you need him for?"

"Don't sound so surprised," I said. "He's needed me since we were six years old and I beat up Willy Clark on the playground for him."

"I remember it the other way around," he said.

"Stop it, you two."

"Anyway," Perkins said, "he knows Brian Taylor. I want to see if he would like to visit Mr. Taylor in the hospital with me tomorrow. Taylor won't say boo to me, but Jack isn't being paid to look into this by the Tour. He's just a guy visiting his friend in the hospital."

"I don't follow," Lisa said.

"I was in Taylor's office in January," I said, "when Victor Silco came in and they had an odd meeting."

"Odd?" she said.

"Bingo," Perkins said to me. "Define odd."

I recounted the entire story—again.

"So he looked upset when you told him to have a good season," Lisa said.

"You're missing the point," I said. "He was so wrapped up in whatever he was thinking that my comment startled him, or something."

"Or something," Perkins said. He went to the fridge and helped himself to a second beer.

"Do you think Victor Silco ran Brian Taylor off the road?" Lisa said to Perkins.

He opened the bottle and shrugged. "I'd like to know more about this Russian golf thing. I ask for information from people in Taylor's office and I get press releases. I want to talk to him about it."

"What has he told the cops?" I said.

"Just about zip. That it'll be great and wonderful. That it'll help the people of the former Soviet Union. That Silco is a generous benefactor."

"You talk to Pete Taylor?" I said.

"His brother, the golfer?"

I nodded.

"Not yet. Why?"

"I'm just curious," I said. "He's funding part of this, too, and he's a nice guy with a lot of problems right now, I think."

Lisa said, "You can say that again."

. . .

The next morning at 8:37, I was not on the first tee, or the practice green, or in the fitness trailer; rather, I was on an airplane, seated next to Perkins, watching him devour a rubber scrambled-egg breakfast—then attack mine. At least we'd gotten to the airport early and boarded hassle-free.

As we flew through golden sun shafts into white clouds, I thought of Nash and hoped he would use his day off constructively. Lisa was to take him to lunch. Although Perkins had promised to have me back in Connecticut by 7 P.M., I wasn't holding my breath.

"What are we going to ask Brian Taylor?"

Perkins drank orange juice from a small plastic cup. "What do you mean?"

"What questions are we going to ask?"

"We're going to wing it."

The plane leveled off. Outside, clouds seemed to lumber slowly past. I thought about Brian Taylor's situation in detail. For the first time, I didn't have golf, or my rookie caddy, or anything else on my mind. By the time we landed, I had come up with one question I wanted answered.

. . .

In the hospital lobby, I stood idle as Perkins went to the information desk and asked where Brian Taylor's room was. Since the accident had been suspicious, they didn't just give us his room number. An elderly woman manning the desk called the room. When she hung up, I saw Perkins speak to her, listen, then frown, shake his head, and speak again.

He approached me, chuckling. "It seems Mr. Taylor was taking visitors but when they rang his room to let him know you were here, he suddenly decided he was no longer up to it. I think that speaks to your personality, Jack."

"Of course. Also tells us he doesn't want to see anyone from the Tour. He figures they might have questions."

"No," Perkins said. "It's just your personality."

"Yeah, I should be used to it by now. What are his injuries?"

Perkins shook his head, indicating he did not know.

"So what now?" I eyed my watch. It was nearly noon. I was hungry and missing valuable practice time.

"We wait."

"Ah. So this is detective work?"

"Tough, isn't it?"

We sat in the hospital lobby. Light filtered into the room through the window-lined walls. Sunlight didn't bolster my outlook. The furniture consisted of two sizes of stiff, wooden seats—adult and toddler. After a while, the sounds became virtually nondescript—the low mumble of people speaking in hushed tones; the click-clack of shoes on tile floor; and the constant incessant electric hum of the automatic front doors—a low, nearly scraping sound to open, followed by a quicker, whirring sound shut. Scratch-whir. Scratch-whir. An old and out-of-shape security guy sat near the doors, reading the paper. Moments later, the paper was in his lap. He was sleeping.

"When you retire," I said to Perkins, "you can come down here and replace that guy."

"He's a former golfer. The sport lends itself to napping."

A short while later, as I sat reading the newspaper for the fourth time, I heard Perkins mumble something then stand up.

He moved quickly and called "Miller" as he went.

A guy paused just inside the electric door. He was beefy, a full half-foot shorter than Perkins, and wore khaki slacks and a crisp white shirt. His tie was pulled up tight. He didn't carry a briefcase, as if he were either on his lunch hour or returning from it.

They spoke briefly, then Perkins waved me to follow.

I caught up and we walked to the elevator, where I was introduced.

"Golfer?" Miller said. "What are you doing here?"

"He knows Taylor," Perkins said.

"Friend of yours?" Miller said to me. He had blond hair and big, dark eyes. He looked like a country boy, a small-town football player, who maybe had joined the service after high school, then the troopers after the service. He had a soft, good-natured face with smile wrinkles at the corners of his eyes.

"An acquaintance," I said.

"He says he doesn't remember anything about the accident. In fact, a couple of kids were in the woods playing and saw it." Miller looked at Perkins. "Gave a real good description of what happened. It all checked out with our crime-scene techs, too."

Perkins smiled.

"Hell," Miller said, "they were better witnesses than most grown-ups I have to deal with."

Perkins snorted. I didn't have to deal with grown-up witnesses or child ones, so I kept my mouth shut and smiled.

. . .

On the hospital's eighth floor, Miller led us into a room that apparently had been the TV lounge. Now it was his office, or he believed it was. It had a small sofa, four chairs, and two end tables. There were two *Clifford the Big Red Dog* books on the floor. Miller's briefcase was in one corner. He opened it and spread papers on to the chairs. Then he closed the door for privacy.

"What do you know about the Russian golf thing?" Miller said to me.

I shrugged. "Brian told me they wanted to 'take golf to the Russian people.' Said a UMiami professor, who I met, named Silco, was a benefactor. That the Tour and Pete Taylor were also involved financially."

Miller nodded like he knew all that. "That's it?"

"That's it," I said.

"All right. As I said before"—he turned to Perkins—"I don't like working with PIs."

Perkins grinned as if he'd heard it a million times.

"But," Miller said, "it's better than the FBI."

"Of course," Perkins said. "That way if I help you solve it—or solve it myself—you can take the credit and get a promotion, maybe even go to work *for the FBI.* If you're working directly with them, you can't take the credit."

Miller didn't like that and stood glaring.

"Apparently," Perkins said, "they haven't gotten involved yet, because, if they were, they'd swat you out the way like a mosquito—"

"Shut the hell up," Miller said. He didn't look country now. Now he looked like he could hold his own. "So you get the point?" he said. "Anyway, I've checked you out. Liked what I heard."

"Thanks for your vote of confidence," Perkins said. "Screw it. I'm alone ninety-nine percent of the time. I'll take any ally I can get."

Miller extended his hand. Perkins shook it. I stood there watching and thinking I'd just witnessed the most bizarre testosterone-driven handshake agreement in the history of mankind. As the two of them considered their partnership and stood looking at each other, the room was quiet. It smelled faintly of sweat and the air was thick with tension. It was not the time for a doughnut joke, so I said nothing.

"Anyway," Perkins said, "we all know Taylor won't talk, but what about his brother or his wife?"

Miller shook his head, a vague *no* gesture.

"They won't either?" Perkins said. "Or you haven't spoken to them yet?"

"Haven't spoken to the brother. Always golfing. Two days ago, I called his attorney and told him we'll drag Peter Taylor off the course in front of millions of TV viewers if we have to. He called yesterday and we've set up a meeting. The wife, Cindy, is very upset, as you can imagine."

"Take Jack to Taylor's room," Perkins said. "I'll wait in the hall for a while, listening to Taylor's answers."

"I'll come back here," Miller said. "He knows I think he's full of shit. You're better off on your own."

"Aren't I always?" Perkins said.

Miller grinned. "An honest-to-God gumshoe," he said and shook his head.

. . .

Outside Brian's room, Perkins gave me several topics to hit. All were obvious.

"Relax," he said. "Feel your way through it."

"That's all you have to say?"

"Yeah. It takes a long time to get good at these things. Just get him to talk on those topics—if you can."

Brian Taylor's room was standard issue—metal bed with guard rails; television hanging in one corner near the ceiling; gleaming linoleum tile floor; dresser; closet; and a private bathroom with one of those thick, heavy bathroom doors that takes two healthy people to pull open. The blinds were up and sun shone onto Taylor's bed.

Brian Taylor did not look ill or badly injured. In fact, when I entered, he was discussing work with a young Hispanic guy who had longish raven-colored hair, eyes like coal, and a small jagged scar on one cheekbone near the eye socket.

"Are you sure you understand the Arnold Palmer Hospital funding?" Taylor said.

The kid wore a red-and-white striped golf shirt with the PGA emblem of a golfer holding his follow-through. He smiled at Brian. "I'm a CPA, Mr. Taylor. I can handle it. You relax and get better."

When Brian recognized me, he looked anything but relaxed. He still had the tan and his hair was evenly combed, parted neatly to the left. His color was good. I extended my hand. He shook it like one who gives thousands of handshakes annually in hopes of receiving donations. It was firm and strong.

And damp.

"Jack," he said, "what are you doing here?"

"I heard about the accident. What happened?"

"I don't know." He sat staring at me, his eyes narrowed, his jaw locked firmly.

I looked at the television. A muted NASCAR race was underway on ESPN Classic. The Hispanic kid stood silently.

"I had to be in Florida anyway," I said. "Thought I'd stop by."

"Why were you in Florida?"

"Business," I said. The interrogation had turned around. Perkins was right: These things take time, and Brian Taylor was in the defensive mode, trusting no one.

"What kind of business?"

"Speaking of that," I said, "they got a designer for the Russian golf course yet?"

"No. Why are you here?"

"I heard about what happened. All the guys are concerned."

I stood next to the bed. My hands hung awkwardly at my sides. I thrust them in my pant pockets. Hospitals had always made me uncomfortable to begin with. Being in one to interrogate someone made it worse.

"No reason for concern. I'm fine." He turned to the young guy. "Emilio, go ahead then. Call me if you need anything."

The kid left. Brian and I were silent for a long time. Then Perkins, flashing a couple hundred teeth, entered and went to the windowsill, leaned his hips against it, folded his arms, and glanced nonchalantly around the room.

Taylor watched him enter, then turned back to me. "Guy must've tried to pass and got a little too close. Thank God for the way Mercedes are made, huh? You have one?"

"No. A Suburban that I never drive."

He nodded, his demeanor friendly now that Perkins was there. "Courtesy cars," he said. "Buicks, right?"

"Yeah. Brian, I want to say: Catherine is in my thoughts and prayers."

That brought a dark cloud over the room; however, I hadn't seen him since she'd disappeared and even Perkins looked somber.

Brian glanced at him. "Officer . . ."

Perkins shook his hand. "I'm a civilian like you. How're you feeling? The doctor told us about your injuries."

That was a lie, although I soon understood Perkins's intent.

"It's just sore now." Brian nodded toward the window. "I'll be out of here soon. I thought you were a police officer."

"Nope."

"Huh," Brian said, tilting his head, staring at Perkins. "You've been working with Chief Miller. You're not a cop?"

"That's right."

Brian was still looking at Perkins, trying to figure it all out, when I said, "I'm glad you're not badly hurt. What's the latest on the Russia venture?"

It got his attention. "Oh, it's moving along."

"Still on schedule?"

"Yes."

I didn't know where I was headed, but there was one question I wanted to ask: Was Brian's role solely to represent the Tour's financial contribution, or did he have personal money invested?

"Your brother's on a roll right now," I said.

"He's been on a roll for a decade, Jack," Brian said. "It's called talent."

Perkins's gaze drifted to me. The look told me we weren't there to antagonize the guy, rather, to get him to speak frankly.

"Not what I meant, Brian. He's hot right now."

"Sure."

Perkins coughed once and stepped forward. I knew I had just been replaced. Subtlety is an acquired trait.

Perkins didn't even attempt it. "Brian," he said, "what happened yesterday?"

"First, tell me what you're doing here. You came to my house and acted like a cop. Now I learn you're not one."

"I'm a private investigator hired by the Tour," Perkins said. "I told you this before. I've been hired to find Catherine. You were so upset, you forgot or you never heard me."

Taylor shifted in his bed. He didn't appear sore. I had been chased into an alley once, roughed up by some thugs, and wound up hospitalized for several days. I knew what it felt like to move in bed with bruised ribs. Brian Taylor was not in pain.

"Miller has a caseload," Perkins said. "I'm giving all my attention to finding Catherine."

"We're on your side, Brian," I said.

He looked at me coldly. "My side of what?"

The room was suddenly silent. I had been there only five minutes, yet Brian was on the defensive. His eyes moved from one side of the bed to the other, back and forth between Perkins and me. I walked to the far wall and sat in a straight-backed chair beneath the television. Perkins stood over him, staring. The dense quiet was broken by someone rolling a cart down the hall outside the room.

"Brian," Perkins said, "I know you're not here by accident. Someone ran you off that road."

"That's not what I remember." He turned away from Perkins, rolling onto his side. It was a juvenile gesture and struck me as odd coming from a guy in line for the commissioner's seat.

Perkins glared at Brian's back for a long moment. Then he looked at me. I shrugged.

"Cut the shit," Perkins said.

Brian seemed to flinch, but did not roll over.

So Perkins moved around the bed to face him.

Brian rolled onto his other side, again turning his back to Perkins. I grinned when Perkins moved around the bed once more.

"For Christ's sake," Perkins said. He shook his head in disgust, went to the windowsill, and leaned against it. "Miller has crime-scene techs that say a guy rear-ended you, forcing you off the road, Brian. They can tell by the markings on the pavement. Plus, Mercedes have antilock brakes. You left skid marks."

Brian said nothing. He continued to lay there, pouting.

"And two kids saw the whole thing," Perkins said.

Still nothing.

Slowly, Brian rolled onto his back and stared at the ceiling.

We stayed like that—me sitting, Perkins at the windowsill, and Brian, on his back, staring at the ceiling—for what seemed several minutes. Then, unexpectedly, Brian began to cry, slowly at first, then an all-out sob.

When Perkins left the room, I followed.

Nik's face was pale after the predawn flight. He put the key in the door and slowly turned the knob. When Katrina ran toward him, his dull eyes livened with the recognition that something was wrong. He felt perspiration bead on his forehead.

In the doorway, holding his bags, he stood listening as she spoke frantically in Russian. Nik took it all in: *the baby.* Then she pointed at Oleg and swore.

Nik stepped inside, dropped the bags, and closed the door behind him, carefully locking it. He turned and gazed at Oleg, who sat calmly on the sofa watching television.

Oleg nodded once. "No doctors," he said and flicked his cigarette ashes to the floor.

Nik scanned the apartment. The sight made him sigh. Katrina was no housekeeper. The kitchen was unkempt—the sink was overflowing with dishes; the living room's tan carpet had several patches of silver cigarette ash; no one had vacuumed. According to his watch, it was 10:55 A.M. He was tired and stiff from the flight. He had done push-ups and sit-ups in the hotel room, but had hoped to come back, nap, then go to a local gym. Outside, windswept sand scraped the windows. His mind flashed briefly to his childhood, to dirt on the wooden kitchen floor, to the sound of it beneath the soles of his shoes. Hadn't he escaped that sound?

"Where is she?" he said.

Katrina took his ropy forearm and ran, leading him to the bedroom. Baby Catherine, garbed in a white T-shirt and wearing tiny white socks, lay on her back in the makeshift crib—a dresser drawer set on the carpet, padded with a folded towel that served as her mattress.

Nik noticed her coloring immediately—pale with pink blotches on her forehead and cheeks. She lay silent, looking up at them.

He unzipped his leather jacket and dropped it to the floor. "Has she been crying?"

"No," Katrina said. "No, and that is not good. She doesn't cry. I wanted to take her to the hospital last night, but Oleg wouldn't—"

"No hospital. She is fine. What are the red spots?"

"I do not know, Nikoli. We must—"

He simply shook his head. She stopped.

"Babies," he said, "are resourceful."

"She is small and weak and she is not eating, Nikoli."

He shot her a look that made her step back slowly.

"I told you," he said, his face like stone, "no hospital." He inhaled and moved closer, his face inches from hers.

Her eyes went to the floor.

"And never call me Nikoli. Ever again."

Gently, he reached out and touched her face. He raised her chin so she would look at him.

"Now come with me to the other bedroom. I have worked hard and need some . . ."—he paused, searching for the word—"recreation." He turned and left.

Katrina stared down at the baby. When she finally followed, tears streaked her cheeks.

. . .

When they had finished and his tension eased, his head lay gently on the pillow and he stared at the ceiling. Nikoli told Katrina to check on the baby. He had no intention of letting her sleep next to him. She dressed silently and closed the door behind her.

The act of sex, he realized, had been the only time she had ever looked him in the eye. That told him a great deal about her. He wondered what her future would hold. He knew she had come to this country as a young girl to live with an aunt who had nothing to give. So Katrina had no one and nowhere to go, which had led to the streets of Miami and prostitution. Some women, Nik thought, have only their children, not even themselves. He was glad she cared for the baby but did not want her getting too attached.

As he lay beneath the sheet, his hand absently went over his torso, moving along the layered stomach muscles that felt like rows of small rocks, up to his chest, his index finger following the crevice between the pectoral muscles, and stopping at the base of his neck, where the Adam's apple bobbed as he swallowed. He got out of bed and walked to the bedroom window. It was long and rectangular, four feet off the floor, he guessed thirty feet above the ground.

He watched the sun burn low over the city, and, for the first time since this had begun, he longed for his life. Certainly he had awakened each day and wished he were off to the gym for two hours, yet he had not *longed* for Miami like now. It was not, however, the type of longing that would have him give up Catherine and return. He wasn't that kind of man.

But, as he stood before the window, he thought of his new home, of the day the contractor had completed it. It had been a Miami contractor, who had estimated the home's value at $2 million. He had built it for Nik in exchange for annual payments (that Nik figured to be kickbacks from the Canadian restaurant chain). The first payment was due shortly. Nik knew of the contractor's reputation. He wanted to make his payment on time. Constantly looking over his shoulder for Vladimir Remeikus and the Lithuanian group provided enough worry. He did not need a crooked Miami builder to join in.

Besides, the house was not something he wanted to conjure anything but positive emotions. He thought back to the day he first entered it. He recalled the feeling of accomplishment as he glanced at the glistening floors, the ceiling lights, the pool that lay before the ocean. He had escaped his childhood, his homeland—which had brought so many down—and had succeeded as a *businessman,* indeed future owner of seven restaurants in western Canada.

The house was his home. It was beyond his wildest childhood dreams. The terra-cotta tile roof was lava red; the walls were off-white; the trim a soft pink. South Florida all the way. Nik loved it. Miami *was* south Florida. South Florida was America—the true land of opportunity. Seven bedrooms, five full baths, an indoor-outdoor pool, a clay tennis court, a four-bay garage, and ocean frontage, which Nik especially loved. He thought of it as owning the ocean he had crossed. A symbolic power lay in that: Not only had he made it here, he had bought everything in his path—including the sea.

It had not been easy. In truth, until Brian Taylor made the transfer, he could not pay the contractor. And, he thought, staring out at the midmorning sun, if he did not get the $16 million back from Taylor, he did not have the strength to begin again.

He would get the money at all cost. It was now or never.

"Subway for lunch?" I said. "I thought this meal was on the Tour."

"Keeping expenses low is good for business," Perkins said. "You should see what I feed my dirt-bag contacts—informants, those types."

"Glad to know I rate above them."

"Just barely. I take them to Grand Openings, anywhere I can get a free hot dog."

"A class act," I said.

Miller, Perkins, and I sat in a yellow Subway booth. The wallpaper was white and brown and had pictures of horse-drawn carriages, men in top hats, and ladies in long gowns. I was having a foot-long tuna on wheat. It came with a Coke and a small bag of chips; I had grabbed Doritos. Perkins was having ham, cheese, and hot peppers, with the drink-and-chips combo, as well. Miller had ordered what looked like a Philly cheese steak. His face was fleshy and, as he chewed, his jowls rolled down past the collar of his shirt. It was 1:30 P.M., after the lunch crowd. There were only two other people in the place: two suits in a booth at the other end of the restaurant.

"Watching you and Taylor chase each other around the hospital bed was worth the trip down here," I said to Perkins. "They teach you that in detective school?"

"I bought you lunch hoping you wouldn't mention that." Perkins grinned and took a bite. A pepper fell onto his shirt. "Goddamn it."

"It's one of those days," I said.

"What happened in there?" Miller said to me. "You guys weren't there very long."

I knew Perkins and Miller weren't exactly pals, but Miller had invited himself to lunch and Perkins had allowed it.

"I tried to find out something," I said, "but Taylor stonewalled."

"Taylor wouldn't talk," Perkins said.

"Wouldn't talk, huh?" Miller bit into the steak-and-cheese. "Now there's a surprise."

With a straight face, Miller had told us he was on a diet moments before placing his artery-clogging order.

Perkins swallowed. "Taylor's into something and he's in deep."

I opted for a simple nod of concurrence. Body language allows one to keep eating. There's a time and place for everything and, after all, we were in an eatery.

Miller said, "No shit. He's scared. We knew that on day one."

Perkins set his sandwich down and sipped his drink through a straw. He shook his head once very slowly, contemplating. "Yeah, we knew he was scared, but there's more to this. He's not scared *for the daughter.* He's scared *for himself.* You can tell. I think he's in deep shit and that's why the daughter is missing. That's why he was run off the road, too."

"Don't believe in coincidences?" Miller smiled.

I was halfway through my sandwich. Neither of them was close.

"Not hardly," Perkins said.

"Look," Miller said, "I see all the same things you do—how he acts, the daughter, the accident—but let's look at the whole picture: Florida ain't exactly . . . Where do you live, again? New Hampshire?"

Perkins had moved out of Massachusetts and now commuted into Boston. New Hampshire doesn't have state income tax and he had told me he wanted to raise Jackie in a small town.

"Yeah," Perkins said. "I know that. I just—"

"Let me finish," Miller said, raising a hand. They were sharing info now, although there was still a rough edge between them. "You know how many kids go missing each year in Florida?"

Perkins shook his head.

"You ever heard of ACIM?"

Perkins said he hadn't.

"It's an organization called A Child Is Missing. There's over fifty-one thousand missing kids in Florida right now. Three thousand people go missing each day in this country. The problem is so big, Florida's state government is putting a million bucks into ACIM. Taylor's situation is sad, but not isolated."

I was quiet. So was Perkins. We were digesting that.

"And car jacking is a goddamned recreational sport in Florida," Miller said. "They ought to sell licenses for it."

"He wasn't carjacked."

"I know," Miller said. "I've thought about this, and I know where you're coming from, but Taylor's accident and his missing daughter don't have to be related."

. . .

At 2:15 P.M., we were back in Brian Taylor's hospital room. He looked thrilled to see us.

The room had an antiseptic odor. The sun was bright and sat in the sky directly across from Taylor's eighth-floor window. The air outside was hot and heavy with humidity. The air conditioner hummed steadily. Brian lay in his bed, watching a car race on television again. The blond women I recognized as his wife was seated in the chair next to the bed.

She had shoulder-length hair, big blue eyes, and a tan nearly as flawless as her husband's—she was Barbie to his Ken. She wore khaki shorts, a sleeveless white blouse, and tan leather flats. Her honey-colored legs were crossed. Her foot bobbed gently up and down as if dangling from a wharf into water. She had half-dollar-sized gold hoop earrings and a gold chain around her neck. The diamond on her left hand was bigger than my first car.

Looking at her, something told me Taylor did not drive a

Mercedes by accident. He'd probably be driving one if it meant a second job stocking shelves at night.

Perkins had met her previously and quickly shook her hand. "Cindy, this is Jack Austin."

She stood and I shook her hand.

"You're an investigator, too?"

"No. I play on the Tour. I came to see how Brian was doing."

"That's thoughtful." She glanced at her husband, who continued staring at the television. Now he refused to acknowledge us.

"I'd like to ask you some more questions," Perkins said to Cindy.

That made Brian Taylor glance over.

"Fine," she said. "Anything that might help find Catherine."

"Thank you," Perkins said.

"I thought things couldn't get worse," she said. "Then some idiot nearly kills my husband. Why can't anyone in Florida drive? Will someone please tell me that? You drive around this state and see how people pass. It's like this car race." She pointed to the television. "Now someone cuts in too soon and . . ." She looked at Brian and shook her head.

Taylor was staring at the television again.

"Can we go out in the hall?" Perkins said.

Cindy shrugged. "Sure."

"No." Taylor clicked off the TV. "You can ask her questions here."

"I don't want to bother you," Perkins said. "You seem engrossed in that race."

Miller and I both knew Perkins wanted to get the wife away in hopes that something might surface.

Taylor wasn't giving an inch. "No bother," he said. "I insist."

The air conditioner continued to hum and Perkins's footfalls were loud as he moved around the bed and pulled the straight-backed chair near Cindy's. They each sat down.

I went to the windowsill and leaned against it, my arms crossed. Cindy did not seem defensive. Brian Taylor was obviously scared of letting Perkins help. She was not. Nothing in her demeanor had changed upon seeing Perkins again or at his request to interview her further.

Miller had not said a word and now leaned next to me. When Perkins began, however, Miller was quickly at Taylor's side, attempting to distract.

"Awful what happened to Dale Earnhardt, huh?" Miller said, nodding at the television. "Is this that twenty-four–hour Dale Earnhardt tribute?"

Taylor was trying to hear what Perkins had asked. Cindy was speaking.

"How you think the Earnhardt kid will do?" Miller said. "His father's shoes are awful big for a kid to fill."

"Yeah, sure," Taylor said.

"Been to any races?" Miller said. "I was at Daytona when it happened. Saw it all. The crash didn't look real bad, just sort of routine. Except nothing's routine at a hundred and ninety miles an hour, huh?"

"Yeah," Taylor said, squinting at his wife. "Can you let me watch TV?"

"Oh, sure," Miller said.

From there, we all listened as Perkins asked Cindy about their daughter. The questions—as one would expect—made her cry. Not a sob, but, as she spoke, tears rolled down her cheeks. She said she had checked the mail each day hoping a ransom note would appear. She said she even checked the mailbox each night before going to sleep. She purchased a second answering machine, although she had not gone anywhere and couldn't have missed a call. Also, she said Chief Miller had someone listening to her phone line. She explained that Miller suggested she continue her normal routine and the state troopers would send an unmarked car to follow. However, she could not think of anything besides Catherine, so she had sat at home, hoping and praying.

As she spoke, I watched Taylor. All color drained from his face. His jaws clenched. Tears streaked his face. He tossed about on the bed like one trying to get comfortable. He shifted and squirmed. Then, finally, he could take no more: "Stop badgering her. You're not even a cop!"

The room fell silent. Perkins leaned back in the chair, his arms folded across his chest. Miller was smiling. Cindy's mouth hung open.

"Cindy, for God's sake, this man isn't even a cop. He's a snoop. You don't have to speak to him."

"He's trying to help, Brian. He's been to Connecticut—all over—trying to help."

"Everyone," Taylor said, "leave. All of you. Leave me alone for a while."

. . .

Cindy looked devastated, on the verge of tears, as the four of us stood in Miller's makeshift office. Miller pulled a chair away from the wall for her. She seemed to collapse into it.

No one spoke, at first. Miller and Perkins were probably waiting for Cindy. I sensed something going on, so I remained silent. Perhaps it had taken a full minute but the dam finally burst.

Cindy, her face making the slow transition from deadpan to perplexed, looked up at Perkins and said, "What's wrong with him?"

I sat in a chair. Perkins remained standing. Miller sat on the sofa, next to Cindy.

"You've noticed a change in your husband?" Perkins said, his inflection making the question a statement.

"Of course. Something is eating him from the inside out. He asked us *all* to leave. I'm his wife, Catherine's mother. She's *our* daughter." Her hands went to her face and she sobbed. "I feel like my whole world has been turned upside down—first, Catherine, now my marriage."

It was tough to watch. Absently, I filled my cheeks and exhaled silently.

"We're trying to help," Miller said. "I hope you know that."

"Yes. I want your help, badly."

"Your husband does not," Perkins said. "Do you have any idea why that is so?"

I had never heard him use such proper diction. I was still thinking about the question I had pondered on the plane: I wanted to know if Brian had fronted any money for the Russian golf venture. I knew Pete was a benefactor. What if Brian was as well? Certainly he did not have the money Pete had. What if something had gone wrong with the deal and he'd been forced to borrow money to cover something? The Russian golf idea was Brian's, or that was how he was presenting it. It was a great one, too, one that could land him—as Tour commissioner—in golf's most powerful seat. To most people, that kind of end was enough to lead one to any means. What was Brian Taylor into?

Cindy was still crying and paused to blow her nose. She looked up, embarrassed. I sensed she was high maintenance, but she did, obviously, love her daughter very much.

"I'm so sorry," she said, "for all of this—me sobbing, my husband acting crazy."

"Do you have any explanations for his behavior?" Perkins said.

I saw her squeeze the balled tissues, her knuckles turning white. "What do you mean? He's under so much stress."

"Yes," Perkins said.

"But, ma'am," Miller said, "so are you."

Something in her face changed. Her eyes narrowed. She looked from Perkins to Miller, to me, then back to Miller.

"What do you mean by that?" she said.

The cat was out of the bag. She knew what the three of us thought: Her husband had gotten into something that led to the kidnapping and to his car crash.

"Please explain that remark," she said.

"He meant nothing," Perkins said. "Both you and Mr. Taylor are under a great deal of stress. How about a cup of coffee? Jack, why don't you take Mrs. Taylor down to the cafeteria and get her some coffee?"

"Sure," I said.

. . .

In the elevator, Cindy and I were quiet. It was tense and the air felt heavy, almost difficult to breathe. For the thirty-second ride down, she stood staring at the floor, motionless, obviously in deep thought. The previous conversation seemed to hang tangibly between us.

"These things can be confusing," I said. I didn't know what else to say and hoped it might lead to conversation. Any dialogue had to be better than the tension of dead air.

She glanced up, as if remembering I was there. "You're a golfer, right?"

I nodded.

She inhaled deeply. "They think Brian is guilty of something."

I was just a simple golfer, just here to visit. I shrugged, oblivious to it all.

The elevator doors opened and we got off. As we moved to the cafeteria, I said, "His idea to bring golf to the Russian people is great. I'm looking forward to helping out."

"You're involved?"

"Brian asked me to give a clinic over there. I've never been. It ought to be great."

The cafeteria had an S-shaped line weaving past a host of items. We opted to head directly to the rows of cylindrical coffee dispensers. Cindy had French vanilla decaf; I took regular, and added two creams and two sugars. At 3:20, the place was nearly empty. Coupled with the sheer size of the place—wide enough to be a very good two-putt; long enough to be an *outstanding* two-putt—it offered a distinct sense of privacy. They know how to build hospitals in Florida.

We sat near a window that looked out at an empty brick patio with plants and a picnic table. Our table was imitation oak and shone under tract lighting. The tile floor glistened beneath the sunlight.

"Who's running the Russian golf thing now that Brian's so busy with Catherine, and now his accident?"

"I don't know." She sipped coffee, then grinned. "Probably still him. He's a self-proclaimed workaholic."

"I can understand his concern. A lot of money has been invested in it. Some of which, I imagine, is his own." I smiled, an attempt at guile.

She returned the pleasantry. The gesture, however, looked forced; it was not the same stunning smile she had greeted me with upon learning I had come to see how Brian was feeling.

"I don't usually know much about what goes on at the office," she said. "And I like it that way. When Brian comes home, I want him to come home, not work. I do know none of our money is invested. I don't like to take financial risks."

I didn't doubt that.

"Two benefactors and the Tour are the investors," she said. "I know that much, because that was a stipulation."

She glanced out the window and watched as a man toting a briefcase and wearing a long white lab coat sat down at the picnic table. He glanced covertly at Cindy, the way men did at Lisa when I was with her, as if they knew she was taken, but still wanted to gawk.

"Stipulation?" I said.

"Yeah. Brian was upset about it. Peter Barrett said the Tour would not get in a situation where it might get left . . ." She gave a flitter with her hand.

"Holding the bag?" I said.

"Yes. He told Brian to find a third party, which turned out to be difficult."

Casually, I drank some coffee. "So he got his brother, Pete?"

She shook her head. "Pete was always in it. He found a man from the Soviet Union to help."

Victor Silco. I had wanted to know how much money Brian Taylor had put in to this Russian golf idea. I had learned the answer: none. I had also learned he had sought Silco to make his generous donation and that the deal was off without Silco—a fact that led to many additional questions.

The card had been written in large block letters. A felt-tipped Sharpie pen had been used. Nik had been careful, dutifully wearing thin leather gloves, not touching any part of the paper or flowers with his bare hand.

He had worked slowly. The wording had to be perfect. Taylor must know immediately *who* had sent the flowers. Indeed, the card echoed the sign Nik had shown Taylor moments before the crash. Yet, at the same time, the wording had to be somewhat vague, inaccessible to anyone but Brian Taylor. Nik knew the result of the crash and the ensuing note might lead Taylor to believe Victor sent Nik in the car that had pushed him off the road. That was fine. Brian Taylor still would have no reason to believe this was Nik's deal, not Victor's. At that thought, Nik smiled.

The humid summer air seemed heavy to him as he crossed the parking lot. Ponte Vedra Beach was not like Miami. No place was, he thought. Miami was home now.

He was dressed in a gray suit and carried the flower arrangement wrapped in tissue paper. A white card rested peacefully in the center of the arrangement. A *Miami Herald* was folded under his arm.

Through dark glasses, Nik eyed all that was around. The hospital bustled with after-dinner visitors. The parking lot was filled and a steady flow of people walking in both directions through the lobby's doors. At the lobby's entrance, there was a cop. He knew there would be one and figured this was not an official police officer, rather a security guard. He had planned to send Victor. The second phone call, though, ended with Victor screaming at him, asking him why, in regards to Taylor's crash. It let

Nik know Victor was likely of no further use, which saddened him. Had he not, after all, given Victor the academic life he lived?

In any case, Nik would make the delivery himself, continuing to pressure Taylor.

The electric doors of the hospital whirred opened. Nik smiled casually, holding the newspaper close to his face with one hand, the flowers in the other. He headed to the information desk.

An elderly woman smiled, gazing up from her seat. "May I help you?"

Without speaking—or dropping the paper from his face—Nik set the arrangement on the countertop, turned, and walked briskly out.

Wednesday morning, as the sun rose, I was already on the practice green with Nash when Lisa approached.

I had returned to our hotel suite shortly before midnight, thus was working on about five hours' sleep. Upon my return, she had told me that while I had been in Florida, Nash had slept in, had an afternoon workout, and had joined her for dinner. Apparently, he had slept through lunch.

Now he was standing next to me on the putting green, showing off by pointing out different pin placements he'd noticed upon running the course earlier that morning. He was also reading some putts. He was working his tail off to make up for the two-stroke penalty. I was impressed.

I was leaning over, making a slow practice stroke, when Lisa called my name.

I handed Nash the putter and went to the edge of the green. Lisa stood with her arms crossed and looked agitated. She was dressed in a porcelain-blue linen jacket and matching cropped pants. Her sandals were the same color. She had long ago refused the golf-shirt-and-khaki-pants attire typical of golf's TV analysts. Indeed, when she left the *Washington Post* for the Tour, she had made some kind of pact with herself, promising to remain serious, to examine the most pressing issues, not simply do the joke-filled commentaries or pat-the-player's-back features viewers typically see. In fact, our original meeting occurred when she asked me to be a part of a live on-air putting feature. She had asked me to stroke a few putts, then had proceeded to explain—on national television—how my stroke illustrated what *not* to do. I had stuck around long enough for the cameras to stop, then had given her a piece of my mind. She had countered by looking me in the eye, using a tone that was friendly and only wanted to help, and offered a putting lesson. After storming off, I realized I couldn't get her out of my head. We went for a light-hearted dinner three nights later.

She didn't look light-hearted now.

"I was in the middle of an interview," she said. "Perkins has been calling around, looking for you. Finally, someone from the Tour staff came to get *me.* I have work to do, Jack. Call him back right now so he'll stop bugging everyone."

"What's he want?"

"I'm not your receptionist, Jack. I don't know."

"How important could the interview have been?" I smiled. "This week's champion is standing right in front of you."

"I was asking Tiger about the Grand Slam, Jack."

My smile widened. "He's so-so."

"I made the damn appointment a month ago"—she glanced at Nash, then looked at me—"sweetie." I sensed *sweetie* hadn't been her first choice.

"Well, tell Tiger he's playing for second place this week," I said, grinning.

"I'll let you do that, Jack." She turned and began walking away.

"Gary McCord thinks I'm funny," I said.

Over her shoulder, she said: "No. He just feels sorry for you. He told me so."

· · ·

"*A deal is a deal,*" Perkins said, as he read the card Taylor had received over the phone. "Based on when the flowers were taken up to Taylor's room, the hospital staff said whoever left them at the front desk must've done so between six-thirty and eight P.M. That's when we were at the airport."

"Good timing."

"Yeah."

"They describe who left them?"

"No. You saw the guards they have there."

"Yeah. How did you get the card away from Taylor?"

"After I dropped you at the airport, I went back and was sitting in his room when the flowers were brought up. Look on Taylor's face gave it away. He went white. I thought he was going to puke. I took it and read it."

"Isn't that a violation of rights—reading people's mail?"

"Probably. You think I give a shit about his rights? His daughter is missing. I think he's at the root of it."

I was in the locker room at the Tournament Players Club at River Highlands, sipping orange juice and sitting in a leather chair. A little-known fact about life on Tour is that players are granted free worldwide phone calls from the locker room, a perk courtesy of AT&T. I was leaning back, holding the juice in both hands. My feet were crossed at the ankles and the phone was shrugged against my ear. I knew Perkins didn't care about Taylor's rights. There was a point at which Perkins went inside himself, to a seemingly primitive level of good and evil, right and wrong. When he reached that point, all bets were off as to what he might do. It was why he was no longer a cop. Perkins had quit after finding a four-year-old rape victim. He had held the little girl as she bled in an emergency room before she had been treated. Then he had sought, found, and beat her father—the perpetrator—nearly into coma. A high-profile pay increase was being sought by the Boston P.D.—and being debated openly in the media—at the time; Perkins was allowed to *retire* quietly.

"Taylor knows that I know he fucked the duck," Perkins said.

"Cindy know about the note?"

"Not yet."

"Miller?"

"Sure."

We were quiet. It was not yet 8 A.M. The locker room was busy. A breakfast buffet had been set up featuring eggs, ham, steak, fruit, and cereals. There were several flavors of coffee and a variety of juices. Five players were making their way through the buffet line. I had grabbed a couple Power Bars and a large coffee on my way to the course and after beating range balls for an hour, the steaks smelled great. Fred Couples was reading the paper across the room. A guy I didn't know, maybe a Monday qualifier or a rookie, was staring at the financial report on CNN.

"Taylor insists," Perkins said, "and I know you'll have a hard time believing this, that he doesn't know what the note means. Says it 'must've been sent to the wrong guy.'"

"It must have been sent to him by name," I said. "If it was delivered to the information desk."

"Of course, and almost every time I walk in, Taylor lies on his bed and cries. I don't even think he wants to go home."

"For Christ's sake."

"I know. It's crazy."

"So what will you do now?"

"Victor Silco never returned my call and there was only one major change in Taylor's life preceding this: the Russian golf thing."

"One change," I said, "that you know of."

"Sure thing, Mr. Armchair Detective. That *I know of*—but those of us who are not armchair detectives know that you go with what you've got and what I've got is the Russian golf thing."

"And the fact that Silco won't talk to you."

"Or at least doesn't want to," Perkins said. "But *you* are a different story."

"Me?"

"Yeah. You would legitimately need information, since you'll be giving that golf clinic you mentioned. Be logical for you to need to speak to him now that Brian is hurt."

"I didn't do so well with Taylor."

"Like I said, I go with what I've got."

"What about Miller or one of his guys?"

"I'm not giving this whole case to him," he said. "Sure, he's running it, but if I keep my distance, I can maneuver. If I'm using his people, I can't."

"I see."

"Besides, Jack, whoever delivered that card did it right under Miller's and my own nose. Taylor won't speak to me. Silco won't return my call. That means whoever delivered the note probably knows I'm on the case—and probably what I eat for breakfast."

"Are you asking me for help?" I said. "Is that how I should interpret this?"

He cleared his throat. "Jesus Christ, I never thought this day would come."

"So *you* need *me*."

"*Need* is too strong a word."

"Strong but accurate."

"You met Silco once . . ."

He obviously had given this painstaking thought.

". . . and he knows you are legitimately involved in the Russian thing. Therefore, it's logical that you would have questions. Dragging him into an interrogation room won't get it done. Not if he's got the balls to walk in there and deliver that note."

"I play at eight thirty-four tomorrow morning," I said. "And I just got back from Florida."

"There's a plane ticket waiting for you at the airport, U.S. Airways. It's the ten forty-five flight. Gets you in Miami at three thirty-one. I'll meet you in Miami."

"Perkins–"

The line went dead. He had hung up before I could protest.

. . .

I had showered quickly and walked out of the locker room, toting a small gym bag and wearing blue jeans, a fresh white golf shirt with MAXFLI on the left breast, and cordovan loafers with tassels. Collared shirt and loafers. I looked so preppy that aside from the jeans, Horizons School probably would have accepted even me.

I headed to the parking lot, where Nash was to drive with me to the airport, then return the car to the course and meet up with Lisa. His instructions were to find her and explain that I was on another day-trip and would, hopefully, be back for a late-night dinner.

What I found in the parking lot was not Nash waiting in the pale blue Buick LaSabre courtesy car I'd been given for the week. At first, Nash was nowhere in sight. Then I saw him, maybe thirty yards away, casually leaning over, his head inside a car, his thick forearms resting on the open window of the passenger's side door. The car was a red BMW 325i. The person behind the wheel had shoulder-length blond hair, gold earrings that hung nearly to her shoulders, expertly applied makeup, and looked great. Even to me.

And her name was Sharon Taylor.

The Beemer was not running. I walked down a row of cars, between bumpers and tailgates, staying hidden from Sharon's view, stopped when I was within earshot. I heard Sharon say, " . . . around four-thirty."

"Got to go," Nash said, pulling himself out of the car and straightening. When he saw me, he went into an instantaneous and defensive street-tough mode. It was a side I had not seen. He slouched slightly, flexing his knees, folded his arms across his chest. He was a big kid and he was, apparently, a tough kid.

"You spying on me?"

Sharon didn't stick around to hear my answer. My guess was she didn't care. The BMW started up and she drove slowly past me. Her gaze was like ice when our eyes momentarily met.

"What the hell is going on?" I said.

Nash brushed past me, heading to the car. I got in the driver's side. When I started it, he leaned forward and turned on the radio, pushing the volume up too loud.

I leaned over and clicked it off.

"Tell me what the hell you were doing with Sharon Taylor."

"I'm eighteen. You got no right asking 'bout my personal business."

"Cut the bullshit, Nash. I'm your legal guardian this summer."

"You're my boss."

The statement and his tone said a lot. Of course, legally, he was right, but I thought of myself as more. I pulled slowly out of the lot, my mind racing. It was mid-morning. The traffic wasn't bad on Route 9, which lead to I-91 and the Bradley International Airport. It was a good thing the driving was easy. My mind certainly wasn't on the road. What the hell was to take place at "four-thirty"?

We traveled in silence for twenty minutes. I contemplated skipping the flight. Brian Taylor and his family were obviously in real trouble. However, although I felt for Cindy and of course her daughter, Catherine, I feared Taylor had brought it upon them himself. I believed Taylor had reached into someplace without looking first and had gotten bit. Nash was nearly in the same situation. Except, he hadn't—I was assuming—gotten into anything. Yet.

He was a kid, a kid I knew only peripherally: I had just witnessed his street-toughness—when all that matters is respect and having the balls to get it; I knew he had dreams; that he had a great work ethic; that he was a good kid; an insecure kid; a kid with vast potential.

He couldn't meet my glare, which flashed occasionally from the road to him. Instead, he sat staring out the window, as if fascinated by the passing scenery.

I coasted to the breakdown lane and stopped.

He looked over. "What are you doing?"

It was my turn not to speak. I stared at him for maybe ten seconds. It made him uncomfortable; he turned back to his window. We sat like that for a full five minutes. This put making my flight in jeopardy, yet I at least had to broach the subject. Maybe I should have done so the first time I'd seen him talking to Sharon Taylor. Hindsight is never skewed. Yet I had no prior experience with teens, let alone in mentoring one. I felt responsible for Nash, however, and now I had witnessed what I believed to be the scheduling of some sort of date.

"What are we doing, Jack?" He still wasn't looking at me.

"Can't look me in the eye?"

He turned and glared.

"Don't feel guilty because I gave you the clubs," I said. "And had you play golf with the most influential man in my life. Feel guilty because you're betraying my trust."

His stare didn't waiver. His jaws flexed. "Your trust?"

"Yeah," I said. "This isn't just a business partnership, golfer-caddy. This is a friendship. I know what's best for you, Nash."

He shook his head slowly, as if I was belittling him. Maybe I was. He was eighteen, but I couldn't let him make so obvious a mistake.

I went on: "And what's best is school and football—in that order. You've got two people—me and Lisa—who give a shit about you, who are trying to help you. You cause a scene with Sharon Taylor and you'll screw up your life, your future."

I hit the gas and pulled back onto the highway. I drove far too fast the rest of the way. When I pulled to the curb at my gate, I got out without speaking, grabbed my carry-on bag, slammed the door, and walked off.

. . .

Since September 11, 2001, they like you to be at the airport two hours early. I wasn't and paid the price. Having no check-through baggage made it worse. Searched, scanned, and finally allowed to board, I leaned my head back as the plane took off. The U.S. Airways flight would not be direct. In fact, I had a fifty-minute layover in Charlotte. They were fifty minutes that could have been spent on the practice range.

The Nash situation only made the travel situation worse. I had to contact Joan Lerman to see if she could tell me anything I didn't know. I could see how a woman like Sharon Taylor would appeal to Nash. Hell, at eighteen, I'd have given my left arm to have an older woman who looked like that attempt to seduce me. However, at eighteen, I had known the difference between right and wrong, between married and single. I knew Nash did as well. You could see it in his manners, in the way he acted around Lisa. He had pulled her seat out at meals and always held the door for her. He had learned that behavior somewhere. When his parents had not contacted me with questions or comments about what I had planned for their son, I had assumed his parental guidance hadn't rivaled Ward and June Cleaver's. Now I wanted to know where he had come from.

When we leveled off, a stewardess brought me a bottle of water. I felt like ordering a couple of good, stiff drinks. When you're young, one of the greatest things about life on tour is the travel, flying city to city, staying in hotels, eating out. Over a decade ago, that was how I had felt. Now, I was just glad for frequent-flyer points enabling me to forever fly first-class, where my legs could nearly stretch out and the food wasn't always like chewing rocks. Players in the upper echelon of golf's financial world—Tiger, Greg Norman, and older legends like Jack and Arnie—own personal planes, jets, which make travel nearly enjoyable. Likewise, other players sign endorsement deals to receive planes—or partial rights to them—in exchange for having their photos in magazines read by those with enough wealth to consider purchasing a jet.

As I sipped my water and watched the clouds float by, I felt a tinge of guilt for my cynicism regarding travel. After all, as a kid, my father had routinely left the house before my mother and I had even woke; during winter months he sought indoor carpentry jobs, but usually had to resort to plowing snow as well to make ends meet. I had the world's greatest job.

I took the Philip Levine book out of the gym bag and leaned my head back against my seat. The book had been in my locker at the golf course and I had grabbed it before leaving. I was making my way slowly through it and hit a poem called "Magpiety." It is about the legend of magpies, how they delve into the affairs of others. It was probably about much more, but I was limited. Still, I read poetry because, when I did, sometimes something hit home. It did this time. Something moved in my stomach. Nash Henley was, after all, eighteen, an adult. He thought

I was snooping around, looking over his shoulder. Was I? Near the end of the poem, a section reads:

. . . You
are thirty-two
only once in your life, and though
July comes
too quickly, you pray for
the overbearing
heat to pass. . . .

Levine, you've got that right, I thought, and closed my eyes. I didn't wake until we landed in Charlotte.

. . .

As I walked up the ramp in Miami, Perkins stood waiting and smiled like a guy selling used cars.

"Hey, buddy," he said and gave me a big, warm handshake.

I stopped short. "This is going to be hard," I said, "isn't it?"

19

The hospital, Nik thought, had such poor security. In fact, he had returned and sat outside Brian Taylor's room reading the paper after delivering the flowers. No one had expected him to do that. No one knew what he looked like, or even who he was. After all, Victor was in charge of the golf venture. Or so they all thought. To Nik's knowledge, no one even suspected Victor of wrongdoing.

Now Nik sat far below Brian Taylor's room, in the cafeteria, sipping strong coffee. He recalled watching the hulking blond man rush out of Taylor's room, run down the hall, and demand to use the phone at the nurse's station. Then he looked on casually as the cop from television—a policeman named Miller, he remembered—had gone down the corridor swiftly, entering the floor's TV lounge, before heading to the elevator.

The coffee was fresh. Nik had asked the Negro woman working the register to brew a new pot. It had looked stale, old, and she had smiled casually, the way he had often discovered Americans, in jobs requiring a servantlike mentality, often did. He never understood that. How could one smile as he pumped gas? Or take pride in washing a windshield, standing back, finding spots he missed? There were other options. Nik had always understood those options. Often he wondered why others did not. Today, he simply smiled, thanked the woman for the freshly brewed coffee, and headed to a table with his newspaper.

The paper did not mention that a little girl had been kidnapped. Nor did it say Taylor had been in an accident. Was that old news, Nik wondered? If so, it would make things easier. The less people thought about Taylor, the less chance that people in positions to discover the money would find it. Still, each time Nik thought of that, of losing the money he worked so hard for, something moved in his solar plexus, like a hand tapping his shoulder, then a whisper asking: *Have they already found the money?*

The thought nearly made him scream. Each and every time it overtook him. It unnerved him, a sensation similar to being watched: He felt something was wrong but could do nothing except move on, hoping to escape the feeling, as if a new locale would reassure him that all was fine, that Taylor had protected the money.

It made sense that Taylor would have protected it. Taylor surely knew questions would arise if the additional money was discovered. That alone should be enough to ensure that Taylor hid it well. Because it would follow that, if the money was found, Taylor would be questioned, his reputation damaged severely. If that were not enough, Nik thought, skimming the

World News section, Taylor must realize if the authorities came for Nik, he would throw Taylor at them like a door prize.

And the baby would die. Of that, there was no question.

20

Lisa no longer sounded miffed when I called that afternoon, at 3:45. Perhaps the Tiger interview had gone well. I had insisted Perkins give me thirty minutes before proceeding to the University of Miami in pursuit of Victor Silco. We were still in the airport. I was talking on my cell phone near the luggage carousel. The location made hearing a challenge; in fact, the runway may have been quieter. However, I didn't want to spend my half-hour seeking solitude. I dialed and put my free hand over my phoneless ear.

I got down to business and told her about the scene in the parking lot and the drive to the airport.

There was a long pause, as she digested it all.

"He never mentioned it at lunch," she said. "Only that you would meet me for a late dinner."

"Where is he now?"

"I don't know. Although, I did learn something about Nash's home life at lunch."

"What?"

"That he has one. He received mail, forwarded from the Horizons School, care of you."

"So he has someone," I said, "somewhere. Can you find Nash before four-thirty?"

"Jack. I'm working. Tell me what you're doing in Miami."

"Perkins wants me to speak to Victor Silco."

"About the Russian golf proposal?"

"I guess," I said.

Lisa didn't say anything. A group of girls stood at the carousel, wearing matching blue windbreakers. They giggled and yelled back and forth. They looked about Nash's age. One stood alone, wearing headphones, her knees bending slightly, bobbing to some rhythm only she was privy to. She had long brown hair, which hung straight down her back, and wore faded jeans and old running shoes. She was cute with her big blue eyes. She was Nash's age and wasn't driving a Beemer or drinking rum and Cokes like she owned stock in Captain Morgan.

"You 'guess'?" Lisa said finally.

I heard exasperation to the point of anger in her voice.

"Jack, this is a practice day, or did you forget? And you're no longer in the top hundred and twenty-five."

"Don't lecture me." My voice sounded tired. I knew my position on the money list. I knew young kids fresh out of college go through PGA Tour Qualifying School each year and would—again—line up this January to take my spot. I knew my putting was suspect, that a couple hours on the practice green were needed far more than a day-trip to Miami.

"He's my best friend, Lisa."

"I assume you're not talking about Brian Taylor."

"I've asked Perkins for help far more often than he's asked for mine. Hutch Gainer can attest to that."

"So you're paying back debts, to the detriment of your career?"

"This isn't August," I said. "I have three full months left. Also, neither of us would think of it as paying back."

"You're like brothers," she said. The anger had left her voice. She spoke now as if realizing something. I knew it wasn't exactly a realization, maybe a remembrance of the lifelong bond I shared with Perkins.

"Maybe closer than brothers," I said. "The point is, someone walked into the hospital right under Perkins's nose and delivered a note to Taylor, which read *'A deal is a deal.'* Taylor's involved in something. Whoever delivered it must know who Perkins is and what he's doing. So, if Silco is involved in any of this, he'd know what to expect if Perkins went to see him."

"Maybe," she said.

I waited.

"All of that assumes that the person who wrote the note is rational. Maybe it was a crazy wandering around."

"Handing out incriminating notes? At one point, Taylor threw his wife out of the hospital room along with Perkins, Miller, and me. He's got himself in a jam."

"So you'll go see Dr. Silco with questions about your clinic and try to slip in some guile while you're there, as well?"

I had no idea what I would do, so I went back to the original topic. "Can you find Nash before four-thirty?"

"I'll try. Then what?"

"Talk to him."

"About the birds and the bees? That's your job, Jack."

"Just see if he opens up. I lost my temper in the car. I shouldn't have. He might not talk to me."

"He's a sweet kid," she said. "At lunch, he pulled out my chair again and thanked me repeatedly for the shirt I bought. What are you going to do about Nash and the Sharon Taylor situation?"

"Call Joan Lerman, once and for all. Try to get a handle on where exactly he is coming from."

And when we hung up, I did just that.

. . .

It took a call to Horizons School to get Joan Lerman's summer phone number. I had spoken to her only once previously. The groundwork for my hiring Nash had begun when I received Nash's letter. Next, I called the Horizons School to learn more about him. I originally spoke to someone who now I could not even remember. Then Joan called back to discuss Nash.

Joan had said she had looked for summer employment for him near the Horizons campus because he didn't want to go home. I had explained that the only employee I have is a caddy and that his timing had been ideal, due to Tim Silver's decision to begin work on his book. I said I was considering giving Nash a chance. Moments later, she had enthusiastically described Nash in colorful detail. Finally, I had met with Nash three times—and had been reminded of my own school days. I had seen the same things in Nash that Joan had seen: inner strength, intelligence, a polite maturity. Moreover, I had seen enough of myself in him to offer work.

Joan's voice was still like melted butter. She sounded like Cher and seemed even more upbeat than during our previous phone conversation. It was, after all, now summer vacation.

Perkins sat staring at me in a row of steel-framed chairs. During my talk with Lisa, he had read a newspaper a traveler apparently discarded. Now he was antsy.

"I need for us to speak candidly about Nash Henley," I said.

"Sure. I was off to the beach. That can certainly wait. I hope nothing's wrong."

"No. Where exactly is Nash from? I'd just like a little more detail."

"Roxbury."

"Do you have a street address? Or is there an alumni directory on the school's Web site?"

She hesitated.

"I know it's personal information, but I'd like to update his parents on his work this summer."

"Won't Nash give you his address?"

"Didn't ask him for it. This isn't a formal report or anything like that. I just wanted to call you for a little background and thought of writing his folks just now."

She seemed to think that over. "He is tough to get information from, isn't he?"

"Yeah."

"I can get you a street address. You have e-mail?"

The Tour provides all players with laptops and Internet access. I told her my e-mail address.

"I want to know more about his home life. What is it like? His parents? He doesn't say much."

"I've noticed," she said and chuckled. "It takes a long time to get to know him. He's got no mother. She died when he was fourteen. No one knows who his father is. Halle Basker, a football coach, took him in after his mother died."

"Adoption?"

"No. He was Nash's legal guardian—but Nash is eighteen now. He told me he didn't want to go back this summer. That's really all I know. I haven't spent a lot of time with Halle. All I know is he came to watch Nash play football, but skipped the parent-teacher conferences."

"I see."

Perkins was staring at me and tapping his watch. I ignored him.

"As far as I know," she said, "Halle was Nash's football coach and the one Nash turned to when his mother died. He called our admissions office about Nash. Got the application process rolling for him to come to Horizons."

"How did his mother die?"

"That is something I don't know," she said, "as odd as that may sound. It's not necessary information in the admission process and Nash won't speak of it. I will say this, however. I sense he was very close to her and, judging from the way he acts—how polite he is—she had a very positive influence. Of course, he speaks much better than some people from his neighborhood. He is extremely intelligent. His writing doesn't nearly reflect his spoken articulation."

"I know." I thought about what she said about Nash's mother.

"If you don't mind my asking, Jack, why are you so concerned about Nash's background?"

I was not about to mention Sharon Taylor. "He's just very tight-lipped. Made me wonder."

Joan Lerman said she'd have someone at Horizons School e-mail me an address and phone number for Halle Basker. Then she explained that she was on Cape Cod for the summer. I apologized for interrupting her vacation and hung up.

Perkins leaped from his seat and we headed out the door. As we did, I thought about what I had learned of Nash, and about all that I had not.

. . .

The Medical Campus at the University of Miami was a $20 cab ride from the airport, plenty long enough to provide me time to think about Dr. Victor Silco. Moreover, it gave me time to get nervous; I was a golfer, not a cop. Although he was an academic, not a thug—so if he had something to do with Brian Taylor's car crash, I might be able to tell.

Regardless, I did not feel like a perky undergrad as I walked stiffly into the science building and located Silco's office. Perkins called the science department beforehand and had been told Silco had office hours from 3 to 6 P.M. It was 5:00 and the office door was open.

Silco did not have on a suit, as he had nearly six months earlier in Brian Taylor's office. He wore a white lab coat. He sat behind his desk, which was piled with papers and books and a stack of manila folders, some of which spilled computer printouts onto the desk. His lab coat was unbuttoned. Beneath it, he wore a white dress shirt with a starched collar. His tie had red and blue diamonds. His thick black hair was neatly parted and his face was still ruddy, although the room's poor lighting made it less noticeable than Taylor's window-lined office had. He wore narrow, rectangular, metal-framed glasses. Taken on the whole, he seemed the picture of academia. He also looked very comfortable in that setting. We were on his home field.

He didn't recognize me when he looked up from his work and asked if he could help. Leaning on his elbows, he took his glasses off and held them dangling above his desk blotter; they must've been for reading only. Silco had a large snake-necked desk lamp. Behind him, hung degrees. The walls were lined with books jutting from nondescript shelving like jagged teeth. The room seemed too small for all it contained. When I said my name and Silco's eyes refocused, hinting of recognition, tension only added to the clutter.

I extended my hand. Silco stood and took it. His was like holding a dead fish. He did not speak, waiting for me to lead.

"I was in the area. . ."

His eyes narrowed slightly, his lips pursed. His back straightened a little. He didn't buy it.

". . . to see someone," I said. "And I had a couple questions about the golf clinic Brian Taylor asked me to put on in Russia."

"I thought the Tour was in Connecticut this weekend?"

In Taylor's office, he hadn't recognized my name. I'm not Jack Nicklaus. Yet, as Loren Roberts is known for his putting prowess, I'm known by golf fans—certainly those serious enough to follow the Tour's week-to-week schedule—as a perennial driving distance leader. Previously, Silco had never heard of me. Now he knew we were playing near Hartford this week. Maybe his interest in the game peaked with his involvement in the Russian venture. Maybe. It might even be logical—but my gut told me that was wrong. His sopping handshake and the look in his eyes when he recognized me did as well.

"I'm in town today on business," I said. "Tournament starts tomorrow."

"I see." He pointed to a yellow plastic classroom chair along the wall.

I dragged it across the linoleum floor to his desk.

"It's good to see you again," he said, as he sat down and folded his glasses into the breast pocket of his lab coat.

His greeting was a little late in coming, but I played along. "You, too."

As uneasy as I had been about this, I now sensed I had the upper hand. He no longer appeared to hold the home-field advantage. In fact, he didn't want me there. My knowing it told me something was wrong. I wondered if the cops had gotten the same feeling when they spoke to him. If not, it meant Silco's discomfort probably stemmed from my knowledge of his January visit to Brian Taylor's office. Something had occurred that day—I had known that from Taylor's reaction when I'd re-entered his office. I had not been able to describe what had happened because I did not know. Yet Taylor was no poker player. His expression and manner had screamed something at me. What the hell had it screamed?

Only Silco knew and his hesitancy now yelled it again—whatever the hell it was.

"So," he said.

"So." I glanced around the office. No need to rush.

Across from me, he shifted in his seat. He didn't like this at all.

I pointed to a degree behind him. "You got your medical degree from here?"

"Yes."

"And now you teach here?"

"I'm a research fellow."

"What are you researching?"

"My field is nuclear medicine."

He had told me that once before. "How does that work?" I was genuinely interested. "Sounds like an oxymoron."

"Mr. Austin, I really don't have time to chitchat."

"Guess I'll have to read up on it on the Internet." I gave a wide smile. The small talk had given me pause to think. "I'm planning some vacation time and wanted to know when the golf course will be ready—when you'd like me to give the clinic."

"That's Brian Taylor's domain," he said. He glanced at a clock on the wall, then leaned back in his chair. He exhaled slowly and his shoulders lowered as if tense air had left him. He did everything but sigh and wipe his brow, thrilled that he couldn't answer my question.

"Oh," I said. "What exactly is your role in the Russian deal?"

"Why do you ask?"

"If I'm to be involved, I'd like to know some details."

I knew it wasn't very strong; so did he. He took his glasses out of his pocket and, with his wrists on the desk blotter, leaned forward and unfolded them. Then he sat looking at them, thinking.

"What does that have to do with your clinic?"

"Will you be in attendance?" I said.

"Probably not." He reached past the glasses and shuffled papers.

"How much money does a project like this cost?"

He looked up from the papers. "I don't know the exact figure. I suspect no one will until the project has been completed."

"Makes sense. Are you and the Tour equal partners in it?"

"Mr. Austin, I don't see where you need to know that."

Where you need to know that. His diction seemed perfect now. No hint of an accent. This benefactor probably had as much contact with the former Soviet Union as I did.

"I need to know it here, in this office." I grinned.

He didn't get that.

"How old were you when you moved from Russia?"

"It was the Soviet Union then, in 1989." He leaned back and looked away and slowly crossed his arms. He was thinking again.

"You miss it?"

"That's a complex question. It was—is—my home."

"But, life must be better here."

He didn't answer that right off. He thought some more. Then his head tilted to one side and he looked straight at me. He was trying to gauge, I think, if I was genuinely interested. I was. His initial pause made me wonder how life could have been better there.

"Life was very difficult for us, but we were all together for a time. It is my home."

"*We?*" I said. "Your family?"

His face told me the bubble had burst. There was something there. I had hit a nerve.

"I really need to get to work," he said. "Regarding the golf question, I'm afraid I can't answer it. You'll have to wait until Brian Taylor is better and can help you."

"How did you hear about Brian's accident?"

"How did I hear of it?"

"Yeah," I said. "It hasn't had much television or newspaper coverage."

"I find your tone offensive."

"Just a simple question."

"I called his office to speak with him. They told me he had been injured in an automobile accident."

"What exactly happened?"

"I don't know the details."

I had tried to get him tangled up, but I wasn't an interrogator. I was a golfer who should've been practicing. Instead, I was intellectually sparring with a college professor, which showed me why I'd been a C student.

"How much money are you putting into this deal?"

He shook his head.

"You must know. It's only a question. I can find out myself by asking a Tour official or probably even reading it in a paper."

"No," he said quickly. His voice was sharp and direct, as if stating a fact.

"It's a secret?"

"Confidential."

"How'd you make your money? College professors aren't usually millionaires."

"I don't ask where you get your money."

I shrugged. "I made it on the Tour."

"And how much do you have? Do you like that question?"

"Like I said to you, it's there for everyone to see. According to my career stats, I'm a millionaire, but it costs a hell of a lot to play the Tour."

There was a beat of silence.

"You invent a cure or patent something?"

"You have pried and insulted me. It's time for you to go." He put both hands flat on the desk blotter as if preparing to stand.

"Too bad about Brian's daughter," I said. "Think they'll ever give her back?"

He shifted in his seat and dropped his eyes. He hadn't simply noticed something on his pant leg and focused on it. The reaction was peculiar. However, it lasted only a moment.

Then he stood and went to his door and held it open. "This conversation is over."

I sat looking at his empty chair. His reactions had screamed that same uninterpretable something. This time, it had been yelled more than once. Not knowing exactly what the hell it was made me angry. Was it knowledge? Guilt?

I sat thinking and exhaled slowly. Everything seemed to be spinning out of control: Nash was heading in the wrong direction. My golf game was, too. Instead of practicing, I had come down here to listen to bullshit answers. I had fallen out of the top 125. A baby girl was missing. Her old man probably knew who had taken her. To top it off, I had the feeling that Victor Silco knew much more than he was saying.

I had had enough. I didn't move.

"Mr. Austin, I really must be getting back to work."

I stood and stopped in the doorway across from him. Inside, I felt as if a hot balloon was rising. If it burst, I would lose it.

"I hope Taylor gets his little girl back," I said, staring at him.

He couldn't hold my gaze. He turned away sharply and shut the door in my face.

. . .

"How'd it go?" Perkins said when I got back in the cab.

"Better than some of my undergrad years."

"Oh, shit," he said. "I roomed with you. I know how those went."

I ignored that. "How tough were the cops with him?"

The cab pulled out of the lot and we were heading back to the airport. A 7:15 P.M. American Airlines flight put me back in Hartford at 10:18. We would be cutting it close and I wasn't looking forward to attempting another last-minute arrival at the boarding gate.

I told Perkins all about my cordial chat with Dr. Vic.

"The cops didn't like Silco much," Perkins said. "It's why I wanted to speak to him myself. After Taylor's daughter went missing, a couple uniforms went in and asked some things. They said his answers seemed rehearsed. Miller said he was told that when they asked a question Silco wasn't expecting, Silco stumbled."

"What did he stumble on?"

Perkins smiled. "A tax question."

"IRS guys are bastards," I said. "I asked about his money, too. He didn't like it."

"No one likes talking about that stuff. What did you ask?"

"Where he got his."

"Jesus, Jack. That's tactful."

"Where *did* Silco get his money? Someone must know. Did he invent a cure or discover something and patent it?"

"What I've been told—which isn't much—is that it's family money from Russia. That's all I know."

"There is no money in Russia."

"I'm sure someone over there has money. Just like someone in Mexico has a lot of money."

"Then, is it dirty?"

"If it is, it was probably made a long time ago because Silco doesn't seem dirty—or shouldn't be if he's dealing with the PGA Tour. Then again, the Tour office says Brian Taylor is handling all inquiries about the Russian golf venture himself."

"PGA Tour Charities Office is a big operation," I said. "Someone surely checked out Silco."

"My read on it: only Brian Taylor."

"You report that to Schilling?"

"Not yet. I'm still looking into it all."

The whole thing made me tired. I turned to the window. "He doesn't like talking about his family. Topic made him uncomfortable."

"How so?"

"I don't know. I asked him and he didn't like it. Same thing with Taylor's crash."

"Jesus, did you accuse him of that?"

"Not directly."

"It'll be like talking to a bolted door tomorrow."

"Tomorrow?" I said. "I thought you weren't interviewing him. Isn't that why I'm here?"

"I have to apologize for dragging you down here. While you were in there, I grabbed a course-offerings list. Silco had a night class yesterday from six to nine. He held the damned class, too. I checked."

"Which means he didn't deliver the *deal-is-a-deal* card."

"At least not himself. I'll go feel him out. Anyway, it means I took you away from a practice day. Sorry."

He had caddied for me, occasionally. He knew Wednesdays were practice and Pro Am tourney days. I knew, as my best friend, he was also following my season. He knew where I stood on the money list. His apology was sincere.

"You've done a lot for me," I said. "Don't worry about it."

He shrugged and slid deeper into the seat, leaning his head back. "This Taylor thing is turning into a real hairball, you know?" He shook his head and let out a long breath. "How's your game?"

"Getting better each day."

"Not today."

"Maybe a day off is good, now and then."

"You used to hit off mats in the field house at Maine. In the spring, you'd shovel a patch off the football field to hit balls. A day off isn't what you do."

The cabby pulled to the curb near my gate.

"I'll hit some putts in the hotel hallway tonight," I said. "Don't worry."

He made a fist and held it up. I stood outside the open door and tapped his fist with my own before heading into the airport.

At 10:35 P.M., the elevator doors parted. Nik entered the hallway, walking briskly, moving confidently toward the uniformed police officer, who sat reading *Sports Illustrated* in a plastic chair next to Brian Taylor's hospital room.

His hair had been combed neatly, Nik's outfit chosen specifically—a white lab coat over a pale blue button-down shirt, matching tie, and trousers. His face held no expression. He walked to the door, put a hand on it, and nodded once, a lackadaisical gesture, one that offered an unarticulated confidence and spoke of routine. The greeting, like his outfit, had been carefully planned.

The cop looked up from the magazine, flashed a raised-eyebrow salute, then gazed down again at his reading.

Nik felt his shoulders lower slightly. He wondered if it were a release of tension. Preparation, he had once been told, was the key to preventing anxiety. Being ready at all times. Ready, he was. Even now; he had selected this precise time—the end of one shift, prior to the start of the next—in an attempt to enter when the staff was at a lull. Previously, as he had watched the huge blond man and the cop from television dash from Taylor's room, Nik had taken inventory: the hospital floor consisted of a long rectangular-shaped hallway that outlined the perimeter of the nurses' station. Taylor's room was two doors from the corner of the hall. There was no way for someone at the nurses' station to see Taylor's door. Preparation.

Suddenly the police officer stood up.

Nik froze, his hand still on the doorknob, ready to open it.

"Everything okay, doc?" the cop said. He set the magazine down on the chair.

"Just making rounds," Nik said. He had not turned his body and stood facing the door. He had, however, met the officer's eyes with his own. His gaze was unwavering.

"Last night no one made rounds," the cop said.

"This man was in a bad accident. A precaution."

The cop nodded, satisfied, and walked away, stopping at a water fountain to drink.

Nik entered the room and left the lights off. He moved quietly to Taylor's bedside. Brian Taylor was sleeping soundly when Nik placed a gentle hand on his shoulder.

Nash was gone.

It was after 11 P.M. when I arrived at the hotel. Lisa was up, waiting for me.

"I couldn't find him this afternoon," she said.

She was sitting at the desk in our suite, wearing gray sweatpants and one of my white golf shirts that fit her like a skirt. Her hair was pulled back and held in place with a beaded band designed for the purpose. She had dark rings beneath her eyes. The a/c was running and the air felt cool.

"When you called during the layover," she was saying, "and said you wouldn't make it back in time for even a late dinner, I went to find him again, see if he wanted to eat with me. He never answered his door."

I set my carry-on bag on the desk in front of her. I kissed her forehead. From the onset, this had been my one fear about Nash having his own room. Of course, he couldn't stay with us. That would no doubt make myself, Lisa, and Nash uncomfortable. I wanted to stay with Lisa, not share a room with Nash, so he had gotten his own room. Yet he was a kid, living alone in hotels, where temptations existed. I had figured a kid in his late teens might have a fake I.D. and get caught trying to enter the bar. That had been my worst-case scenario. Naive me. I hadn't planned on anything approaching the Sharon Taylor situation.

"I called his room and left a message. He has not returned my call. I was," she paused momentarily as if the weight of what she was about to say hit her, "waiting for you to go inside his room. After the Hutch Gainer thing, it seems easy to think the worst."

"Sure. That's understandable."

She was as tough as anyone, but had been kidnapped and witnessed the shootings of two men—by me. It's something you never get over; rather, you maneuver around it mentally as best you can. Maybe being the shooter had been easier than what she had gone through. I would never know what had been said to her during the hours before I intervened, would never know how it felt to have her hands bound by a man with lust in his eyes and a gun in his hand. They had not hurt her. Physically.

"Stay here," I said. "I'll get inside his room."

. . .

The hotel manager gave less hassle than I expected. Maybe he could tell I was in no mood for debate. I had planned to work on my putting in the hallway. The speed, of course, of the carpet would not be nearly as fast as the greens I was to face the next morning, but I could work on the rhythm of my stroke. Those plans were now nixed. I was worried about my game and, moreover, feeling extremely guilty. Had my actions on the drive to the airport pushed Nash away?

There were two ways the situation could go: I could simply fire him and not have to deal with the distraction. Yet he was more than a caddy now. He was a kid I wanted to see succeed, which was probably why I'd lost my temper in the first place.

Or I could find him and address the situation.

"What's it like playing golf for a living?" the manager said. We were in the elevator, going up to Nash's room.

"Best job in the world."

"That's what I thought."

He was maybe twenty-five, small, with an athletic build like a flyweight boxer. He was balding and looked remarkably awake at almost midnight.

"You hear people talk about the pressure. But seeing the golfers around here"—he made an inclusive motion with his hand, indicating the hotel—"no one looks stressed."

"I enjoy every day of it. You never know how long your career will last." I had, in fact, made that statement many times before. This time, however, my mind flashed to my place on the money list. My own clichéd response hit me like a fist.

We got off the elevator. At Nash's door, the manager knocked three times. He looked at me. I nodded and he slid the key in and opened it.

We stood in the dark, momentarily. The air felt cold against my bare forearms, as if the air-conditioning had been cranked up and left on. I felt for the wall switch and snapped on the light. The room looked unused: The bed was made, the bathroom was organized—no soap had been unwrapped; the plastic cups were still in wrappers. It was as if Nash had never been there.

"When do the maids come in?"

"Between ten A.M. and two P.M."

We walked around the room slowly. It wasn't a suite. The examination took only a minute. Nothing about the room told me where Nash was. All his belongings were gone. He had only one suitcase and the clubs I'd gotten him. Someone could've packed it all for him, although it looked as if he'd left under his own accord.

I stood alone in the hall after the manager locked the door and returned to the lobby. I replayed the car ride to the airport in my mind several times. I had lost my temper and, apparently, Nash had fled, although he had said nothing to indicate he might leave.

As I started back to my room, where Lisa would be waiting, I felt like a child molester. Had I run the kid off?

. . .

"I had an idea while you were down there," Lisa said, as soon as I opened the door. "And I was right. There was a note for you at the front desk. Someone is bringing it up."

The note was in a sealed envelope. It was addressed to me, by name only. JACK AUSTIN had been script across the front in large block letters in black ink. The note was on a piece of hotel stationary. It was from Nash:

Deer Jack,

Thanks for what youve done for me. I really let you down and thought it would better if I went. So I am. Tell Lisa thanks to. You both our nice.

Nash

I read it aloud, then handed it to Lisa. Her eyes fixated, she stood and walked to the sofa, where she sat on the armrest, still staring at the paper. The silence in the room was nearly tangible. I went to the sliding-glass doors that opened onto a cement veranda, and used the cord to pull open the drapes. The glass was dark in the light's reflection. I walked out into the night's brisk air and stood, leaning against the iron rail, looking out at the parking lot, thinking.

I heard Lisa's footsteps. Then she was beside me.

"He's obviously dyslexic," she said. "My God, he speaks so well."

I looked at her.

"All right. No small talk. Where do you think he went?"

"I don't know. Home? If he even has a home to go to." I turned around and leaned my hips against the rail. My arms were folded; my feet were crossed at the ankles. I was staring at the cement floor.

"I blew this," I said. "Big time."

"What are you talking about, Jack? You got mad at him, as you would your own son or even a good friend. That's not blowing it. That's trying to help."

"I am responsible for a teenage kid this summer and I don't even know where the hell he is," I said. "Joan Lerman is supposed to e-mail Nash's home address. He lives with a coach—a guy who got him into the Horizons School—named Halle Basker."

I went back inside, found the laptop the Tour provided and logged on. The address was there. Lisa was sitting next to me on the sofa. The computer was on the coffee table before us.

"Why don't you go to bed?" I said. "You've got to work tomorrow."

The realization came slowly to her. "You're withdrawing from the tournament?"

"Of course," I said.

"I know this is important, but can't you call this Halle man?"

"And ask him to solve my problem?" I shook my head.

She didn't say anything for a long pause, then wet her lips, thinking through what she was to say. I knew it would be something heavy.

"Why don't I go look for Nash?" she said.

"You?"

"Jack, you're on the verge of losing your card."

I said nothing.

"You could wind up on the Nationwide Tour. Your Tour card means everything—our life together." The words had come in a rush. We both leaned back and contemplated them.

I shook my head. "I'm withdrawing. I've got to find Nash and set this right."

I went to the desk, opened the phone book, dialed the airport, and had Nash paged. Then I dialed U.S. Airways. I asked if Nash Henley was a passenger on any flights. They told me I couldn't obtain that information and said the policy was industry-wide. If he was at the airport, Nash never answered the page.

He figured Brian Taylor would try to yell, so Nik had covered Taylor's mouth when he leaned over him and whispered "A deal is a deal" into Taylor's ear. The reaction illustrated in Taylor's eyes—they squinted opened, followed by a flutter, then burst wide, as if the eyes were attempting to leap from the sockets—had been nearly gratifying to Nik. After all, Taylor had *his* money. However, unlike the money, at this moment the power *had* changed hands.

Nik was in control. He knew Taylor was fully aware of that the moment Taylor felt the knife blade's cool edge resting upon his throat.

Nik whispered the four words again.

"You're not Victor," Taylor said, muffled beneath Nik's hand.

"No."

"Who?"

"No need for that."

Taylor did not respond and Nik knew he was considering. There wasn't time for contemplation.

"I have Catherine," Nik said.

He felt Taylor's body stiffen, then surge up. Nik leaned on Taylor and pushed his hand firmly over his mouth. Carefully, he pushed the knife against Taylor's throat.

"Not a fucking word, Brian. Yes, I have her. She is fine. When the money is in the account, she will be returned."

He felt Taylor's mouth move under his hand, an attempt to speak. Taylor's saliva mixed with perspiration from his lip. Nik's palm was wet. He let Taylor talk.

"How do I know she's fine?"

"Because I'm telling you she is. She is only a means to the money."

"Did Victor send you?"

"I'm here to work out the rest of the deal. Why is the transfer late?"

"People are watching," Taylor said. "Cops, a private cop, even a golfer. It's a lot of money. It's hidden, but to move it will take time—"

"No." Nik had said it even before Taylor finished. He was shaking his head. He felt his hand pressing the knife against Taylor's flesh. The move hadn't been conscious, yet a trickle of blood appeared. Taylor flinched and closed his eyes. It made Nik smile. Was Taylor preparing for the end?

The knife handle was slick in Nik's sweating palm.

"No," he said again. His voice was suddenly gentle. "No. You will transfer the money now or Catherine . . ."

He pressed the knife against Taylor's throat again. This time the effort was conscious. Then he straightened, slid the knife inside the lab coat, and looked at Taylor for a long second before walking out.

. . .

Katrina sat staring out the window of the El Paso apartment. The heat rose from the pavement crystalline and shimmering. Five years previous, she had arrived in this country hoping for much more than she found. She was nineteen, mother to four. They were currently with her aunt, who had been the first in her family to leave Russia.

Katrina could still remember her aunt's letters from the United States. They would arrive and Katrina and her mother and sister would gather around to hear of the joys of her aunt's new life, to hear what America offered. The letters spoke of wonderful people, both helpful and kind; of gourmet foods and specialty shops, grocery stores with dozens of breads; of Miami's weather; of cars fast and new, cars people could buy and pay for over several years. Also, the letters spoke of work, attractive jobs where one could get ahead.

Katrina's mother had urged her daughters to join their aunt in the United States.

Katrina had gone. Her sister and mother remained behind, afraid to leave. Katrina had sought a change, a new life, a chance. More than anything, *that* was what she had sought—a chance at a better life.

Now, as she rocked the baby and thought of Oleg, sitting behind her as he stared blankly at the television, she wondered if she had ever really *had* a chance.

The information provided in those letters had not described what she found. Yet her aunt had never admitted the lies. Even to this day, Katrina thought, she would not confess they had been lies. To the contrary, she told Katrina that she had suddenly fallen on hard times. However, the first night Katrina was in the United States a thin black man named Jerome appeared at her aunt's apartment door, his eyes appraising Katrina like a window shopper. Later Jerome reappeared at the dirty, barren apartment, this time with a fat balding man with foul-smelling breath. Katrina knew he was drunk.

Even now, rocking the baby, she could recall her aunt sobbing and rambling uncontrollably that night, her voice pleading, accidentally leaping back and forth from Russian to English. The sobs and hysterics had not mattered. Katrina, then fifteen, had spent her first night in America on her back, beneath a fat man who sweated profusely, and said over and over, "Say you like it."

The words were like thunder claps that had never ended.

Afterward, Jerome had given her $20. She had taken it and sat slumped in a corner of the apartment, crying. She had cried until her aunt had returned, dressed in clothing unlike anything Katrina had seen before but in clothing to which she herself was now accustomed.

Katrina was ashamed of how she had lived, of what her mother and sister would have thought. During the past several days, she had spent much time in this seat, rocking the baby, watching the heat-baked pavement—and thinking. She had nothing to say to Oleg. Surprisingly, he had said nothing to her, apparently caught up in Nikoli's orders, as if hoping for future employment, she thought. So she had sat with the baby, listening to its hoarse breathing, and evaluating her past and present. America *had* been a chance at a new life. She blamed herself for not grasping it with both hands.

For two of the last four years, she had lived from high to high. It had started with drink, then painkillers a john had offered, then heroin. Then more heroin. It had taken waking in a hospital room, her mind focusing on its first startlingly clear image—her mother—for Katrina to kick heroin. She had not kept in touch and didn't know if her mother was even alive but the imagined vision of that woman, who had such high hopes for her, was a wall Katrina had hit head-on. Katrina knew she was not the woman her mother had been, not the mother to her own children that woman had been to her. In fact, little by little, her income had been at first absorbed by the heroin, then, finally, her prostituting had been in return for heroin only. At that point, she had no longer even provided for her children, a task her own mother had been willing to go to any means to accomplish.

All of that, however, ended two years ago. Now there was no heroin. There was the same work, but she had left Jerome, set up a new clientele, even moved to another neighborhood and had her aunt helping care for her children. The apartment wasn't much better. Yet she worked out of a motel room and, more importantly, was no longer working for anyone. She worked for herself now. For her children.

Then Nikoli had appeared and asked her to take a trip. He had offered what she might make in two months. She knew of him. He had succeeded. She had jumped at the chance to go with him, to be with him. In that regard, she knew she was similar to Oleg.

Now she was holding a baby, a sick baby who needs care, she thought. She, too, was a mother. Nikoli had taken the baby. She did not know from whom or why. She knew only that he had taken the girl from her mother, that somewhere a mother was looking for her baby. Katrina knew also that the baby was sick. She looked down at the four-month-old blonde. The child's breath was warm against her stomach.

"Oleg," she said.

The man on the couch did not move.

She stood and walked closer to him. He was asleep.

Katrina inhaled deeply and let the air out slowly. She moved to the door, unlocked it carefully, the deadbolt making a light *click,* then she went out into the hundred-degree heat and shut the door behind her.

I felt bad waking him, but Tim Silver was a longtime friend and former caddy. He had studied his way out from a starting place similar to where Nash had begun, the place where Nash may well have returned. Silver was holed-up in Plainville, Massachusetts, a town near Foxboro, where the Patriots play, working on his book about life on the Tour.

"Openly gay" didn't fully describe him. He was, however, tougher than most expected. It always fascinated me how he could, with Lisa, for instance, discuss women's shoes and how stylishly she dressed, even make cracks about my butt; then, as if pulling a switch, sit at the end of a bar next to Perkins and not look out of place. More than anything, though, aside from Perkins, he was my most trusted friend.

He picked up on the sixth ring. "What the fuck do you want, cutie? It's almost two A.M. You drunk?"

"Not hardly. How's the book coming?"

"You woke me for that?"

"No."

"Book's going good. I'm writing the chapter about how all you cute khaki-wearing golfers are in love with me."

"Funny, I don't remember much of that during your caddying career."

"Still in denial. How's Lisa?"

"Fine."

"How about Perkins? Guy has biceps to die for."

"He's still married."

"Aren't they all . . . ?" His voice trailed off, as if he were thinking longingly of Perkins and his arms.

"Want to go to Roxbury tomorrow?"

"That's an hour away. What for?"

"I need to go. I've never been and I hear it's tough."

"You saying you need a black guy to get you around?"

"No. I need someone I can trust who knows the area, but, since you mentioned it, you being black probably won't hurt, unless you blow it by hitting on someone."

"I'm always hitting on someone, Jack."

"Ever hear of sexual harassment suits?"

"I'm a flatterer," he said. "Can't help it. Tell me what's going on."

I did. It took half an hour.

When I was finished, Silver paused, then said, "A good caddy doesn't cause distractions, Jack. Look how Tiger fired Fluff."

I was getting sick of hearing those comments. The golfer-caddy relationship had long been a peculiar one. Wives caddied for husbands; kids caddied for their Tour dads.

"For Christ's sake, Tim," I said. "Ryne Sandberg, the Cubs's second baseman, retired and has caddied for a buddy who played the Tour."

"I know," he said. "You're the one hitting the shots. Nash is a good kid, too—asked a lot of questions when he followed us for two weeks."

"He's a *kid* and he's disappeared back into a place his school told me he might not make it out of."

He sighed. "You need me, whitebread."

"I know. I owe you for this."

"A dance in the bar of my choice. Preferably one where men can hold hands and order a sloe gin fizz."

"I don't owe you that much," I said.

. . .

Thursday morning, Lisa was up before me. That wasn't new. She usually ran at 5:15 A.M. each day. Today she didn't look ready to run. Didn't sound ready either. In fact, she was on her hands and knees vomiting into the toilet. That *was* new. She was never sick.

I knelt beside her and rubbed her back.

"Jesus," I said, "I feel awful leaving you."

She pulled some toilet paper off the roll and wiped her chin. "I need a day alone to rest anyway. I'm going to call in sick."

"Never seen you do that." I shook my head.

"Never felt like this in my life. Must be lingering from the night I had food poisoning."

"It's a bug. Better kick it now or you'll have it all summer."

"Get going, Jack. Take a shower. I'm fine."

I took a quick shower while Lisa called CBS brass to tell someone she wouldn't be able to host the opening round of the Greater Hartford Open. The TV analysis team featured Lisa, a cohost in the tower above the eighteenth green, and three on-course commentators. Someone would be given the chance to cohost the telecast in her absence. That told me she was really sick. It was equivalent to an injured baseball player letting someone play his position for a game. What if the backup hit two homers? She had never called in sick before—and I'd known there had been days when she had not felt well.

I watched her carefully as I dressed. She had returned to bed.

"Take a light jacket," she said. "It's supposed to be cool."

"I'll bring one," I said.

"You think Nash flew home?"

"That would be my guess."

"He loved flying," she said. "He told me he'd like to take flying lessons some day."

"And he'd have a hell of a time trying to rent a car. He's not twenty-one."

Her eyes were dark. Her voice had sounded weak. "Why don't you go see a doctor, Lisa?"

"I'm going to," she said.

. . .

It was sunny when I left Connecticut. The two-hour drive to Plainville was fairly easy. My mind, however, was still racing. I should have been playing the Greater Hartford Open. By no means was I in a comfortable position on the money list. In fact, the last time I had been outside the top 125, I'd been forced to play the final six events and make an eight-footer on the seventy-second hole of the final tourney to slip into the hundred and twenty-fifth spot, thus retaining my card. The experience had left me physically exhausted: rising each day at the crack of dawn to fine-tune my swing and stroke, playing eighteen holes and working hard to focus on a single shot at a time, working, grinding to stay in the present, then, finally, sleeping—doing that for six consecutive weeks, all the while hoping my game would ignite. It did not, so I'd been forced to stand over that eight-foot bender and make the stroke of my life. As tired physically as I had been when it was over, the emotional stress left me completely spent. Afterward, I did nothing for a month. The stress-induced exhaustion had also given me a bad aftertaste following that season. All in all, it had been an experience I vowed never to relive. Now I was getting close and that weighed heavily on my mind.

I was listening to a sports talk-radio show. The local PGA Tour event had them chatting golf. The discussion focused on whether or not Phil Mickelson would win the next major. A caller pointed to Ernie Els, having won two U.S. Opens and a British already; thus, he could beat Tiger, head-to-head. My name wasn't mentioned in the same breath as those other players. In fact, it wasn't mentioned at all. I turned off the radio.

My plan for the day was simple: Grab Silver, then find Halle Basker. From what Joan Lerman said, Halle was a good bet to have heard from Nash, or maybe to hear from him in the near future. Maybe Nash wasn't in Boston at all. Maybe he and Sharon Taylor had run off. Judging from the note he had left, I didn't think so. I thought he would either return to Boston or go back to the Horizons School. Doubtless, Joan Lerman would find out and let me know if he showed up there.

Silver was waiting outside his duplex in Plainville. He was obviously still punctual—a prerequisite for any caddy. He was built like a gymnast, about five-foot-nine. He had a shaved copper-colored head and a goatee. He stood, a foam Dunkin' Donuts cup in hand, wearing a white silk shirt with a black leather string tie that had silver tips and a silver emblem where the knot should have been. He wore black jeans and black leather cowboy boots.

I got out of the Buick and shook my head slowly, appraising the garb. "Want me to call you Butch?"

"Butch?"

"Butch Cassidy."

He grinned and shook my hand. "Like I said, as payment, you're the Sun*dance* Kid."

"With a sloe gin fizz," I said. "Nice one. I walked into that."

"So your game has gone to hell without my caddying." He moved to the driver's door. "I bought two coffees, but you're late. I drank the first already. Now I'm into the second."

"Thought you guys like espresso or latte," I said.

He ignored that and shook his head sadly. "You made the mistake of thinking I was replaceable."

"You quit," I said, and grinned. "Remember? Said you wanted to write your tell-all book. Besides, listening to which players you thought were cute didn't do a hell of a lot for my concentration."

"I've been in Mass. all summer. Give me the address and let me drive."

I tossed the keys to him. It was midmorning. The sun was still shining. It was eighty-five and muggy. A bead of perspiration rolled down my back, although when you play Memphis in June every year, no place seems all that humid.

Silver got in, put on a jazz radio station, and adjusted the air conditioner.

"In all seriousness," he said, "what is going on with your game? Nash followed me for two weeks. He saw the best in action."

"Yeah," I said. "He has seen the best: Stump Jones has taken him under his wing."

The trip from Plainville to Roxbury would take almost an hour. We took Route 1 to 95 North.

"Just not playing well," I said.

"I know that much from reading the scores in the paper. What's the problem?"

"Mediocre in all areas right now."

"Nash a good caddy?"

"Yes and no. Before this summer, he'd never played golf."

"Never played golf before?" he said. "He never told me that."

I nodded. "He caddied at a country club. He works hard and, on the course, he says all the right things. More than anything, it's like you said: He's not the one hitting the shots."

"Jack, I know about the letter he sent you, but why'd you let him on the bag in the first place?"

We were on 128 South now. His tone expressed sincere curiosity. I felt we were heading toward a conversation that would make his book. The difference between the two journalists I knew best, Silver and Lisa, had always fascinated me. Where Lisa wanted the facts to report before anyone else, Silver wanted the facts to trace back and see *why* something happened. Immediacy was not what interested him; cause, however, was.

"A lot of people ask why," I said. "Kid reminds me a lot of myself."

Silver pondered that for a few seconds. Finally, he turned from the road to me. "What the hell are you talking about? He's a kid from the hood. You're a preppy golfer from Maine. This is your career, Jack."

I sighed. I had been tired of it last night. Lisa had even mentioned the Nationwide Tour. I not only needed to play, I needed to do well. I knew that better than anyone. Nash had come on strong after the penalty. He had gotten the pin sheet and done well with yardage, too. He was trying, but this trip wasn't about me looking for my caddy. This was about me finding the kid I was responsible for. If he wanted to stay, that was up to him. I wanted to find him and see—as he had mentioned in the note—*how* he had let me down, and be certain he was okay.

"More to it than meets the eye," I said.

"Apparently."

We took Route 3 and 93 North. If you've never driven in and around Boston, one quote from a golfer during the Bank of

Boston years ago says it all: Asked about his round, his comments fell along the lines of: "I'm just glad I didn't get killed on the way from the hotel this morning."

We were doing nearly seventy-five to keep up with traffic.

"The prep school Nash went to is for kids with learning disabilities," I said. "I've got dyslexia."

"Still?"

"You don't outgrow it, and there's no cure."

"That's why you add your score with the calculator." It wasn't a question. He was putting it together.

"Yeah. I can do the math. Though, when my paycheck depends on it . . ."

"Which brings us back to my original question. This is a big risk. Why take it?"

"As a kid," I said, "I had a really tough time in school. This kid is obviously in the same boat."

"That's it?"

"When I was eight years old, we used to read aloud in class," I said. "I couldn't do it. It was something I can't really describe, some problem going eyes to brain to mouth. I could read—hell, I'm still a slow reader—but it was reading aloud that I had real trouble with." I shrugged and made a dismissive gesture with my hand.

Silver had glanced back and forth from the road to me as I spoke. I had said something he'd not heard before. I had mentioned being dyslexic and Nash having it, too, but nothing this personal.

"I used to try to count and match the paragraphs with the kids ahead of me and see which one I'd have to read," I said. "No matter how hard I tried to memorize my section, I'd still stumble."

"Humiliating."

Again, it wasn't a question. We were quiet for a while, listening to Miles Davis.

Then Silver said: "This explains the poetry. I used to ask why you read it, and you never really answered. Reading poetry is a fuck-you-all thing, an I-can-do-it thing, isn't it?"

I didn't answer.

"Why haven't I ever heard this stuff before, Jack? We've been friends a long time."

"No reason to talk about it before."

He looked back and forth, from me to the road, several times, his eyes narrow. Then, staring straight ahead, he nodded to himself. "Probably a lot of that shit stuck with you."

Everyone has bad childhood memories. Mine were no worse than others'.

"On the course, what's going on?"

I told him about the penalty.

Silver took Exit 18, Massachusetts Avenue.

"Otherwise," I said, "he's done fine. Goes over the pin sheet, does yardage, and does the little things—compliments me a lot. I know, as pros, we shouldn't need it."

"We all know you guys do," Silver said.

"Nash has had a lot of similar experiences," I said, simply.

Silver nodded.

In fact, Nash had not gone into the specifics of how his affliction had manifest itself. His remarks, however, told me the results of those unarticulated tribulations had obviously been similar to my own.

"Okay," he said. "I see what's going on. You can relate to this kid, but you gave him a shot and he quit. Why are we chasing him? You planning to adopt?"

"Kid needs help," I said.

"So does your golf game. My question stands."

"I might have driven him away," I said. "No, I did drive him away."

"You haven't changed, although I never thought you would. You tried to help. It didn't work out. You can't let it go at that."

"Kid's note read as if he failed me," I said. "Maybe it's the other way around."

"I can see why the kid wouldn't want to work for you." His eyes brightened and he grinned. "You're a pain in the ass to caddy for. That goddamned counting on the practice green—one . . . two . . . three . . ." He broke into a laugh.

We listened to John Coltrane for a while. You can take Mass. Ave. to the Harvard Bridge and visit Cambridge, see Harvard, take in the Boston Symphony. Or you can turn onto Huntington Avenue, go past Northeastern University, and enter Roxbury, which is what we did. Silver turned down the radio and concentrated on his driving.

He zigzagged from side street to side street until we pulled to the curb near a faded two-story clapboard house. The street was narrow and lined with cars of various years and makes. The sidewalk was cracked. A nearby storefront window was broken. Three kids, wearing Yankees caps over what looked like black pantyhose on their heads, leaned on a wall near the car. One wore an Atlanta Falcons jersey, half tucked in. The other two wore hooded sweatshirts. All three wore jeans with the crotch at their knees.

Silver eyed them, then said, "Most people would say to hell with this kid, but you're still doing things your fucked-up way. Let's go."

. . .

The apartment door opened until the short chain caught. Through the crack, Halle Basker looked like a football coach. He also looked like he could easily take the biggest guy on his team. Where Perkins was muscular, Halle was just plain big. His expression was acrimonious. His skin was a deeper hue than that of Nash or Silver. His face had liver spots and his neck was speckled with tiny brown warts. His fleshy arms protruded from a white T-shirt, pulling the fabric taut. The shirt's collar was dark with a sweat ring and his armpits were yellowed with dried perspiration. He wore faded dungarees and was built like a beer keg on stilts; maybe six-foot-three, closer to 300 pounds than 250.

"Yeah?" he said.

I told him who I was and that I was looking for Nash Henley. His eyes went to Silver.

"Who's this?" he said. "You a cop?"

Silver was dressed like the Lone Ranger; however, maybe Halle thought because he was there with a white guy he had to be a cop.

"No, man," Silver said. His voice had taken on a dialect I'd not heard him use. "No five-oh here. Just helping a friend."

"So you the golfer," Halle said to me. "You the one bought Nash the fancy clubs, huh?"

I nodded. Halle's voice was full of mockery. He didn't like me. Yet he knew of the clubs. He obviously had heard of them from Nash, maybe even seen them himself. The question was: How long ago? I also wondered what Nash had told him that made him so antagonistic. Maybe nothing. Maybe this was a race thing. Maybe it was a money thing. I didn't much care. I was there to see Nash.

"You look more like a football player," Halle said. "So what you want?"

I had told him already, but said, "Where is Nash?"

"What, you go and lose him, did you?"

"Yes."

He grinned. Joan Lerman had described Halle very differently than I would, given this meeting. In fact, the more he grinned and mocked me, the more I felt the urge to let my right fist help him overcome that tendency.

"You the great white hope, going to show Nash how he can live. Now you looking for him." He shook his head side to side and chuckled. "I told him golf's a white man's game. No place for a tailback. Told him he ought to be at Clemson getting ready for practice."

"He's not going to Clemson," I said. "He's going to Curry College, here in Mass."

"The hell you talking 'bout?"

I shrugged. "That's where he's going to college."

Halle looked at Silver, who raised both hands palms up, then back at me.

I nodded, sadly. It was my turn to mock.

"How about you let us in and I tell you what I know?" I said.

He closed the door. I heard the chain release. Then the door opened. Over Halle's huge, sloping shoulders, the apartment was dully lit. It smelled of bacon. All that I had admired in Nash—pride, obvious work ethic—was lacking in what the place showed about its owner. It was not the poverty I'd noticed outside. I had grown up working-class, understanding poverty to be only a few short steps away. Given that proximity, I'd always had empathy for the poor. This was different. The apartment was disheveled, filthy.

A worn carpet that had begun life, maybe a decade earlier, white, was stained and tattered. We moved down a short, dark corridor, past a closet, its sliding door broken and leaning against the wall. The kitchen was to our right, the linoleum floor was torn in several places, the sink stacked six dishes high with food stuck to them. Silver and I continued down a short hallway to the living room, which also had carpet that, at one time, had apparently been white but now was a dirt-stained tan. Likewise, the walls were tinged with yellow as if Halle or the previous tenant had chain-smoked.

Halle pointed to a sofa. I sat on a soiled cushion. Silver bent and wiped cigarette ashes off the cushion before settling his western attire into place. Halle remained standing. The clubs I had gotten Nash leaned against the wall.

"Why ain't he going to Clemson? What, you got him playing *golf* now?" He nodded at the clubs.

"He didn't get in," I said. "Curry College is a good place. The people at Horizons helped him with that choice."

"What kind of football team they got there?"

"I don't know."

"They ain't Division One."

"No," I said. "Three, I think."

"Three?" Halle began pacing. "Three? What, you crazy? Nash is D-One material. Kid always been. Then the NFL. I seen that in him since he playing Pop Warner. Why I sent him to Horizons. Scouts from Boston College, from the other Big East schools, going to prep games now. B.C. coach said for Nash to get the SAT score up. I told him to do that. Didn't he do it? He ain't smart, but I told him he don't have to be."

"He is smart," I said. We were talking about Nash. Halle, though, used *I* a hell of a lot. "And he'll get a good education at Curry. If he's good enough, he'll get noticed. If not, he'll graduate with a real degree."

"'*Real degree.*' Shit. He go off for one summer and get messed up in golf. Now he going to a preppy college, listening to preppy golfers."

The sofa was beneath a window. The glass hadn't been cleaned recently, but sunlight fought its way through, splashing onto the floor before us.

"Why don't you care if the kid gets an education?" Silver said.

Halle looked surprised that Silver had spoken. "What side you on?"

"No side. Just a question, man. Why don't you care?"

I noticed his dialect thickened again as if he turned it on and off as deemed necessary.

"Kid needs an education," Silver said.

"Hey," Halle said, "don't come in here like a Tom telling me what the boy needs. I been his agent. . ."

He paused and looked at me. He knew I'd caught the slip. He tried to recover.

". . . his friend. I been looking out for him a long time. . . ." He paused again to regroup, shifting from one foot to the other. Then he plunged his hands in his pockets. "Since he fourteen."

"Like Don King looks out for Mike Tyson," I said.

Halle looked at me. I don't think he got it.

Meanwhile, Silver had stood up, moved directly in front of Halle, and was motionless, arms at his sides, fists clenched, looking up at him.

"No one calls me a Tom," Silver said.

The situation was getting out of hand. That was bad for two reasons: Silver was out-weighed by maybe a hundred pounds; and, I wanted to get to the bottom of Halle's "agent" slip, which seemed to clash with the fatheresque picture Joan Lerman had offered.

I yelled, "Hey." Both men looked at me. "Silver, sit down. Halle, why did you send Nash to Horizons? You his agent? His guardian? Both? What's your interest in him?"

Silver came back to the couch. He and Halle glared at each other for a long time.

Halle sensed I was accusing him of not considering Nash's best interests.

"His coach," he said.

"And he lives with you," I said.

"Kid got to live somewhere."

"But you don't send every kid on your team to prep school."

"Nash ain't every kid."

"He's a special player?"

"Yeah. Strong, fast, can spot the holes, keeps his feet moving. You can't teach them to keep their feet going. A natural. But having him here killed my social life."

"I'm sure," I said. "B.C. coach wanted his SATs up so he could recruit him?"

Halle nodded.

"And you, being his agent, sent him to Horizons hoping he'd raise those SAT scores."

"Not his official agent yet," he said.

"Now that you find out he didn't raise them, you are concerned—only because your cut of his NFL career might be in jeopardy, if Nash isn't playing on television every Saturday for the next four years."

"Bullshit," he said. "I care 'bout that kid."

"Sounds like you care about your social life and Nash's NFL career," I said. "Tell me where he is."

"Don't know."

"Did you see him today?"

He looked out the window above us, folding his huge dark arms across his torso, tilted his head, thinking.

I waited.

"He's obviously been here," Silver said, "unless you've taken up golf."

Halle looked at him, a glance that told me that if I left the two of them alone for ten minutes, Halle would rip Silver's limbs off.

"When did he get here?" I said.

"Late last night. Left this morning. Didn't say where he's going."

"And you didn't ask," I said. "What did he say?"

"I asked if he been doing the Clemson off-season workouts. That punk looked me in the face and say he been. All I done for him and he stand there and lies to my face."

"He's got no one," I said. "Probably just realized he'd never even had you."

Halle looked at me. I motioned to Silver. We left the apartment and Halle staring after us.

. . .

The smart play seemed to be to wait. Nash left his clubs at Halle's. It was a safe bet he had left his other things there, too. After all, that was his "home." So, parked curbside, farther down the street, we sat and waited near the open gate of the chain-linked fence that ran the length of an apartment building. The fence separated the building from the sidewalk. Its gate hung open, slanted, connected to the fence by a single hinge. A cracked and faded tar walkway led to the apartment complex, which now lay sprawled before us, its sun-splashed windows lined with black wrought-iron bars. On the dirt grounds between the fence and complex, a teenaged girl held the hand of small child and looked at Silver and me apprehensively. Momentarily, she was joined by a guy her age wearing a checkered red flannel shirt, unbuttoned, over a gray T-shirt. He wore a bandanna on his head. She said something. He glanced at us.

"You live in tough neighborhoods," Silver said, "you become very careful. He's probably her boyfriend. That baby may be the only thing either of them has."

"How'd you get out?" I said.

He turned away, looking through the windshield. "My mother." He said it simply, a statement of fact. Then he repeated it: "My mother."

The engine idled. We had on the air conditioner. I sat on the passenger's side. Silver was quiet behind the steering wheel, listening to R and B now. I imagined twelve-year-old Nash impressing Halle with his athletic prowess, mistaking the coach's praise for support and concern, and eventually moving in with the coach at age fourteen. I was no psychologist but I guessed he would have sought that much-needed paternal bond—which his life had certainly come to lack—somewhere. As if on cue, Halle had appeared. Thus, Nash had turned to him, needing a parent. Now Halle informed me that his all-mighty "social life" had suffered. Pity the invasion of his privacy. Yet he wanted Nash to raise those SAT scores so the kid could play big-time college football—then the coach/agent/mistaken father figure could cash in on NFL dollars. Given the last four years of Nash's life, the kid turned out pretty damn good.

Our wait didn't last long. Nash appeared maybe a hundred yards down the sidewalk with three other boys about his age. He was dressed in a white warm-up jacket that read HORIZONS FOOTBALL, maroon sweatpants, and Nikes. The other kids wore jeans—crotches to their knees—and various sports jerseys. One had an Atlanta Falcons shirt with Michael Vick's number seven; another wore a Dallas Cowboy shirt; the third a Chicago Bulls jersey, number ninety-one, a tribute to Dennis Rodman. The kid in the Cowboys shirt had a black hat on sideways.

"There's Nash," I said.

Silver nodded. "Those others look like gangbangers. He in a gang?"

"I don't think so. I don't know all that much about his past. Sort of piecing it together as I go."

"The story of your life," Silver said.

It was nearly 1 P.M. The sun was high and distant above us. Nash was squinting into the sunlight. He paused slightly when he saw the car. In retrospect, I believe he never thought I'd come for him. In any case, he kept walking. When he could see us through the windshield clearly, he paused. Our eyes met. I opened the door and got out. Silver cut the engine and followed.

"Nash," I said.

"What're you doing here?"

His three buddies stopped near him, looking antsy. They also looked tense and ready for just about anything.

"I want to talk," I said. "That's all."

"You get my note?"

"Yeah. That's why I want to talk."

Nash nodded to Silver. Silver said, "Hey, Nash."

The kid in the Falcons jersey said, "Nash, who this guy? Want us to move on him?"

Nash's reply was slow in coming. Across the hood of the car, Silver shifted his weight from one foot to the other.

Nash shook his head. "I got to talk to this guy. I'll meet you later."

The three friends departed and Silver sat in the car, the engine idling again.

"I'd like you to come back," I said.

Obviously, Halle was no caretaker, but the decision was Nash's. If he returned, there was a lot I needed to discuss, like Sharon Taylor, what was going on between them, and what Pete Taylor knew. Yet I feared if I moved too fast, he'd flee. I wanted to help, so I let only those words hang.

Nash left them there, dangling between us for a few moments. He turned away from me and looked at the apartment house, his eyes rising slowly to the second floor—the floor on which Silver and I had met Halle.

"Thought you had the tournament today."

"I withdrew."

He turned back to me. "Why? We were—you were—close to that cut off, that one twenty-five."

When I didn't say anything, his face told me he knew why I had come.

He glanced at the car and Silver, then to the apartment house, then down the street. A guy sat leaning against an abandoned building, drinking from a paper sack. A breeze blew a paper bag across the pavement.

Nash looked down for a long time. "You withdrew to get me?"

"Yeah," I said.

"I never slept with her, you know?" He was still looking down. When his eyes rose slowly and met mine, he held out his hand.

I took it and shook firmly.

Something moved in my stomach. It felt like the release of a long-clenched fist.

I exhaled.

"So that was what Nash told you?" Lisa said.

I had just recalled the highlights of my conversation with Nash to Lisa. Nash and I had dropped Silver off and returned to Connecticut.

"The drive took two hours. He told me everything."

"And that's everything?"

"I have no reason to think he'd lie. He wouldn't have returned if he was having an affair."

"No, it wouldn't make sense for him to come back. Besides, I don't think Nash would lie to us."

"He's not the type," I said. "In the parking lot, when I'd seen him with Sharon and I questioned him, he got mad, said it was none of my business, but he never denied anything."

I was leaning back in the sofa in our suite. She lay across me, her shoulders in my lap, head resting on the armrest. In front of us, an empty pizza box was open on the coffee table, three empty Pepsi cans beside it. Nash had left for his room a half-hour earlier. During our low-key dinner, Lisa had merely kissed his cheek and welcomed him back. Otherwise, she made no mention of his leaving.

"Nash told me Sharon came to his room one night, saying she wanted to talk," I said. "He says he knows it was stupid but admitted he let her in."

"It would be easy for a kid to be—to be seduced by Sharon Taylor."

"He told me she kissed him but he stopped things. Yesterday, when I heard the conversation in the parking lot—"

"The meet-at-four-thirty conversation?"

"Yeah. Nash said that meeting never materialized. Said he took off before it."

"So, what do we do about Sharon Taylor?"

"Not a lot we can do. Let it go, unless she approaches him again."

"If she approaches him again," Lisa said, "I'll deal with her myself."

"Sounds like a maternal instinct."

"Don't patronize me. It's sick. She's married and he's a kid."

We were quiet for a while. I clicked on the television. The hotel offered the Golf Channel and Lee Westwood continued his climb back after dethroning Colin Montgomerie as Europe's top player, then falling from grace. Westwood was leading the Volvo PGA Championship, with Monty three shots back.

"This is a replay," Lisa said. "The Volvo was played in May."

"It turns me on when you talk golf." I grinned.

She ignored me. "Was Halle Basker that bad?"

"He was that bad."

"Then Nash will have to spend college vacations with us," she said matter-of-factly. "We *need* a family."

Lisa turned back to the TV screen, the statement floating between us.

It was nearly 7 P.M. I was tired. I had planned to go to the fitness trailer to workout. To say her last remark caught me off guard was like saying the *Titanic* had only minor mechanical flaws.

"A family?" I said. "Didn't we discuss that last year?"

She sat up beside me, her knees together, feet planted firmly on the floor.

"Marriage, Jack. We discussed marriage, and how we couldn't fit it around our careers. How, if you lost your card, I wouldn't see you. The more I think about it, the more awful that sounds—selfish, self-centered on both our parts."

"That wasn't the only reason, Lisa. You know that. It's us—what we're like—not the careers. Our jobs are extensions of us. We're both very driven people."

"People change, Jack. Sometimes change is good. People grow."

"Growth is different from change."

She stood suddenly. Still dressed for work in a white silk blouse and black slacks with matching flats, she looked great. Her expression, however, did not. Any male having dealt with the opposite sex knows he is inherently stupid by comparison. I now sensed I had made the fatal error men begin making at roughly fifteen and continue making until death: I had opened my mouth and followed my own words—the significance of which, of course, I failed to comprehend—into a place that was deep and dark and unforgiving.

Lisa's expression told me she comprehended my miscue fully. "So, you think I'm some workaholic woman, too focused to have a marriage or a family?"

"I don't think—"

"If that's what you think, you don't know me."

Then she was gone. The bedroom door slammed behind her; the lock clicked into place. Moments later, the door reopened.

A pillow and blanket landed beside me on the couch.

. . .

Friday, Nash and I were on the range early. I had missed the cut the previous week and unfortunately was taking this week off. The result would be my name appearing far above the hundred twenty-fifth spot on the money list. One of the great things about the $3- and $4-million purses we play for each week is that, with one top-ten finish, you can leapfrog a bunch of players. By contrast, the ability to make that amount of money so quickly was now something I loathed—I could only watch others earn it this week.

As the 7 A.M. sun rose, spectators filed to various viewing positions on the course. Nash and I were in line on the range, hitting with players who were warming up. I was not warming up. I was working. There is a difference. The most obvious one is that when I work, my hands bleed. Hitting 500 balls in a single day will do that. Hitting balls now was not the same as it had been when I was a kid. Then, I could hit a hundred balls in an hour. Now, each ball required my preswing routine: two practice swings; then, standing behind the ball, visualizing where I wanted it to go and the swing needed to produce that result; and, finally, hitting the shot. Five hundred balls would take until late afternoon. Then I planned to workout, shower, and work on my short game after dinner.

Padre Tarbuck approached. Before storming off the night before, Lisa had mentioned that he was in second place at four under par, trailing Tiger and, of all people, Pete Taylor, both at minus five. I had not spoken to her since last night's episode.

"Where the hell have you been?" Padre said.

"Here and there."

"What kind of answer is that?"

"A vague one."

"What kind of statement is that?"

"An equally vague one."

He shook his head. "Anyway, when I heard you had withdrawn, I figured you hurt your back again."

I told him my back was fine. He looked like he always did, as relaxed as if he was on vacation. Since he was a former priest, I figured maybe he felt as if on a permanent vacation. He still had the stubble of a short beard that makes me look hungover, but, on him, women think it's sexy. He wore black Reebok shoes, matching pants, and a white shirt with creased sleeves that had obviously been ironed. His visor read REEBOK. He used to dress in Titleist and Footjoy garb.

"New sponsor?"

He grinned and winked. Then his expression turned serious. "Oh, the reason I stopped by was they're looking for you in the clubhouse. You've got a phone call."

"I'll get the messages later," I said. Lisa wouldn't call. She'd talk face-to-face. She was that type. If it was Perkins, stories of Brian Taylor could wait. My game no longer could.

"No time for phone calls?"

"No," I said. "I need to work."

"Sweating like a bastard. Working your ass off?"

"I have to."

He gave a nod that suggested he knew what I was referring to: The money list is something we're all conscious of. A nonexempt player's position on it affects seemingly all areas of one's life—those out of his control, such as which events he plays—and those in his control, like how often and hard he practices, how much sleep he gets; it may even dictate his mood in the locker room. Padre knew all this. He nodded solemnly and walked off.

. . .

It was nearly 1:30 when I broke for lunch. I was no longer a participant. The locker room, however, was spacious so, despite withdrawing, I had kept my locker, since I would be there practicing all week. The locker room was carpeted and had leather furniture and coffee and card tables. My locker was pine, and on the inside of the door, two messages had been taped. One was from Perkins, from whom I had expected to hear, assuming he would call either to see why I wasn't playing this week or to update me. The second call was one I would not have expected under any circumstances. It had come from Brian Taylor. I stared at the hand-written note for several seconds, then dialed Perkins, who answered immediately.

"Why would Taylor call you?"

"I half expected to hear from his brother, Pete Taylor," I said.

He asked why. No one was within earshot. I told him about Nash and Sharon.

"Jesus Christ," he said. "Where's Nash now?"

"Having lunch with Lisa. Silver asked about you."

"I bet he did. He's a nut. I can never figure that guy out. Sometimes I think he's straight."

"Just because he's gay doesn't mean he's not tough," I said.

"I know that. But when he's gay, he's *really* gay."

Most of the morning tee times had yet to finish their rounds; while some of the late times had already gone off. There were only a handful of players in the locker room. One guy I didn't know—perhaps a rookie or a Monday Qualifier—sat in front of the television. Hal Sutton was in a leather chair reading a newspaper. I was at the phone table. I wasn't a contestant, but didn't want to screw around with a payphone or go back to the hotel to make the calls.

"Anything new with Brian Taylor?" I said.

"Nothing. I went to see your buddy Dr. Victor, though. If we keep pushing, something'll give there."

"Like what?"

"I don't know. Maybe the kidnapping and his Russian project aren't related, but the guy is a stress case."

"What are you going to do?" I said.

"Miller's got a couple tough cops questioning him today. Then I'll go back for another visit."

"You've got no plan?"

"Just push until he cracks."

"That's how you get yourself sued," I said.

"Which probably explains why I'm private."

"Well, I'm going to call Brian Taylor back. I'll let you know what comes of it."

We hung up. Then I called Taylor. Cindy answered and said he was at home and feeling better.

"Both physically and mentally?" I said.

It took her a while to respond. "He's been through a lot."

"You both have," I said and left it at that.

She got Brian and I heard him ask for privacy. Through the phone, I heard a door close.

"Jack," he said.

"I'm returning your call."

"Yes, ah, thanks. . . ."

I waited. He didn't say anything for maybe five seconds. Clearly he was thinking. Did that mean he was reconsidering this conversation? That in itself would mean he had something that, earlier, he had wanted to share. I knew I had to get him talking or I'd lose my chance at information I sensed to be important.

"Brian," I said, "you called me at the course. What is it?"

"Um, sorry to bother you. It's just—I need—needed—to talk."

"About what?" I leaned back in my chair and crossed my feet

at the ankles. I had not changed from the khaki pants and golf shirt I'd worn on the range. The sweat was drying. I could smell the salty odor. "What did you call for?"

His breath sounded heavy. He remained silent, thinking and, I assumed, reconsidering.

"You can trust me," I said. "I'm trying to help you get Catherine back."

"No."

"No? You don't need help?"

"Jesus, just lay off." It was a short, curt sentence—and followed by silence.

"Lay off what?" I said. I knew he meant my Victor Silco visit. There was nothing else he could be referring to.

I heard him sigh into the phone.

"You've got to lay off," he said. "You met the guy accidentally. Let it, for Christ's sake, go. She'll be returned, but you've got to let up. And your friend from Boston, too."

He hung up before I could ask him the rush of questions that seemed to pour over me: Who had I met accidentally? Silco? That day in Taylor's office? Of course. However, how did he know she would be returned? Was the kidnapping part of some deal? Everything pointed to Victor Silco. And Taylor had just admitted he knew the person who had his daughter. So why hadn't he called the cops? Why hadn't he gotten her back? Why wait, if he didn't have to? Or did he have to? What exactly was going on between Silco and Taylor? Brian's brother, Pete, was also involved in the Russian golf venture. Could he be involved in his niece's disappearance?

The locker room came back into focus. I needed to be alone. I needed to think.

. . .

The curtains in front of the sliding-glass doors were open, the sky patched with clouds. I was back in the suite with the air conditioner cranked up, lying on the bed, my thoughts so deep they could have been meditation.

Brian Taylor.

My January visit to his office. There, I had met Silco.
Catherine's vanishing. Now kidnapping.
My trip to Silco's on-campus office.
Then I backtracked. I recalled Brian's face when I returned to his office following Silco's departure, then my exchange with him: Brian Taylor wished me luck. I had offered him the same. Except my reply left him looking like I'd called his bluff. I had never before described his expression that way. It had never before occurred to me as such. Yet that was how he had looked. Had I called his bluff? Had he seen, on that very day, the events that would unfold?

Those were questions to which I had no answers. I knew only one thing: Dr. Victor Silco was involved in Catherine's disappearance. I could smell that. I could taste it. I now knew it.

I would share all these thoughts with Perkins. He was, after all, looking into that end of this. What of Pete Taylor, of his role as a contributor to the Russian golf deal? It would be awkward due to the Sharon-Nash ordeal, but I could chat with Pete myself.

"What do you mean Katrina is gone?" Nik said to Oleg. The door remained open behind him.

Nik stepped inside the main room of the two-bedroom apartment. The television broke Oleg's silence. Still wearing a windbreaker and carrying his garment bag, Nik walked to it and turned it off. Oleg remained standing in the center of the living room, still and silent.

"Where has Katrina gone?"

Oleg made a gesture Nik could barely decipher as a shrug.

It had been nearly midnight when the cab dropped Nik curbside in front of the Wayne Inn on North Mesa Street in El Paso, Texas. The apartment building had stood before him, various apartments lighted in checkerboard fashion.

"And the baby?" he said. "Where is she?"

Oleg did not answer.

"Where is the baby?" Nik stepped closer to Oleg.

"Katrina took her."

"No." Nik dropped the bag. It landed heavily near his feet.

"Please sit," Oleg said. "Let me explain."

"Explain?" Nik said. He moved very close to Oleg. His voice grew quiet, almost a whisper. "Do explain. Tell me where Catherine is. A lifetime of work rides on your answer."

Oleg stepped back again.

Nik went to the door and slammed it. He turned back to Oleg, his chest heaving. His eyes took in the condition of the apartment. It was worse than before. Judging from the condition, Katrina had been gone some time. Near the Lay-Z-Boy, the earth-colored carpet was spotted with cigarette ashes. Also near the chair, Nik saw a beer can, empty, lying on its side. Oleg followed his gaze to the can.

"I had only one," Oleg said.

Nik heard the hopelessness in his voice. The man surely was aware any attempt at recovery was futile, he thought.

"Nikoli, it is not my fault."

But it was, Nik knew. He leaped at Oleg's throat before the man could move.

Then they were on the floor, Nik's knee on the man's chest, his hand clenching Oleg's neck. The skin on Nik's face seemed tight. His chest felt hot. His eyes were bloodshot. His forehead creased with strain. He heard his teeth grinding.

"The baby," he gasped, "is all I have. Where—is—she?"

"I—" Oleg's breath rasped.

The man could not speak. Nik knew that if he did not let go, he would kill him. Oleg was a shooter, not a fighter. He felt Oleg clutch and scratch at his arm, as if batting weakly at a taut cable. He pressed his knee hard into Oleg's chest, then stood, leaving Oleg on the floor, gasping.

When Oleg sat up, his hand went to the holster on his back hip.

"Oleg," Nik said, his voice effortless, his tone flat. He shook his head slowly.

Oleg looked up at the nine millimeter Nik pointed at him.

"Sit," Nik said, "on the couch and tell me what happened."

Nik reached down and helped Oleg to his feet, reaching behind him, taking the man's pistol from the holster as he did. He tucked Oleg's gun into his own belt and saw the concern on Oleg's face, an expression that illustrated a knowledge that he was no longer of value. Nik also saw that Oleg made the realization of what the future might hold.

"When you calm down," Nik said, in an effort to ease Oleg, "I'll give your gun back."

He motioned to the small sofa in front of the television. Oleg sat. Nik stood before him and listened as the man explained that he had woken to find Katrina and the baby gone.

"What time was that?" Nik said.

"Maybe two. The day you left." Oleg wore soiled blue jeans with black shoes and white athletic socks. He had not shaved. His white T-shirt had yellow circles at the armpits.

"Two?" Nik said, making a circular motion with his left hand. His right hung loosely at his side, the pistol tapping lightly against his thigh.

Oleg sighed. "In the afternoon."

"In the afternoon," Nik said. "I see. So you were napping and she took the baby and strolled out. Now she may be in Juárez, Mexico. Excellent work."

"Nikoli, her things are still here. That means she'll be returning."

"No," Nik said firmly. "She will not return."

"Why do you say that?"

"Don't speak anymore," Nik said.

He realized the gun had come up, the barrel pointed at Oleg. The blood drained from Oleg's face, turning it from pale to nearly gray. Nik lowered the pistol. He needed to think.

She was not coming back. He had frightened her during their last discussion, when they had spoken of the baby's condition. He had seen fear in her eyes. He knew she had been upset when they'd had sex because, although her eyes met his, they had not remained there. He knew, also, she was attached to the baby. Yet he had thought she felt a loyalty to him. Hadn't she wanted to prove herself trustworthy? She had jumped at the chance to join Oleg and him. Originally, Nik had thought she held hopes that an affair might land her a residency in his beachfront home. He had been happy to exploit that misperception—as long as it kept her obeying him, caring for the baby.

Now, Nik knew the baby had come first. She had been frightened when Catherine had gotten ill. Had she fled to a doctor? That would be disastrous. Surely every hospital in the nation was on the lookout for a missing baby televised on CNN.

In any case, Oleg was to have watched over things. He had not.

"Follow me." Nik led Oleg to the bedroom.

Nik moved to the faded dresser on the far wall. Oleg remained in the doorway and Nik stood, his back to him, and opened the drawer. Inside, was a silver case.

Opening it, Nik called over his shoulder, "Where do you think Katrina has gone?"

"I don't know . . . ," Oleg said, his tone defeated, his voice growing quiet.

Nik heard the man's voice trail off. He knew Oleg accepted his failing. He only hoped he would accept his punishment equally well.

"You don't know?" Nik said, turning to face Oleg.

The man shook his head, his eyes registering the exchange of pistols, knowing full well what the silencer meant. As Nik raised the handgun, Oleg opened his mouth to protest.

Nik simply shrugged, squeezing the trigger.

. . .

Nik returned to the living room and sat, his head spinning. Catherine was gone. Oleg lay splayed in the hallway, dead. Things had gotten out of control. No. He fought that thought. True, he no longer had the little girl. Taylor, however, did not know that. Not yet. If he moved quickly, he could still get the money. He would move soon. First, he had to regain his composure, had to think everything through.

How had things gone wrong? During times like these, when Nik sat staring blankly at an uncertain future, his past formed a dark storm overhead. He wondered briefly about Vladimir Remeikus, about the Lithuanians. He wondered if they were coming for him, for the money he had taken. He also wondered if he would ever get a full night's sleep, unbothered by thoughts of Remeikus, thoughts of his past actions and the fears to which those actions led.

He clutched the phone in one hand and punched the number to a Connecticut hotel. When the front desk answered, Nik asked for the room of the blonde who had first mentioned Brian Taylor's Russian golf plan. It was nearly 1 A.M. Surely the husband was there, but Nik had to speak to Sharon, had to find her—at all cost.

Sharon Taylor's voice was groggy when she picked up.

"Where will you be next week?" Nik said.

Her voice a whisper, she told him. "Will you be coming?"

He told her he would.

"I can't wait," she said.

He hung up and headed back to the airport, thinking of the plan that had spawned all this.

And counting the people who knew of it.

"Something interesting just emerged," Perkins said.

Prior to his call, I had been sitting on the loveseat in my suite, wearing gray sweatpants and a pale blue Maxfli T-shirt. My attention had alternated between the Philip Levine book in my lap and sets of thirty push-ups. Lisa had not come home from work yet. Nor had she called to make dinner plans. Thus, I had eaten room service—three tuna sandwiches and a bottle of Heineken—and stuck the tray outside the door.

"Your boy, Dr. Silco," Perkins was saying, "has a brother that Miller just discovered."

I waited. Outside, the fading sun was nearly horizontal with the sliding-glass doors that led to the veranda.

"Guy lives in Miami and came to this country after Victor."

"He a doctor, too?"

It made Perkins chuckle. Perkins was not the type to laugh. Apparently, my question bordered on hysterical.

"His name is Nikoli Silcandrov. He's Victor's older brother, has a mansion on the beach in Miami. No one has yet figured out where he got his money."

"Seems to be a family trait," I said.

"Yeah. He's been here a little more than a year."

"What's he say to Miller about the money?"

"Nobody can locate him. House is empty. But—and this is a major *but*—Victor's boss remembers a guy showing up at the U of Miami looking for Victor. Physics chairman said the guy looked 'threatening.'"

"People describe you that way."

"I am threatening," he said. "That guy might have been Victor's brother. The chairman also said Victor left the office that day with the guy and took the next week off to attend a conference in Korea. Cancelled lectures and research for a week. Plus, he tried real hard to downplay it."

"How so?"

"When the chair asked, Victor said only that he was 'pursuing academic matters' at the conference in Korea."

"Where has this brother been?" I said. "Why didn't anyone go talk with him before?"

"The name change. Silco shortened his name."

"Shortened it," I said. "Or deliberately changed it?"

"Miller and I thought of that, too," he said. "Anyway, that Korean conference strikes the department chair as strange because he says when professors attend conferences they usually seek reimbursement. Victor did not."

"He's got money," I said. "He doesn't need to be reimbursed."

"Exactly," Perkins said, "and—with us finding this brother—it's becoming more clear where he's getting it. Anyway, the chairman also said attending academic conferences is something one typically puts on their résumé for review. Victor made no mention of it."

"Uh-huh," I said. "And Victor struck me as a real academic. He seems to take the academic life very seriously. You'd think he'd want people to know of all his accomplishments."

"You would," Perkins said. "This means something, Jack. We don't know for sure who the guy Silco went to Korea with was, although I'd bet my life's savings it was the brother. Every instinct I have says so."

"Working on that hypothesis," I said, "the question becomes: What was the conference on?"

"That is what everyone, including the chairman, is trying to find out. He said he'd get back to me on it. Said without the usual paper trail—forms for release time, expense forms—it'll be tough to find out exactly what Victor was doing."

"At least the guy sounds helpful."

"They were thinking of hiring Victor full time. He's on a research grant right now. If anything is wrong, they want to know about it before any offer is made."

"So, Victor didn't want anyone to know what he was doing in Korea," I said.

"Silco's research is in nuclear medicine. You know about the North Koreans and nukes, right?"

"Apparently, they're trying to stockpile them," I said. "You think Silco is selling nukes or research to the North Koreans?"

"I don't know. I'd like to know what he was doing there. If that was the case, it would attach a real foul smell to that money he donated to the PGA Tour."

That thought made me sigh. "Would explain why Brian Taylor handled the donation himself."

We were quiet, each considering that.

"Anyway, I've got something for you," I said and told him about the Brian Taylor phone conversation.

The phone line went silent.

"That spineless fuck," Perkins said. "He knows who has her."

"I've been thinking a lot about my coffee chat with his wife. I don't think Cindy knows anything."

"I agree. I think Taylor got into something. It didn't shake down the way he expected and now someone has his balls in a vice."

"Except," I said, "it's not his balls. It's worse."

"Yeah, the little girl. So he knows Silco—or someone Silco hired—has her and he's not trying to get her back."

"Got to be something more to it," I said. "I know you'd get Jackie back if it meant your life."

"Yeah, I would. That should be instinctive, so we've got to look at why he's crying instead of talking. The only logical reason is that Victor told him if he says anything, the girl suffers."

"Makes sense," I said. "But I can't picture Victor Silco kidnapping anyone."

"Desperation can make people do unexpected things."

"He seems mostly put out by this," I said. "I don't know. He just struck me as more tired of all this than anything else. I know he was bullshitting me in his office, but. . ."

I heard a key scraping. The door opened and Lisa walked in. She nodded once, then made her way to the bedroom. She closed the door behind her.

"Silco always struck me as nervous," Perkins said. "Maybe too nervous to take a baby. I don't know. I'll think it over on my way to Connecticut."

"You're coming back?"

"Got to report to Tour Commissioner Peter Barrett. He called me. Miller's going to be here anyway—they're bracing Victor about his brother as we speak. First, I'll meet with Miller, hear what Vic said about family ties, then head north. I think for now we keep Brian Taylor's call to ourselves. I'll run it by Miller. He's smart enough to know that if Silco knows Taylor called you he might get scared, and we don't want to jeopardize the baby."

"You're just coming back because you can't stay away from Silver," I said. "Can you?"

"Finally figured me out," he said.

. . .

I tapped on the bedroom door. Lisa said to come in. She was sitting on a chair near the window, reading a book titled *Ethics: The Lifework of a Journalist.*

"Want to talk?" I said.

"We need to. I apologize for flipping out last night. I had no right to do that."

"What's going on?"

I sat at the foot of the bed, a couple feet from her chair. She had changed into khaki short-shorts and a sleeveless button-down denim top. Her thick black hair was held in a bun atop her head. She looked as beautiful as always, yet there was something else there as well. She looked deeply unhappy. It was something I not only saw in her eyes, but sensed with all my being. For the first time in our relationship, I felt like she was slipping away, like something had suddenly come between us, formed a gap so large it might never be bridged. For the first time since we'd met, I felt like she was holding something back, as if she felt something but couldn't or wouldn't articulate it.

That scared the hell out of me.

I couldn't imagine life without her. We'd nearly married a year ago. After Lisa had been kidnapped and following the shootings of two men, we had both gone off to work the next dawn. I had long felt the fact that we'd gone on as usual—I to the course; she to the TV tower—following such an earthshaking experience, spoke volumes about us as people. It showed me that as committed as we were to each other, we were also—and maybe equally—committed to our professions. My love for her never had, and I believed never would, waiver. Yet, I felt we were better off keeping our relationship as it was: together forever, but unwed. A year ago, she said she agreed with that position.

Now, as she sat with her book held before her as if symbolically placing the object between us, I knew she no longer felt as I did. Something had changed and changed suddenly.

"Tell me what's going on."

"I just need space, Jack." She looked at the open door leading out of the bedroom. "Can you give me a few days?"

"I don't want to lose you."

She said nothing.

When she pursed her lips, I heard her inhale deeply.

"Space," she said. "I need space."

I nodded slowly. Then I left.

28

Monday morning, Nash and I stood on the practice green at the Westchester Country Club, home of the Buick Classic. Perkins had come back from Florida and I had been staying with him since Lisa had requested space. Perkins and Nash had gone for a five-mile run earlier that morning. I had declined. I hadn't seen Lisa in several days and didn't feel much like running. I didn't feel very much like playing golf, even; rather, I felt like beating balls on the range until I hit a 400-yard drive or swung hard enough to force a trip to the chiropractor. Neither seemed logical, so I was putting.

I certainly needed the practice. I was a hundred fifty-fourth in putting—1.806 putts per hole. Although my driving distance still ranked in the top-ten at over 292 yards per swipe and my driving accuracy had remained where it typically was—I hit the fairway 67 percent of the time—my place on the money list had risen to 133, eight places out of exempt status. I had been around long enough to know putting is the difference between success and failure on Tour. My current predicament was a perfect example: The previous season—during which I had finished an even one hundredth in putting, averaging 1.777 putts per hole—I had finished ninetieth on the money list. Now I was a hundred fifty-fourth in putting and a hundred thirty-third in money. There is a direct correlation between those statistics.

As I stroked ball after ball, the adage "drive for show, putt for dough" never seemed more true.

Besides, practicing and analyzing my statistics meant I wasn't thinking of Lisa.

"Jack," Nash said, "Stump asked if we want to practice with them today."

Only half the field had arrived Monday, but the green was bustling. It was already in the mid-eighties with 98 percent humidity. At this rate, the heat could play a factor in the outcome of the tourney.

A friend and former winner of the Buick Classic, J. P. Hayes, nodded from across the green. I waved.

"What do you think of Stump's offer?" I said to Nash.

"Don't like it," Nash said. He looked uneasy and paused to see if Hayes was going to approach. He didn't. Instead, Hayes leaned over to hit another putt.

"Nothing happened between you and Sharon," I said.

"Man, I told you that already."

"Then you can learn from Stump. It might be a little uncomfortable for you, but I say we play with them."

"Man," he said and sighed.

"Besides, my game needs someone to really challenge it."

. . .

Pete and I had decided on a wager: $100 for the front, $100 for the back—total strokes. I threw in a side bet: $100 for fewest putts over eighteen holes.

The first hole at Westchester is a par-three, 190 yards. The sun was directly over the green, which meant that I was hitting a blind tee shot to the two-tiered putting surface.

I had a five-iron.

Before I take the club back, I always focus on one swing thought, a line from legendary Texas-based teaching pro Harvey Penick: *Trust your swing.* Besides, with the blazing sun making this a blind shot, what else could I tell myself? My follow-through was abbreviated. The ball must have hit the front of the green because I saw it on the second tier. From my vantage-point, it looked maybe ten feet from the hole.

As it turned out, I had a fifteen-footer for birdie, but was inside Pete's ball. He was looking over a twenty-foot, right-to-left birdie attempt that would bend at least three feet.

"Three hundred bucks," Nash said as we watched Pete line up his putt. "That's a lot of money."

It was a statement that offered perspective: Nash was from a different place, one that I had recently seen. I said nothing.

"We've got this hole in the bag, Jack," Nash said, a thin line of sweat trickling down the side of his face. "That's a long putt."

"Pete's won two U.S. Opens," I said. "If anyone can make it. . ." Although, in truth, I felt pretty good about the hole. I thought I could jump on Pete early.

When Pete's ball rolled into the cup—center cut from the time it left the blade of his putter—he looked over and grinned at me. It wasn't a malicious expression or one of arrogance. It was a look that simply said he loved this—competing, having his back to the wall, and responding. I had read a remark by hockey player Wayne Gretzky and had never forgotten it. Most people, Gretzky said, fear success; they don't believe they can live up—game after game, round after round—to their own best performances. Truly great athletes, though, thrive on reaching the bar they have set, then setting new limits. Pete, too, thrived on that pressure.

I stood behind my ball, then lined up the putt from the opposite side of the hole. I was putting uphill. The line appeared to be straight. Fast greens will always offer more break than slow greens. Likewise, if you hit a putt too firmly and knock it through a break, you leave a very long second putt, something no one wants. For this reason, putting on greens as fast as the ones played on Tour, it becomes easy to play breaks that aren't there. It all makes straight putts the most difficult for me. *Trust your stroke.*

I took two practice strokes, trying to judge the speed. Finally, I eased the blade behind the ball, then pulled the trigger.

My fifteen-footer landed atop Pete's ball in the cup. No blood.

. . .

Westchester's second hole is a 408-yard, par-four. The key to this hole is to get your tee shot in the fairway, which slopes left to right. If you hit it right of the fairway, you're in deep rough and can be blocked from the green by trees. So I hit a three-iron into the heart of the fairway, leaving around 160 yards to the green. Pete hit his three-wood out past my ball.

Nash and I moved down the fairway, walking maybe twenty yards behind Stump and Pete. Nash was drinking Gatorade. He had a towel wrapped around his thick neck. He had on khaki shorts, a white Maxfli-logoed golf shirt, and a dark Maxfli hat. His Oakley shades were on and I couldn't see his eyes. Sweat ran down his cheek.

"How'd you leave things between you and Halle?" I said.

He shrugged, staring straight ahead.

"You don't know? Or you don't want to talk about it?"

"I don't care about that guy," Nash said.

I obviously had as much use for Halle as I did roach turd. However, the man was Nash's guardian, so I would keep my opinion to myself. I believed Lisa had gone overboard in saying Nash would have to spend vacations with us. He might not even want to, although I had the feeling that Nash had learned the truth about Halle upon his return to Boston. If that was the case, I figured Nash would no longer be staying with the man. He was a proud kid. If he thought Halle had seen only NFL dollars in him, Nash would feel used. If he felt used, he would not return, and I wouldn't blame him one bit.

"Halle thought you were going to Clemson," I said.

Nash had the bag on his right shoulder. As we walked, he adjusted the clubs as if they had to be in a certain order. I had no organizational pattern for clubs in my bag. I knew he was trying to divert his attention. I let the topic drop. We continued on, silently.

The clubs clinked quietly as we walked. Finally, Nash said, "When I went in to get my things, he told me you said I was going to Curry. Why'd you do that?"

"Because you don't have to lie to him. You're doing what's best for you."

"You really believe that, don't you?"

"I do."

He finished the Gatorade and stopped walking. He set the bag down, opened the large front pocket, and dropped the empty bottle inside. When he had rezipped it, we walked on. I had on a red-and-blue striped shirt and khaki pants. I could feel the pants sticking to my thighs in the heat.

"Halle called me a dumbfuck," Nash said. "Told me to go off, be a Tom for you."

My tongue moved along my upper teeth. It was what I did when I wanted to make sure I kept my mouth shut. Nash had lived with Halle for three years; he hadn't known me nearly as long. I knew to never speak ill of a person's parents; for, even the son of a serial killer will have strong feelings for a parent. Halle had served as Nash's father figure long before I'd come on the scene.

"You know that's not the case, don't you?" I said.

Nash grinned at me. "Actually, he called you whitey."

"How nice," I said. "You're not dumb. I hope you know that."

He said nothing.

At my ball, Nash and I reviewed the yardage: 148 yards to the front, 161 to the pin. I pulled my seven-iron, took two practice swings, and put the shot ten feet beneath the cup. Nash gave me a high-five.

"Thought you were in a slump," Pete said. "You're sandbagging me." Then he grinned. "Nice playing, Jack."

I said thanks and Nash and I moved to where Pete was preparing to hit his approach.

"What are your plans for the end of the summer?" I said. "Will you go back to Halle's before preseason?"

His head swung around. Beneath the Oakleys, his eyes locked on mine for a single sharp moment. Then he focused on the green as he walked. "I got some friends," he said and shrugged. It was street toughness again. I knew my question had implied something I had not meant.

"Nash, I just figured you'd want a little down time before you start preseason. I only ask because I'd like you to know you can stay with me—caddying or when I'm home, with me there."

"And Lisa?"

Something tightened in my midsection. Upon visiting my native Maine, Lisa had fallen in love with the state. I owned a tiny cabin in northern Maine; however, we spent much of the previous off-season in an oceanfront house I purchased about a half-hour from Portland. Lisa owned a place in Maryland, but had it for sale.

"Of course," I said.

I didn't sound confident. Last fall, Lisa commented on how she loved the scent of the ocean, how opening the front door offered the rich odor. I thought of how, on warm days, she cracked a window to pepper the house with the scent.

My mind ran to Lisa and to the next off-season.

"You guys are fighting, huh?"

I looked at Nash.

Pete played his second shot to within five feet of the pin. He had been only a hundred yards away. Still it had been an outstanding effort. I called to him and gave a thumbs-up gesture.

"None of my business," Nash said.

"No. It's not that, and you have a right to know. You're used to doing stuff with the both of us. We're just spending a little time apart right now. Doing some thinking."

"I hope you guys don't break up. I like her."

"We won't, Nash."

We were quiet as we strode to the second green.

"How old were you when your mom passed away?" I said.

"Fourteen."

"How'd it happen?"

I heard him inhale deeply.

"Not something I like to talk about," he said.

"I understand."

We walked to the green, where I would putt first.

It was ten feet and would break right to left. Being right-handed, the right-to-left break fit my eye much better than did a left-to-right. I judged the break to be six inches. I followed my preswing routine: two strokes, then set myself to the line over which I wanted the ball to roll, then I stroked the putt. It dropped into the heart of the cup.

. . .

On the fifth hole—a 565-yard, par-five that rewards a good drive into a tight landing area—I walked down the fairway with Pete. Stump had cornered Nash on an issue regarding raking sand traps. I was taking advantage of having Pete to myself.

He was maybe four inches shorter than I, and twirled his three-wood as we went, rolling it finger to finger like a baton. He had never been arrogant or elitist and, with two U.S. Open titles, probably had a right to be. I didn't understand his marriage—or how he had gotten hitched to someone like Sharon—but respected the man's gentle demeanor and kindness. His charitable organization was legendary. More importantly, Pete's active role in that organization had been well documented.

"How's the Russian golf thing going?" I said.

He was looking down, still twirling the club, and shrugged. I thought of my phone conversation with Brian Taylor.

"It's still on, isn't it?" I said. "Looking forward to going over, giving my clinic."

"Oh, certainly. Still on."

We were quiet until we reached Pete's drive. He quickly selected a long-iron and hit a layup.

"I really think it's great, what you and Brian are doing," I said as we walked on again. "You guys are making golf even more global."

"Spreading the word," he said and smiled.

"I know I don't have the portfolio you do," I said, "but if anything like this comes up again, I'd love to offer financial support, if I can."

Truth was, I didn't have nearly the kind of money to do something like that. For all Pete knew, though, I had invested in Microsoft as a rookie and now had an eight-figure portfolio.

"I hear of anything, I'll let you know."

"What's a project like that cost?" I stared absently down the fairway like it was just a curious question.

We had reached my ball. Nash and Stump were waiting for us. I had ripped my drive well over 300 yards and had around 250 to the front of the green. Pete had hit his second shot to within a hundred yards of the green.

I had played the Buick Classic for many years and had always enjoyed the course. The 6,722-yard layout seemed to fit my game—it rewarded length, though only if you were accurate; the rough could kill you. The course offered risk and reward. To win, you had to drive the ball well, since you had no chance if you were playing from the rough all week. An example was the tenth hole, a 314-yard, par-four. I could reach the hole with my driver, but the green is heavily guarded with trees that leave the putting surface nearly inaccessible if you hit into them. Risk-reward.

Pete was in deep thought. I figured he was either calculating a figure for me, or hedging because he did not wish to answer. In any case, I had to worry about my shot. It wasn't that $300 would break me. It was pride and trying to turn my game around. This was a place where I had always played well. If I had to enter any tournament after missing a cut in the last one I had played, this was the one. In past years, this event provided me six top-ten finishes and nine top–twenty-fives. Also, winning a money match versus Pete—who, as nice as he was, I knew to be a fierce competitor, one who would rather slam his finger in a door than hand money over to me—would give me a confidence boost. Therefore, I focused. We were even, with Pete lying two. This was a great opportunity for me to go up one or more strokes.

I stood over the ball. As I did, the head of the three-wood bobbed up and down behind it as I fidgeted. After several seconds, I brought the club back, then down and through. I had mimicked my practice swing exactly and caught it flush. The ball landed on the front tier of the green and rolled to the third tier, stopping about twelve feet left of the hole.

"Nice shot, bastard," Pete said with a smirk. "Even stuck the thing on the right tier. What do you weigh, two hundred fifty?"

"Two-ten," I said. "Six-one."

"Got me by thirty pounds and probably fifty yards, but don't go counting your money. I'll play this in three shots and stick the approach inside yours."

He winked and we headed to his ball. It was the friendly competitive nature that I had long felt separated our professional sport from all others. During my tenure on Tour, I had seen two cases where players leading tournaments called penalties on themselves, causing one to be disqualified and the other to lose by a single shot. Likewise, anyone in need of help can ask a fellow player for a lesson and whoever is asked will make time to help, despite knowing full well that if the player he tutors turns his game around, it might cost him and his family money.

Pro golf is rooted in a gentlemen's atmosphere, one of first-class behavior and friendship. The first U.S. Open was held in 1895. The PGA of America was formed in 1916. In 1934, more than thirty years before the PGA Tour would be formed, a group of players decided to schedule a handful of events at various clubs. Paul Runyan won the money title, earning $6,767. In those days, players traveled together to cut expenses, ate meals side by side, formed a real camaraderie. I believe that bond, by and large, remains intact. I will admit, however, with $5 million purses, some of that camaraderie has been lost, although not as much as people would expect.

I was still hoping Pete thought enough of me to answer my original question.

"I hit before you could answer me," I said. "What's a project like that cost?"

Pete looked from me to Nash. It was the first time the two had made eye contact. Or the first time that I'd noticed, anyway. Then he looked at Stump, then back to Nash. Finally, he shrugged, a gesture that said *To hell with it.* Then he looked at me again.

"To be honest with you," he said, "Brian is trying to make it bigger than it's going to be. At least bigger than it's going to start out, given my donation. The economy over there is a disaster and—this is just between us—I'm not sure those people want golf. They're worried about where their next meal is coming from, not about playing golf."

"I thought this was your idea," I said. I knew it had not been, but he was talking openly. I wanted to keep it going.

"Who said that?"

I held my palms up.

"No. This is Brian's deal. Don't get me wrong, I think it's

great to offer golf. All I'm saying is that he's talking about having a Tournament Players Club over there, eventually. I'm thinking more along the lines of a muni course."

"Your way makes sense. A small municipal course—nothing fancy—would allow more people to be able to afford golf." I had grabbed a bottle of water on the tee and sipped some.

"Which was the philosophy when this concept began."

"Philosophy changed?"

"We've been friends a long time, Jack," he said.

I glanced absently at the trees that lined the fairway.

"What's it been, ten years that we've been out here together?"

"Yeah," I said. The water was ice-cold.

"I love my brother, but this is going to his head, a little. A Tournament Players Club over there? Come on."

"I heard he's the next commissioner. This is good for his résumé."

"If it's done right—and I've done this stuff before. I'm not losing my shirt in this deal so he can get a promotion. This began with matching six-million-dollar donations and the Tour kicking in the remainder—I think, like, fifteen million dollars—bringing the total to the high-twenties. Brian is looking to get Nicklaus to design the goddamn course now. You know what Nicklaus's fee for something like that would be?" He rolled his eyes.

"Well," I said, "Brian has his money in this too, right?" Cindy Taylor had told me one answer. I wanted it verified.

We had reached Pete's layup shot. All four of us paused. Pete surveyed his lie, then turned back to me. "Brian doesn't have money. He makes a good living. Period. But"—the corners of his eyes wrinkled and he smiled and shrugged admittedly—"neither of us married low-maintenance women, if you know what I mean. On top of that, Cindy wants everything Sharon has. The Tour pays Brian well, but not"—he looked as if he were trying to find a gentle way to say it, then he shrugged again—"but not what I make, you know?"

It was awkward to hear Pete mention Sharon in front of Nash. It told me he knew nothing of her extracurricular activities—or at least in regards to Nash.

"Must put some pressure on Brian," I said.

"Never affected our relationship. He's my kid brother, my best friend. Cindy's a pain, but then whose wife isn't? I think headaches are part of marriage."

To that, I said nothing. Cindy hadn't seemed that bad when I'd had coffee with her, although she had admitted that money concerned her. Some people are concerned about it in an effort to be responsible. According to Pete, Cindy worried about money in an effort to keep up. That told me Brian Taylor was probably under a lot of financial stress.

Pete selected a club—it had a lot of loft; probably a nine-iron or a wedge—and Stump took the bag and moved away. Pete went into his preswing routine, focusing on the pin as if memorizing every inch of the fairway up to it. He leaned over and threw grass into the air. No breeze. He was more intense than he had been on any shot up to this point in our match.

As I watched his ball land inside mine on the back tier of the green, I thought about what I had just learned about father-of-the-year Brian Taylor. I also thought about Pete's opinion of marriage, which made me think of Sharon and, in turn, Nash.

. . .

Pete and I walked to the eighteenth tee all square for the front with me trailing by two strokes on the back—and by two putts on the side bet that I had so wisely suggested. We had carried the $100 over from the front nine, doubling the back nine's value. Through sixteen greens, Pete had twenty-five putts to my twenty-seven. All in all, I was thrilled with the way I had putted. However, that wasn't enough—I still wanted to win.

The eighteenth is 526 yards, a par-five, dogleg left. It had provided many great finishes. If you can drive over the dogleg—and cut the corner—you can reach the green in two. Again, risk-reward.

Pete had honors and took the safe route—a drive into the heart of the fairway, leaving a two-shot approach. I was going try to put my drive over the trees at the corner and cut off maybe fifty yards. If I could execute the tee shot, I'd be able to reach the green with my second shot.

I took two practice swings with my driver then addressed the ball. My grip was firm. I waggled the clubhead to release tension in my arms. Nice and slow, I thought, make a smooth, rhythmic swing, but that isn't what the tension in my hands and arms produced; instead, the ball flew low and very hard into the trees at the corner. Without a gallery, I heard the ball thrash about in the pines. Needles and pine cones dropped to the ground. I knew it had not come out the other side; there were too many trees. I used some choice words to describe the effort and slammed the driver into the bag so hard it bounced up, nearly hitting Nash in the chops. Pete didn't say anything. He knew we were engaged in full-out battle now. Nash seemed shocked at my reaction and was quiet.

Nash and I quickly located my ball. It had come to rest between two large pines. The good news was that it was not blocked, so I could advance the ball toward the green. Also, it was sitting up on a bed of pine needles. The bad news: I didn't know if I could get it all the way to the fairway without hitting a tree limb. I trailed by two strokes, so I certainly didn't want to leave the ball in the woods with my next swing because Pete would be on the green in three for sure.

I had to try to reach the fairway with my second shot to have any chance.

I selected a three-iron and was taking practice swings—making low, abbreviated, punchlike strokes, hitting down, causing pine needles to scatter and dance upward. I was trying to get a feel for how hard to swing. I wanted the ball to fly no higher than three feet in the air, land, and run down the fairway.

"What do you think?" I said to Nash.

"Don't know. We're down by two."

I nodded and turned my attention back to the ball. I crouched to look at the pine needles it lay upon. The groundcover seemed very thick. The last thing I needed was to swing and learn the bed of needles had been even thicker—softer—than I'd thought and chunk the shot only a couple feet forward.

"Jack," Nash said.

Still crouched behind the ball, I looked up. "What's up?"

"You asked what happened to my mother," he said, then he glanced out at the fairway.

I stood and moved closer. "Yeah? I understand if you don't—"

He waved me off. "She overdosed. I found her on the floor in our apartment. It was real bad for a long time—nightmares and stuff."

Unconsciously, I had pursed my lips and was nodding slowly. He had told me something he had not told even the Horizons people. I didn't want to do anything to embarrass him or make him uncomfortable, although I felt like giving the kid a hug.

"Thanks for trusting me," I said. "You ever need to talk. . ."

"Yeah," he said.

I didn't know what to say and I knew Nash didn't want to discuss it further. I addressed the ball.

I brought the clubhead back slowly, only to my waist, then fired down—not hitting behind the ball but, rather, hitting the ball on the downswing—before hitting the pine needles, making sure I didn't sweep under it. The ball came out hot, landed in the fairway, and ran twenty more yards. Nash and I moved to it, quietly. Pete had hit his second to within a hundred yards of the green. I was up again.

The eighteenth green is multitiered, but the pin was in the front. I had 198 yards to the front edge—a smooth four-iron. Sweat was rolling down my face. I could feel it bead at my nape, run down my back. I had drunk two bottles of water and eaten three Power Bars during the round, but the five-mile hike, coupled with the mental fatigue of cerebral grinding over each shot, left me spent. It was only Monday. If it didn't get cooler or less humid, I might have to pace my practice schedule this week. Maybe limit myself to only nine holes on the days I worked hard on the range.

I hit the four-iron crisply and put the final approach shot to within eight feet. My ball was directly behind Pete's, so he'd get a good read watching my putt. I had to make mine—and he'd have to three-putt for me to tie.

I was crouched behind my ball.

"Greens are running fast," Pete said.

"Yeah." It wasn't something we could discuss during the tourney, but during a practice round, we could share information. This was not news to either of us, though, after seventeen previous greens. I knew he was making conversation.

"What are you doing for dinner?" Pete said.

"Nash and I are on our own tonight. Lisa's working." It was a fib, but I didn't want to get into my love life—or have him schedule us for another meal with Sharon.

"Sharon's busy, too. Want to grab a bite somewhere?"

"Sure," I said. "A buddy is in town from Boston. He'll probably join us."

"The big blond guy, the cop?" Pete said. "I met him. Interviewed me about Catherine. He's a good guy."

I nodded. The fairway, just short of the green, sloped away from the putting surface. If you spun your approach shot too much it would roll back off the green and funnel into the collection area below. I knew my putt would break toward the collection area. The question was: How much would it bend? I stood at the bottom of the green and glanced up toward my ball. This perspective gave me the line. I visualized it and locked it in as I moved back to the ball, took my two practice strokes, then addressed the ball. I pulled the trigger. The ball hit the left edge and skidded along the perimeter of the cup—and lipped out.

A tap-in par.

Pete had a two-shot lead and was putting for birdie. I did the gentlemanly thing and conceded the hole and the match.

"Thanks, Jack," he said. "It was a real good match. You're playing too well to be missing cuts."

"Yeah," I said.

"See you at dinner," he said.

I looked him in the eye and shook his hand as I gave him $300. It was an experience I didn't want to get used to. I wanted a rematch.

29

They met in the hotel parking lot at 4:30 P.M.

On the phone, Nik had asked Sharon Taylor where she was staying. He had grinned when she had openly told him. Still blabbing, he had thought.

He knew she was there with her husband, so he waited patiently at the established time, sitting in the idling dark-blue Ford Taurus rented at the Budget counter at the airport. He wore blue jeans, a cherry wood–colored leather belt, topsiders, and a button-down white shirt—the top two buttons undone, exposing a trace of dark hair, his gold chain, and offering a glimpse of thick pectoral muscles. He wore dark glasses and leaned back deep in his seat. As he waited, he looked at no one. A monotone voice offered a weather forecast on NPR.

As he watched her approach the car, he thought she looked exactly as he had remembered: the soft blond hair; the thin legs, long and smooth beneath the short cotton sundress; the heavy breasts; and the waist, no larger than his thigh; her eyes, as intense as they had been when they had made love, which had been often for several months.

But that was before he had taken Catherine. He did not know, and had not speculated, as to how Sharon might react to seeing him again. However, when she smiled, Nik knew she had either been too stupid to realize it was he who had taken the girl, which made him wonder if coming here had even been necessary, or had she simply been too oblivious, too wrapped up in her own world, to put it all together? Regardless, he smiled back.

She opened the passenger door and slid in next to him. Nik

was already accelerating out of the lot when she leaned over to kiss him.

"That can wait," he said, his voice flat, void of the interior conflict that raged.

She sat back in her seat and he heard her make a *Tsss* sound. Still a spoiled American princess, Nik thought.

"Didn't you miss me?"

"Of course," he said. "But your husband could arrive."

"He's playing golf," she said. "As usual."

Nik reached over and placed his right hand on her thigh. "We'll play something more fun," he said. "I promise."

. . .

They stopped to get sandwiches, wine, fruit, and a container of mustard-based potato salad, then drove to a park and now spread the picnic out before them. Sharon poured herself a glass of white wine and drank it down quickly.

"This is romantic," she said.

"You look so beautiful," Nik said. "I have missed you."

His own words took him back in time. He remembered how easy it had been. He had complimented her—a serious and subtle attempt to flatter—at the gym. Upon her reaction to his kind words, he had immediately sensed her neediness. She was a lonely, bored, and, Nik had thought, desperate housewife. Moreover, as he had looked at her in her black spandex tights beneath a red thong, he had known she was there for the taking. And *take* was what Nik had always done.

They had spent the very next afternoon in bed.

Now she sat on the grass beside him, gushing at the compliment. Nik saw the gold wedding-engagement set on her left hand and appraised its value. She was money, he thought. She had so much, yet at the same time, so little self-esteem. It was what happens, he thought, when money isn't earned. He thought of Victor, who himself was very weak.

"Where have you been?" she said. "I tried to call."

"I have been working."

"On what?"

Nik sipped some wine. "Just working."

A young couple strolled past them on the paved walkway, holding hands. Nik saw Sharon's eyes go to them. They had never discussed Nik's involvement in the golf venture, which she had originally mentioned to him. He had assumed, as he had stared down at Oleg's corpse in El Paso, that she had realized he was behind her missing niece. Yet, as he watched her now, he thought that she might very well have no idea it had been he who had kidnapped Catherine.

Sharon drank a second cup of wine. Nik saw her face flush a little and he vividly recalled her drinking.

Time, he thought quickly. Over time, she might not only put two and two together, but—and even worse—over time there was the chance that she would slip and say something to lead others, who were doubtless more competent, to the correct conclusion. He saw her pour herself a third cup of wine and shook his head sadly. And then there was her drinking.

The sun was low in the sky and ducks moved on a pond not far from them. Nik saw a small boy and girl feeding the ducks, their parents at their sides handing them bits of bread. He watched as the young girl laughed and jumped up and down when a duck snatched a piece of bread in its hard beak. The young girl shrieked with laughter.

"Have you seen Brian Taylor?" he said, turning back to Sharon.

She drank from her plastic cup again. He had purchased inexpensive white zinfandel. Sharon shook her head. Then she said something that Nik recognized immediately as a statement that would forever change her fate.

"You must know that I wouldn't say anything, don't you?" she said. Her face was red now. She looked hot like one who had spent an afternoon drinking champagne under a flaming sun.

Nik stared at her and said nothing.

"Victor looks just like you. Besides, he knows nothing about golf and told me he hadn't been to Russia in fifteen years. I didn't ask, just figured you were behind his donation."

"Is there anything wrong with that?"

"No. But I want to know where Catherine is."

"I have no idea. I had nothing to do with it."

"I'm glad to hear it," she said.

He watched her drink more wine and wondered if she really believed him. At this point, though, he knew it didn't matter.

The silence between them was nearly tangible for a short time. Then Nik drank slowly from his cup as well.

"Drink some more," he said. "Things always turn out fine."

He saw her puzzled expression and poured her more.

It was late afternoon. I had left Nash with Perkins. They were going to work out and I was sitting on my bed, reading the Philip Levine book. A poem entitled "The Escape" began:

> To come to life in Detroit is to be manufactured
> without the power of speech.

I loved this particular book, *The Simple Truth,* so much because I got something out of each poem, even if only capable of a surface reading. Regardless, the first lines of this poem pretty much summarized the way I was feeling. Lisa had requested space, not dialogue. Why space? What did *space* mean? Was she reevaluating my role in her life? Or her role in mine? Space for what? Had I cramped her?

What exactly was going on?

A year ago, we had agreed to continue living as we were: traveling together, staying together, eating together, laughing together, talking together. What had happened? For me, there had been no change; however, try as I might, I couldn't stand in

Lisa's place. I didn't know what she was thinking, or dealing with, and it was killing me.

I stood and went to the patio. Perkins's room was no suite, although it had a patio with plastic furniture. I sat and the legs of the chair scraped on the cement floor. I couldn't see the golf course from the patio. It seemed all of Westchester County had a small-town feel. As a Maine native, I was accustomed to "weekenders" and could envision tourists browsing the nearby streets. The distant sun was at three o'clock.

I stared down at the book on my lap. *The Simple Truth.* The title now seemed ironic. I didn't know the truth to anything—Lisa's feelings, Brian Taylor's garbled life, young Catherine's whereabouts, Victor Silco's involvement in it all. The truth, I thought, staring into the sky, was far from simple. I wondered if it ever had been simple or ever would be.

Behind me, I heard Perkins open the door. I went inside. He seemed to explode into the room, never looking at me, his words coming frantically: "They found her."

"Who?" I said.

His eyes never met mine. So focused on his own thoughts, he seemed to forget I was present. He leaped over the corner of the bed, sat on the edge, and grabbed the phone off the nightstand, before clarifying: "Catherine, Taylor's daughter. They ID-ed her this afternoon in a Texas hospital."

ID-ed, I thought. My gut reaction was: *ID-ed her corpse.* "Is she okay?" I said.

He nodded. Then he was speaking to Miller.

From the phone conversation, I gathered that a mystery woman brought Catherine to an emergency room. She'd been caught on surveillance cameras, but had since disappeared. Doctors and hospital officials had spent a couple days trying to locate the infant's assumed mother. Then Catherine Taylor's identity had become apparent. Several things became clear as I eavesdropped: Little Catherine Taylor was ill; Perkins and Miller were desperate to locate the woman; and they were going after Victor Silco hard now. If he hadn't had her, they were convinced he knew who had. I agreed with them.

. . .

In the hotel restaurant, we were waiting for Pete Taylor to arrive. Nash had ordered an appetizer—baked mushroom caps. He was drinking Coke. I was having a Heineken. Perkins, to my surprise, drank coffee, black. We were staying at the Courtyard by Marriott in Rye, New York, about a mile from the Westchester Country Club. The hotel restaurant was spacious, bright, very busy, and loud with a cacophony of voices and the clacking of silverware and flatware. It was Monday night. Not many Tour players had arrived. Most of the clientele looked like business people. I saw five or six players. Scott Hoch sat across the room. We nodded to each other.

"Who's that?" Nash said.

I told him. "Guy's the most consistent player I've ever seen," I said. "Might not win every week, but he doesn't miss cuts."

"But it's all about winning," Nash said.

I liked that comment. Kid was a competitor.

He ate a mushroom and offered me one. I declined. He motioned to Perkins. When Perkins declined, I knew he was working. Perkins was dressed for work in his gun-concealing sports jacket. He was leaning over his place mat, jotting something into a notepad. His focus reminded me of Lisa's single-mindedness.

I asked what he was doing.

"Making lists. It's what I do when I'm putting things together. When Brian Taylor called, he asked you to lay off, right?"

I nodded.

"Even-tempered?" he said. "Or did he appear frightened?"

"Desperate," I said. "He seemed more desperate—exhausted, nearly broken."

Perkins set down the pen. "Then why is Catherine back? Taylor knew who had her—most likely Silco or the brother. He also called you to ask us to back away. And you say he sounded desperate."

I nodded.

"If he was desperate, things must have looked bad. So why does she suddenly appear? Makes no sense."

"The woman," I said.

"Silco is not married," Perkins said. "To our knowledge, not even dating."

"His brother?"

"No one knows a thing about Nikoli Silcandrov."

"So who is this woman?" I said.

"Who the hell knows," Perkins said. "Stick to football, Nash. It's much easier."

"I plan to," Nash said.

"You going to talk to Victor Silco again?" I said.

Perkins shook his head. "Miller is down there. Besides, Peter Barrett told me the Tour is flying the Taylors in for a—his words, not mine—'celebratory press conference.'"

"Can Catherine travel?"

He shrugged. "All I know is Brian Taylor will be here tomorrow. I have a lot to discuss with him."

"Anyone locate brother Nikoli yet?"

Perkins chuckled.

The waitress reappeared. We ordered our meals. Across the room, I saw Lisa enter. She wore an apple-green U-necked shirt with a matching paisley-print skirt, and large gold hoop earrings. She looked great. She went to a booth at the far end of the room, failing to see me.

She was not alone.

A young reporter I recognized from the *Dallas Morning News* sat across from her. The young reporter was male. Tall, thin, clean-cut, nice looking—and male. He was dressed for a date in shirt and tie.

"What the hell?" I said. In hindsight, it had been only the second time—excluding the golf course—I'd swore in front of Nash. The first had been in the car. My mind was running hundred-yard dashes, with my tongue fighting to keep up.

Perkins followed my stare. I heard him say something under his breath. Nash sighed.

"Probably a business dinner, Jack," Perkins said.

"Space," I said. "Space? What the fuck does *space* mean? A date?"

"What are you talking about?" Perkins said.

Nash sat looking across the room at Lisa.

"Jack," Perkins said.

I turned to him.

He nodded toward Nash. I knew what he was saying: *Not in front of the kid.* He was right, but if I had worried about losing Lisa before, now I was terrified. The terror was coupled with anger.

"Don't over-react," Perkins said. "You and I both know Lisa. It's probably a meeting."

"Ace," I said, motioning to the *Dallas Morning News* kid, "is dressed to score."

"He's dressed for dinner," Perkins said. "Settle down, for Christ's sake."

My elbows were on the table. I ran my hands through my hair, my head shaking back and forth. My face felt hot. My hands were cold. The combination told me I was due for a migraine. Soon, I would see fuzzy, multicolored triangles in my peripheral vision. Then my hands would go ice-cold. If it was a particularly bad migraine—and I was no doubt due—my hands would go numb.

"I've got to get out of here," I said and stood. I threw my cloth napkin in my chair and left.

. . .

I never made it to my hotel room. From behind me, I heard the quick-paced click-clack of someone running in dress shoes. Then I heard my father's name called—"Mr. Austin." I turned back from the elevator doors and looked at the person. I had seen him somewhere, although I couldn't place him. He kept moving toward me. Standing and moving had done me good. My hands were still cold, but my head no longer burned. The peripheral triangles had yet to appear.

"Mr. Austin," he said again. He was dressed like a golfer in khaki pants and a pale blue shirt with the PGA emblem on the breast. The small jagged scar under his eye gave him away. Emilio, the young CPA I'd seen briefly in Brian Taylor's hospital room.

"Mr. Austin," he said, "I need to—if you have a moment—can I talk to you?"

"I'm not in a real good state of mind," I said.

He tilted his head, trying to figure out what I meant. We were in the hotel lobby. People were coming and going. Sergio Garcia, the 2001 Buick Classic Champion, paused as he walked by, slapping me on the back. I offered a friendly—albeit forced—smile. Then Sergio saw Emilio and his eyes lit up. Emilio focused on something near his shoes.

Sergio extended his hand and Emilio took it.

"*Que pasa, amigo,*" Emilio said.

Sergio said something back in rapid Spanish. Emilio only nodded and Sergio hesitated, apparently sensing Emilio's discomfort. He gave Emilio a friendly punch on the arm and moved off.

"You look like you swallowed a thumbtack," I said and stepped away from the elevator to let several people on.

"I need to talk," he said.

. . .

We were in the hotel room. Perkins wasn't one to order and not eat. In fact, I assumed he hadn't cancelled my meal and planned to eat it, too. Emilio sat on the stiff wooden chair at the desk and leaned forward, his forearms resting on his thighs. I sat on the bed, pillow propped between my back and the headboard, legs splayed before me. I wondered what Lisa was doing having dinner with the cub reporter.

"The guy you were eating with," Emilio said.

"Nash?"

"No, the other guy. He's working for the Tour, trying to find Catherine Taylor, right?"

I nodded. "They've found her. Now they want to know who had her."

He tilted his head again.

"What about Perkins?" I said.

He took in a deep breath, held it, then blew it out slowly like someone savoring a Cuban cigar. Except he didn't look like he was enjoying this. The pause had been to compose himself.

"I don't know if I should even bring this up," he said, "but something is not right at work."

I had only seen him in Taylor's hospital room. "What's your capacity at the Tour Charities Office?"

"I just started a few months ago. I'm Mr. Taylor's assistant director."

"You're a CPA?"

"Yeah. I was a CPA before. I like golf and this opened up. I oversee financial accounts and donations. Mr. Taylor puts the deals together. I'm in charge of the accountants and the like."

His narrow shoulders were pinched high with tension. When he shrugged, it looked painful. We were quiet. He sat staring at his feet again. He seemed very young and scared.

"Why were you asking about Perkins?"

"I thought of asking Mr. Taylor himself," he said. "But it seems like too much money for him to have missed. I mean, how could he have missed it? But, I just started working there. I don't want to jeopardize my job. I mean, he's a nice guy to work for, and—he's just—he is a *nice* guy. I wouldn't want to say anything to the investigator to get Mr. Taylor in trouble, so I thought I'd mention it to you or Pete Taylor. Then, I saw you. I mean, I can't be sure, but it's so much money. How can it not be accounted for?"

"What are you talking about?"

He didn't answer. He stood. He didn't head for the door. Instead, he paced back and forth in front of the bed, thinking. I knew he was about to tell me something important. I waited. When he spoke, the words seemed to rush out:

"Mr. Taylor told me he would handle the Russian golf accounts himself. Then he got in the accident. I do the majority of the accounting myself. There're two guys under me, but I'm hands-on. Anyway, I discovered some interest that had accrued that I couldn't account for. It was a large amount. I traced it back. It just doesn't look right. I should have known the money was there. But Mr. Taylor never mentioned it, which makes no sense because we keep very tight books."

"Could it have been an oversight?" I said.

"No—not Mr. Taylor—not an oversight. That's the thing that

bothers me. I don't think I was supposed to see that interest. He'd have mentioned something. Also, there's a second account."

. . .

"There were two donations," I said into the speakerphone. Perkins had gotten the phone from the front desk. We had Miller, still in Florida, on the line. Perkins had pulled the desk away from the wall and slid it between our beds. The phone sat on the desk with Perkins on one side and me on the other.

"Emilio said Victor Silco made the six-million-dollar donation," I said. "We all knew about that one. Then there was a second donation."

"For how much?" Miller said.

"Emilio hasn't crunched all the numbers," I said. "But the amount accrued a lot of interest. Enough to stand out."

"And that office does a lot of business in its own right, doesn't it?" Miller said.

"More than fifty million dollars annually."

"Emilio says he thinks it's more than ten million dollars," Perkins said. "And Taylor told Emilio that he'd handle the Russian accounts himself." Perkins was excited, practically yelling into the phone. "You see what's going on here?"

"I see what it looks like," Miller said.

I didn't completely follow. There was more money than the public knew about, Taylor's little girl had been kidnapped, and now she was back.

"The second account," Perkins scoffed, "is deemed 'cost overruns.' What does he think we are? Idiots?"

"Maybe it *is* for cost overruns," Miller said.

"Jack said the same thing. You two need to be more cynical. Emilio said they haven't even been billed for anything yet—haven't even broken ground, haven't selected the land, haven't hired a soul yet."

"Planning ahead?" I said.

Perkins looked across the table at me and just smiled. His expression said: *Poor Jack. How naive.*

"Theoretically," Miller said, "I guess that could be the case."

"It's not the case," Perkins said. "Catherine was kidnapped for a reason. That reason—all three of us know—is related to the fact that ten or more million dollars was being run through the Tour Charities Office."

"'Run through'?" I said.

"Dry-cleaned," Perkins said.

I heard Miller sigh. "Tell me, one more time, about that phone call you got from Brian Taylor?"

I did.

"It looks an awful lot like Victor Silco is laundering money through the Tour," Miller said. "And that Brian Taylor is helping him."

"What about Catherine?" I said.

"Maybe she was insurance," Miller said.

Perkins was nodding like a school teacher who had finally drilled home a point to recalcitrant students. "To see that Taylor helped him."

"How do you explain her being returned?" I said. "The money is still in the account."

"Yes, it is," Miller said. "That's the wild card right now. In any case, it's time for Dr. Silco and Mr. Taylor and us to chat with some IRS guys and maybe even the FBI people. I'll talk to Emilio myself, tomorrow."

There was a beat of silence, then Miller said, "Perkins."

"Yeah?"

"Great work. You're goddamned good."

Perkins said nothing. I knew it was as close to a sincere thank you as Perkins would get, or as close to a you're welcome as Perkins would give.

So I moved on. "What's the latest on the daughter?"

"She's in the hospital in Texas. They're moving her to Florida tomorrow."

"Where's Taylor?" Perkins said.

"El Paso, with his daughter," Miller said. Through the phone, his voice was hoarse with static. "Perkins, tonight just relax about this. That money could be legit. I don't think for a moment it is, but we can't go forcing confessions."

"You think I'd do something like that?" Perkins grinned mischievously at the phone.

"I talked to some Boston cops," Miller said. "Let's all take a deep breath. I think Taylor knew who had his daughter and why. This money, though, might be something else. It could be legit, or he could have set it up airtight."

"If that was the case," I said, "why would he have called me?"

No one answered that question.

"Where's Nikoli?" I said.

"Houdini?" Miller made a noise that might have been a chuckle.

Perkins had made a similar sound earlier. Maybe keeping your sense of humor was a prerequisite to survival as a cop.

"He has vanished," Miller said.

. . .

After we hung up, Perkins went down to the fitness room, saying he had to blow off steam. I sat on the balcony and thought about it all. Taylor told Emilio he alone would monitor the Russian golf funds. Suspicious? Sure, although this venture was his ticket to the Tour commissioner's seat. Wouldn't that be reason enough for him to want complete and total control over the operation? Still, even if that were the case, why not tell his head accountant how much money there was? Emilio had gone on to tell me Taylor and the Charities Office always kept immaculate records. Cost overruns for a project not yet started? Possible, yet the contractor, the golf course designer, hell, not even the land had been chosen. What had they overrun? Coffee filters? Something wasn't right. Taylor's infant daughter had been kidnapped. There were millions of dollars no one could account for. Or could Brian Taylor? Would he in fact produce documentation legitimizing every last penny?

Why had Catherine been returned? Wouldn't Silco logically hold her until Taylor did something with the money or the interest? Why then had he instructed the woman to return her? Or had she done that on her own? How was she connected to Silco? To Catherine? What would the ramifications of Catherine's return be? If Silco held Catherine as a marker on Taylor, what happened now that he'd lost his marker? To Taylor? To that money? Moreover, who and where was that woman? El Paso was on the Mexican border. If she didn't want to be found, good luck finding her.

The sun had set. It was 8:30. Lisa's dinner was no doubt over. I wondered where she was. After fifteen more minutes, I was still wondering about her, about the guy had dinner with. What was she doing? I went to find out.

. . .

My knock had been followed immediately by footsteps, a pause, then the rattling of the safety chain, and finally the door opened.

"Jack," she said, "what are you doing here?"

The suite yawned behind her, as if calling me back. She stood before me in green reversible athletic shorts and a white tank top. Her feet were bare, her toenails rose colored. Her hair had been pulled back and hung in place with an elastic ponytail holder.

"Is he here?"

I said it simply. I needed an answer, or so I thought.

Her original expression had not been warm. She hadn't been on the verge of leaping into my arms and saying, *You came back for me.*

Now, however, she looked at me, saw something in my eyes or my demeanor, and she made one of those long, slow exhales that says, *What am I gonna do with you?*

My face felt hot again. This time it wasn't anger or the onset of a migraine. I was way out of line and I knew it. I felt as if someone slapped my face to wake me from a dream; however, unlike even the worst nightmare, my appearance here and—worse still—my opening remarks would have dire consequences.

Truthfully, I had gotten that same exhale a lot as a kid. In fact, my mother had perfected various degrees of *the sigh.* I didn't, however, like receiving it as a thirty-five–year-old man. Especially from Lisa. I might have mentioned this to her, except, since the moment I had knocked, I'd known I had erred.

I couldn't just run up here and demand to know who she ate dinner with. My flushed face screamed of embarrassment.

The look on Lisa's expressed pity.

"Gregory Small?" she said. "Is that who you're asking about? The kid I had dinner with?"

So there we were—me, standing before the gaping door and, I assumed, visibly shrinking in upon myself like a turtle milliseconds before the impact of a tire. That, however, would have been a much less painful death—at least instantaneous.

But I was deserving. I had brought this upon myself. For that reason alone, I knew Lisa or the golf gods or fate or whatever it was that since the beginning of time had forced men to make asses out of themselves in front of women would not let me off easily.

And Lisa looked more than ready to oblige fate, smiling warmly.

"Is that whom you're asking about?" she said, using *whom* as if on television, making this a formal proceeding.

"I waved at you in the restaurant, but you didn't see me." The last several words left my mouth in slow motion. The remark was so feeble, so pathetic, I found myself actually turning around to make certain no Tour players or Perkins had heard.

On one level—a straightforward man's-man level—it was pathetic. Conversely, on another level, the relationship level, my weak repartee clearly placed Lisa far above me on that who-misses-who-more scale. And wasn't that what really counted? After all, I had an iron will, right? I could go months without Lisa. She, on the other hand, would break—and tell me what the hell "space" meant, once and for all.

"It was a dinner meeting," she said. "The kid asked me to look at his résumé, give him some advice. Wants to move into television."

I didn't say a thing.

"You're not jealous, Jack."

"Just wanted to make sure you were all right," I said.

She looked at me for a long pause, then reached up and touched my cheek gently. "That's sweet."

Her touch felt good, the way it always had. There was something reassuring in that. Then her mouth widened into a smile and I had the feeling I was being mocked or pitied.

"Let's meet for breakfast," she said.

"Okay."

She smiled again and closed the door.

I'd known she'd break. Jack Austin, possessor of an iron will.

When I turned to make my way back to my room, I froze at the sound of heavy footsteps. Not the slapping of sneakers on pavement, but the echo and vibration of sprinting through a hotel corridor. Behind me, I heard Lisa reopen her door, then her voice ask what was going on. People in hotels take note of the sound of sprinting—an instinctive self-preservation when residing several floors above ground.

The pounding footfalls neared, finally rounding the corner of the hall. Perkins was sprinting full bore, his eyes vivid and focused.

"Sharon Taylor," he said. His breath was controlled when he stopped before us. "She's been murdered."

"I'm calling for Mr. Taylor, please," Nik said, calmly into the phone. Indeed, he thought, given all he had been through, all he had done in the past forty-eight hours, he was calm.

Tired, frustrated to no end, yet calm—for calm was all he could be. He had worked a lifetime, maybe many lifetimes. Now, with the loss of the baby, everything had been jeopardized—his money, his way of life, and perhaps more importantly, his dreams.

He knew dreams were, after all, the things men traveled upon. He had ridden his across an ocean, out from the life his father had lived, ridden his dreams away from the very existence in which he had been destined to dwell. He would not, could not, surrender those dreams. To hold on to them, however, would take all the fortitude he possessed. This phone call was the second test of that resolve. He knew he had passed the first when the sound of fragile bones snapping seemed to echo in his ears like the cracking of porcelain.

"May I ask who's calling?" a man's irritated voice said. It sounded frustrated, Nik thought. From his own fourth-floor room, Nik had witnessed the media's descent on the hotel—due to Catherine's return and the death of a golf champion's wife. He assumed Brian Taylor and his fair wife had been inundated with requests and the man's irked tone did not alarm him.

"My name is Vladislav Tretiak," Nik said, smiling playfully. It was the name of a legendary Russian hockey player but served him well now. "I cover world affairs for the *Toronto Star.*"

"One minute, please," the voice said. "I'll see."

Nik leaned back in the wicker chair, crossed his ankles, and admired the tie he had chosen. It was maroon, silk, and went nicely with his dark suit, he thought. A briefcase lay near his feet. A typical American businessman. He smiled, glancing, through mirrored sunglasses, at the others around the room.

One day earlier, Tuesday, he had carefully noticed the arrival of Brian Taylor, had watched as Taylor was led to a conference room in the hotel by Florida police chief Miller and the big blond man whom Nik had seen in the hospital, and a host of others wearing suits, obviously cops, maybe FBI. Some men had held briefcases. One had carried a laptop computer. Nik had left a corpse in El Paso. Now Sharon Taylor's body had been found. Newspapers. Television. Radio. He had failed to realize how well known her husband was. The crush of media attention had been unexpected. Yet it made no difference. Sharon drank too much and her promiscuity had led to information Nik had found vital. Why couldn't another slip of the tongue lead to further information that in time might incriminate him?

He had done what had been necessary. Again, calm, rational. He had considered all aspects of the situation, all sides of the equation, then, he thought, had acted in a logical manner.

But also on Tuesday, Victor had arrived. With a small Latino, young and wiry, Victor had been brought to the same conference room Brian Taylor had entered. Nik had been seated (out of view from the main door) in the hotel lobby—first, garbed as a businessman reading the sports page and sipping coffee; later, as a tourist in sunglasses and bright shorts and a button-down flowered shirt—when Victor had walked casually through the lobby with Miller, down the first-floor corridor, to the conference room.

Victor had not seen him. Nik, however, had known instantly that Miller was leaning on both Taylor and Victor.

Now Nik was leaning right back.

"Hello," Brian Taylor said into the phone.

In the busy lobby, Nik was careful not to display emotion. However, the voice he heard sent a jagged bolt of electricity through him. It was the same voice he had listened to in the stillness of the hospital room.

"This really isn't a good time for interviews," Taylor was saying. "The Tour has a media department. I can give you—"

"Brian," Nik said, slowly.

Taylor fell silent. Nik heard Taylor's breath catch and sensed the man's tension as if a tangible strand were channeled through the phone.

"Are you there?" Nik said.

"What do you want?"

"Only for you to know that I gave Catherine back in good faith."

Silence.

"And, that I can reach out and place a hand on your shoulder—or touch your family—at any time."

Nik gently placed the house phone back in its cradle. Then he stood, flattened the wrinkles across the front of his slacks, and smiled warmly at a woman moving toward him.

The woman moved quickly past.

The lobby of the Courtyard by Marriott bustled with people who looked like executives, as well as those dressed casually—golfers or fans, Nik thought. The tournament was to begin the following morning. He had waited until this particular day,

Wednesday, this very evening hour in fact, to call Brian Taylor—from only six floors below.

Due to Perkins's announcement of Sharon Taylor's death, my breakfast with Lisa never materialized. She was running after the story. A 10:22 tee time enabled me to breakfast with Nash, loosen up on the range, and putt before my round.

We had spent the majority of the two previous days doing much of the same. As I made my way to the first tee, I felt good about my game. Even amid dire straits, I stay positive; however, this was the first time in weeks I truly felt like I was excelling in all aspects of the game—including the club between my ears. I had played well against Pete Taylor and shot subsequent practice rounds of sixty-nine and sixty-seven. Thursday morning, I was ready to play and ready to go low.

I was slated to round out a threesome made up of Brian "Padre" Tarbuck and a young second-year player out of the University of Georgia, Grant Ashley. It was an amicable, chatty threesome. Considering the results of my last two events—missed cut and withdrawal—I was thrilled with the draw.

A large gallery was in the bleachers near the first tee. Years ago, the moment you set eyes on a PGA Tour gallery, you were fully aware you were at a golf tournament. On this day, however, approaching the tee box, I viewed the collection of spectators and thought the group could have formed to view *any* American sporting event—football, baseball, basketball, or soccer. People of all ages, races—and, to the best of my estimation—all economic levels had gathered. The makeup of the Tour's membership had expanded since I'd started, although still overwhelmingly white. Yet the demographic of the fan base had exploded. The change had been wonderful to witness. My original meeting with Brian Taylor flashed into my mind, as did my statement to him: *Everyone should be exposed to golf.*

What had led to this leap in popularity? Tiger? TV coverage? Yes to both. Moreover, the exposure—however generated—had allowed the game to sell itself. It had. As I moved to the first tee, I saw such a collage of mixed faces that I could've been participating in America's *other* game, baseball.

Padre was smirking when Nash and I reached the tee. He extended a hand and I took it. He gave a huge shake, squeezing hard.

Players are grouped in categories, ranging from major championship winners to Monday qualifiers. Because of this, Padre and I were rarely paired together—he had won twice. Grant Ashley, an accurate driver of the ball, was small and had a southern accent that matched his name well. He was a class kid, one who respected the game and the forefathers of the Tour.

"This is a treat, buddy," Padre said. "When was the last time we played together?"

I told him it had been a year or two and introduced him to Nash. Players and caddies shook hands all around, then a man standing on the side of the tee box introduced us. An elderly man with thinning silver hair sat in a folding chair near the tee box. His name was Peter Schultz. He was a former Masters champion and had fought heroically in World War II. He was being honored this week by the Tour. Before hitting, Padre shook Mr. Schultz's hand, a gesture of respect and appreciation for what he'd done for the game. Grant and I followed suit.

We all parred the first three holes. As in my match versus Pete Taylor, the fourth hole—a par-four, 419 yards—proved a true test. The fairway was tight, the landing area narrow. I hit the blind tee shot to the center of the fairway, using a three-wood. Grant hit driver left, into the trees. Padre hit a three-wood as well, but into the right rough. Tournaments are never won on Thursday; they can easily be lost during the opening round, though. I was in good shape on a hole for which a birdie might yield two strokes against the field.

Grant was surveying his shot. The spectators lining the edge of the fairway had formed a V to provide him room. The mouth of the V gaped at the fairway's edge. Grant punched back, through a cluster of pines, to the fairway, leaving himself another hundred yards to the green. Next, Padre—shoes hidden beneath the four-inch rough—choked down on what looked like a six-iron and swung like one of those long-drive champs you see in no-name golf ball ads on television. If you don't believe touring pros are "athletes," you haven't played courses that sinister golf course superintendents water and seed like scientists trying to discover how thick six-inch grass can grow. Forcing your club through rough—that doesn't simply grab your iron but pulls the damn thing out of your hands, snaps it, then hands it back—tests the strength of your forearms, biceps, shoulders, even your back and legs because you need to drive down and through the ball with everything you have. You walk five miles per round and make demands on your back that defy logic. Padre was a lean man, strong and fit, and got his ball out of the rough and onto the green, thirty feet or so below the hole. I admired the shot and respected the level of conditioning and work ethic it had taken to produce it.

Next, Nash and I did the math for my shot: 145 yards to the green; 161 to the pin—but the green sloped back to front. The slope meant two things: I didn't want to carry the ball to the hole because it would spin back, maybe even roll off; and I didn't want to be long and leave a downhill putt. A seven-iron typically would have been the club from that distance, yet I pulled the eight, positioned the ball off my back foot, and hit a low Paul Azinger–like punch. It skipped on the collar, hit, and rolled to eight feet below the cup. It had been a shot I didn't have as a rookie, one that I had spent three weeks one winter playing in brutal Texas winds to acquire. The results of that effort now gave me a chance at birdie.

Padre putted first and left himself ten feet. The former priest swore under his breath as he marked the ball. A small gallery of "Padre-ites" stood near the green, some wearing skirts so short they may have bordered on illegal. (I tried not to notice.) Padre didn't look interested in the skirts, or the legs. He stood on the edge of the green and made practice strokes, trying to work the kink out.

Grant had been the last to play to the green and had stuck a pitching wedge inside my ball, his third shot.

I knelt behind the cup and examined the line from the hole back to my ball. The perspective from the hole to my ball had always helped me. I didn't plum-bob; however, I felt like the view from the other side of the cup offered a truer read. It had become part of my preputt routine. I had less than ten feet, straight, uphill. I addressed the ball, made two three-second strokes, then pulled the trigger. The ball had been stuck firmly but pulled, running past the left edge. I tapped in for par and remained at even. Both partners made bogie.

. . .

I went out in thirty-three, making six pars and three birdies. I stood on the seventeenth tee at three under par. The seventeenth hole at Westchester is a par-four, 374 yards—seemingly not long by Tour standards. Except the hole plays entirely uphill and there is a bunker fifteen feet deep in front of the green. The hole plays to an average score just slightly over par. Since I had been playing Westchester, it had been my personal nemesis. I knew that for the decade I'd been coming to Westchester, I'd left a tournament's worth of strokes on the seventeenth. Lisa, however, had gone a step further, crunching the numbers. She once told me a statistician friend at CBS figured out that in twenty-eight tournament rounds, I had played seventeen at ten strokes over par. I knew why this was so: I had failed to drive my ball in the fairway. In ten years, I had missed the cut only three times. I had hit driver, three-wood, one-iron, even two-iron off that tee. Yet I just couldn't seem to get comfortable on the tee box. Overall, I loved the course. However, this one hole—specifically the view from the tee box—did not match my eye.

So, when I hit driver and made birdie, I knew I was truly having a special round.

On the eighteenth hole, I was four under par and the third name on the leaderboard, trailing leaders Phil Mickelson and a rookie named Mike Miller, who were tied, by two shots. The eighteenth hole epitomizes the Westchester Country Club's layout. On paper—a par-five, 526 yards—it appears reachable in two, but the rough is brutal and your tee shot must be precise to have any chance of reaching the green in two. Likewise, a front right bunker guards against shots that fall short, while there is no room behind the multitiered green. Long is dead; short is dead. So when you pull your fairway metal or two-iron with hopes of reaching the putting surface with your second swing, your mind is doing gymnastics contemplating the risks.

My mind was doing some sort of tumbling routine as I stood on the tee and took my two customary practice strokes. If I made eagle, I could tie Miller and Mickleson. That *if*, however, loomed large because I couldn't drive with my three-metal. I couldn't play my drive in a manner that conceded this as a three-shot hole. That was too conservative. I was in second place and wanted first. Although my performance on this hole against Pete Taylor had led me to concede the hole and the match, I had my driver out. Like Wayne Gretzky said, you can't fear success.

My driver didn't let me down. My tee shot landed on the far end of the dogleg, leaving an excellent second shot with which I could attack the green.

Conversely, Grant Ashley was on his way to a seventy-six by this point. He hit a short drive into the right rough. Padre had made routine—but frustrating—pars all day and was at even par. He would be playing the hole in three shots.

"Pays to be a big hitter," Padre said to me as we moved down the fairway.

My play hadn't changed the dynamics of our gallery any. The Padre-ites remained undaunted, following his every move, cheering loudly for strong play, offering long sympathetic *Ooohhh*s when his birdie putts missed.

"You need to get married," I said to him. "Break some hearts. It's like playing golf with a rock star."

"I hope you know I take my past in the priesthood and my religion, even today, very seriously," he said.

"Of course," I said.

He looked around to make sure CBS on-course commentator

David Feherty was out of earshot. "I read something about a guy who'd gone to an all-boys school, got out, and realized how wonderful women were." He broke into a full-faced grin. "I'm experiencing something along those lines."

I slapped his back.

After Grant hit his second, we moved on.

I had the three-iron out and was working the club back and forth, rhythmically, thinking good thoughts, visualizing the ball flying straight over the left side of the fairway, hitting, and stopping near the back left pin placement.

I asked Nash for a water bottle. He took one from the bag and handed it to me.

"You haven't said boo all day," I said to him.

He shrugged. "Don't want to distract you. This is the best score you've had."

I nodded slowly, drank, and handed the water back to him. I thought there was more to it. He had been quiet since I'd told him about the murder of Sharon Taylor. I knew he had lunched with Lisa the day before. I knew Lisa would broach that subject, so I had not. Nash and I had developed a friendship and he had opened up to me. I didn't want to mention Sharon and have him think I did not believe that nothing physical occurred between them.

But all of that was not my second shot to a tough green with a chance to tie for the lead. The yardage book told me my drive had gone over 300 yards, leaving a three-iron to the green. I loosened the Velcro back of my glove, pulled it on tightly, and clenched and released my fist, stretching the leather. It was a quirk—like Sergio Garcia waggling his club ten or fifteen times before a shot, or like Fred Couples adjusting the shoulders of his Ashworth shirts prior to one of his smooth-as-buttermilk swings. I couldn't explain it and never realized I did it until Lisa mentioned it over dinner one night. Lee Trevino said he yawned to take in extra oxygen—and make his opponents think he was relaxed enough to take a nap—during pressure-packed situations. Maybe my fidgeting with my glove was similar.

Regardless, it kept my hands busy while I focused on this shot. Then the ball left the face of the three-iron and flew low and straight down the left side of the fairway before fading back, landing short of the green, leaping a trap, and running to the back tier.

I was putting for eagle and a chance to go to bed tied for the lead for the first time that season. Nash said nothing but made a fist and extended it. I tapped his fist with my own and we moved to the green.

Things quickly got better. Padre had landed his approach maybe two feet behind my ball, so I could go to school on his putt and learn what my own would do. He saw me eyeing my line from the opposite side of the hole and grinned, saying nothing. I had twelve feet with a slight left-to-right break that I would play four inches outside the cup.

Padre played the line I had seen and missed by two inches. After he tapped in for his eighteenth consecutive par, he glanced at me as if to say, *Learn from that, buddy.*

I did—playing six inches of break—and nailing the putt, center cut.

Nash pumped his fist and exhaled. After we exchanged high-fives, he sighed. "After the penalty stroke two weeks ago," he said, "I didn't want to screw anything up today."

"You wouldn't be out here if I thought you might," I said. "Relax and enjoy it."

"I'm starting to," he said, which—considering our very first round together—was very nice to hear.

But after a sixty-five, just about anything would have sounded great.

. . .

I was in the TV tower above the eighteenth green, seated between Jim Nantz and Lisa, whom I had not seen since Monday night. With heavyweights Lisa and Nantz, CBS had beefed up its golf coverage, offering some Thursday-Friday rounds as well as weekend coverage. Nantz introduced me, then Lisa asked the first question.

"Great round, Jack, your lowest score of the year in fact. How do you explain it?"

Being interviewed by Lisa always felt awkward. There was no discussion I could think of that we had not shared. Now she was asking me routine golf questions in front of a national TV audience, which seemed surreal, as if I were watching from outside my body, pointing and chuckling at us both. Given the current state of our relationship, this dialogue seemed even stiffer.

Yet I played along. "I love the course. I grew up in the northeast and this is hilly, tight, with tough greens, like the courses I played in college."

"Really had the flat stick going today," Nantz said. "How have you turned that part of your game around?"

"I've been working all summer on it. Trying to slow the stroke down—à la Loren Roberts. Also, I played a nice practice round with Pete Taylor earlier this week, which helped me build a little momentum. I'd like to send my deepest sympathies to Pete."

"Yes," Lisa said, "Pete Taylor has obviously withdrawn from the event following the death of his wife."

Then we cut back to live golf action for which I offered insight into the break on the fifteenth green that I'm certain only my mother viewing at home found fascinating. Then Lisa and Nantz thanked me for coming to the booth.

As I took off the headphones and they broke for commercial, I said to Lisa, "We never did make that breakfast date."

"How about dinner?" she said.

. . .

Aside from my time in the TV booth, I'd seen Lisa only on television since Perkins had stunned us with the news of Sharon Taylor's murder. In the ensuing hours and days, I had learned Sharon had been left partially covered in a nearby park. Also, that her neck had been snapped. "Like ringing a bird's neck," Perkins had said. "Somebody just twisted—snapped it cleanly."

I was thinking about that as I sipped a Heineken and waited in the dining room at the Westchester Country Club at 7:30 P.M. Why would Sharon Taylor be murdered? This wasn't New York City. To the contrary, this was suburban New York. The Tour, like any walk of life, had seen tragedies before. Stuart Appleby's late wife, Renay, had been lost when hit by a car outside a London train station. However, Pete Taylor's wife, Sharon, had been murdered. Her neck had been snapped, according to Perkins, who had shared that the police reports indicated the corpse had been dragged—given the heel marks of her shoes—a short distance, where she had been dumped and partially covered with leaves and tree limbs.

I thought back to Monday evening. I had departed Monday night's dinner hastily, although Perkins had said Pete never appeared for the meal that Pete himself had scheduled. During our golf round, Pete had told me Sharon was busy, then suggested we eat together. That meant he knew about her plans for the evening.

Lisa sat down across from me quietly, bringing my focus from Sharon Taylor's demise back to the present. Lisa's smile was broad and genuine. I'd seen the forced version lately. I preferred this one.

"You look great," I said. She did. White slacks that fitted over her thighs smoothly, and a fawn-colored silk shirt. Her hair was pulled back and held in place with a headband. The headband made her look young and she didn't wear it often, though I liked the look and had once told her so.

"You, too," she said.

I nodded modestly. I had chosen navy blue Docker pants and a pale blue golf shirt with white stripes. Navy blue wasn't really temperature appropriate, but fashion must be served.

A waitress took Lisa's drink order: a Diet Coke. Lisa glanced at my beer and smiled.

"Celebrating?" she said.

"First rounds don't mean much, but it beats being on the cut bubble."

"They mean something."

"You've been busy with the murder. I saw you wrote a piece for the *Washington Post*."

She nodded. "My old editor called. Said they had no one who could make it out here and they didn't want to run the AP file story, so I wrote a short article. I've only gotten six hours' sleep since Monday."

"You're amazing," I said. "What's the latest on the Sharon Taylor murder?"

The waitress brought me a second Heineken. Lisa declined another Diet Coke, but asked for slices of lemon to add to her ice water.

"Pete Taylor has been interviewed by police several times since Monday night," Lisa said and shrugged as she held the lemon above the water and squeezed. Then she dropped the lemon slice into the glass and stirred slowly.

"Pete?" I said.

"The husband is always the first suspect in a wife's murder."

"Yeah, but what about everything else going on—Brian, the Russian deal?"

She looked up from her glass. "Jack, everyone knows their marriage was dysfunctional. The cops are very tight-lipped about this, but there's something they're not saying. I think I'm very close to finding out what it is. Where has Perkins been?"

I shrugged. I didn't know. I assumed he was with Miller; however, I'd spent the previous two days practicing and attending the memorial service for Sharon Taylor. I had tried to find Pete Taylor, but had not succeeded. Now I had even more questions about the murder: What about the connection to Brian Taylor's project? Also, Miller had said Victor Silco was going to be in town. Where was he at the time of the murder? What about Victor's brother?

But we were there to talk about us. I leaned back in my chair. "Let's talk about us, Lisa."

She inhaled deeply. It wasn't a sigh, but sure didn't offer confidence in the future or this conversation.

"I've been thinking about us a lot," she said. Her forearms were on the table, her hands resting gently at the sides of her glass. "I've got a lot on my mind, Jack."

"Besides work."

"Besides work."

There are times in each relationship where it seems everything hinges on a moment, one brief yet crystalline segment in time when crucial statements are made and decisions flourish or falter.

"Tell me."

She bit her lower lip and took a long deep breath. When she blew the air out, her shoulders lowered. "I'm pregnant, Jack. I just want you to know. I want you to take some time to think it all over. I will, too. Then we can discuss it further."

"Lisa—"

She held her hand up. Her face flushed. "I can't discuss this right now. Please forgive me, Jack. I love you. I have to go. I'll call when I can discuss it."

Then she was gone, out of the restaurant. I stood slowly, tossed my white linen napkin into my chair, and left.

I had entered the restaurant tied for the lead in a golf tournament—and, naively, believed that was the most important thing in the world. I left knowing I had created another human life and not knowing what to do with that knowledge. For two hours, I sat on the balcony outside my hotel room with *The Simple Truth* and read poem after poem, thinking. Near the end of the book, I hit "My Sister's Voice" and read the poem several times. A particular section hit me in the gut:

> . . . I found no answer,
> or learned never to ask, for
> the wind answers itself if you
> wait long enough. It turns one way,

then another, the trees bend, they
rise, the long grasses wave and bow,
all the voices you've ever heard
you hear again until you know
you've heard nothing. . .

That about summed it up. I felt like the guy in the poem—wandering, listening to the wind, but mostly wishing I had answers to my questions. Lisa and I discussed marriage once, deciding it was not right for us. Was that still the case? People change and grow with the events of their lives.

I was thirty-five. I had spent years driven to perfect my own abilities, enhance my skills—those necessary to knock a small white sphere into a hole in the ground. Certainly golf was much more, but at that moment, the game, my career, seemed trivial. During my youth, throughout high school, then college, I hit range balls until my hands blistered, taped and bandaged them, and the following day, did it again; I had putted, chipped, hit bunker shots until my glistening arms were covered with fine sand; lifted weights, ran, done countless sit-ups and push-ups, and played thousands of rounds of golf—all to become the best player I could be. *Me. My* career. Developing *my* abilities.

I felt ashamed. I was nearing middle age and, to date, had spent my life concerned primarily with myself. Of course, I loved Lisa and thought of her often. Yet she—probably more than anyone I knew, in fact—could take care of herself. Yes, I had tried to give back to my parents and had tried to help others, like Hutch Gainer. But I had helped Hutch to protect the game *I* love.

This was different.

Fatherhood would be hitting the ground running. Fatherhood would be immediate responsibility. A tiny infant, a baby, a child, a teen, then an adult.

I had no nephews, no nieces. I had never even changed a diaper. Sleepless nights. Parent-teacher conferences.

But also pushing a stroller at sunset. Holding a child's fragile hand. Watching him or her sleep. Teaching him or her to talk, to act, even sharing my love of golf and poems. Above all, it would mean unconditional love.

Many people whom I knew had kids. I'd seen the work involved, seen guys try to perform in golf tournaments after staying up all night to rock crying infants. I'd also seen a look in their eyes when they showed people wallet photos in the locker room, heard something in their voices when they spoke of them.

I thought back to Perkins holding up Jackie for Lisa and me to see shortly after Jackie'd been born. The man who—at times—I knew to be the coldest human being I'd ever met, someone who could look a person in the eye and squeeze a trigger, had held that baby with a gentle love of which I'd not known him capable; and his expression—sagging eyes, affected oval-shaped mouth—told me he would gladly give up his own life for this child, with whom, in reality, he had yet to spend even an hour.

My mind ran to Lisa. Did she want the baby? What would she say? No wonder she needed space. *She* was pregnant? Golf's most serious journalist? I had never imagined it. It had never even crossed my mind. I thought we would certainly be together forever, although our "together" differed from conventional "together." No marriage. No white picket fence. No children. Work and play. Things change suddenly. A baby.

A baby?

By the time I reached high school, my father had taught me most things I needed to know to succeed in life. Many of those lessons had come via his example—watching him rise at 4 A.M. to squeeze in two extra building projects each summer; hearing his diesel pickup rumble to a start, then seeing headlights flash across my bedroom ceiling, while I still lay beneath blankets as he left to plow driveways following a winter storm. Other lessons had been stressed during conversations on the golf course; before dawn in a canoe, fishing; walking with shotguns, hunting birds.

Now, I thought back to those times, tried to smell Maine's autumnal woods—chimney smoke, crisp outdoor air hinting of winter—and I could almost hear our footsteps crackling among fallen leaves. I remembered how I had listened to each word my father said as if he had stood on Mt. Olympus: to treat others as I wanted to be treated; the key to living a long life was to find one thing you enjoyed and do it, regardless of pay; I should marry my best friend, as he had done.

Dyslexics often see things in black and white, right and wrong. The Philip Levine book lay on the plastic chair next to me, still open to "My Sister's Voice." *All the voices you've ever heard / you hear again until you know / you've heard nothing.* Maybe I had heard nothing because nothing needed to be said.

I knew what I would do and what I wanted to do. What I needed now was to know if Lisa felt the same way.

. . .

Perkins moved like a tornado. Without closing the door behind him, he had burst into the room and onto the veranda, telling me I was to meet with law officials, Brian Taylor, Victor Silco, and him. Upon hearing my news, he froze in midfrantic rush.

The sun was finally setting. Now Perkins sat very slowly on the plastic chair next to mine, his eyes locked on my own.

"Pregnant?" he said. "Lisa?"

"Yes." I leaned back, crossed my arms, tilted my head, and stared at him uneasily. What was he thinking? The common reaction would have been a congratulatory slap or handshake.

"She's too busy to be pregnant," he said. "Jesus Christ, she's about to blow the top off this investigation, Jack."

"What are you talking about?"

"I mean, she knows—probably better than Miller and me—the details of this case. You tell her anything?"

"Until Emilio came to me, I had nothing but unsubstantiated information and a strange phone call. Lisa doesn't deal with unsubstantiated, so I never had anything to tell."

He leaned back in his chair and shook his head. "Well, she's on the warpath. She has Emilio, too."

"For a story?"

"Christ, yeah. I honestly think it was a relief for him to talk to Miller about that extra interest he found. Hell, he went from fearing Taylor's wrath to acting like he wants the guy's job. He brought in a goddamned paper trail for us to confront Taylor with."

"How did Lisa get him as a source?"

"Jesus, how does she do any of the things she does?" He leaned back and clasped his hands atop his belt. He had on jeans and a white T-shirt that read NEW ENGLAND PATRIOTS under a dark blue blazer. He wore loafers.

"She probably hounded the kid until he agreed to go on record," he said. "Or gave her the same papers he gave Miller."

I thought back to her handling of Pete Taylor during our first meal with him and Sharon, how sympathetic Lisa had been, how laid-back. Then I recalled the way she had chased the Hutch Gainer story—like a shark following the scent of blood. She was a true journalist, not an ambulance chaser, not a cream-puff either. When the story was corrupt, and she felt it needed to be told, no one was tougher. She never gave up.

"FBI guys are furious," he said. Below us, lights were coming on as the day's last rays faded. "She's airing a story tomorrow pinpointing where the money is that's earning all that interest. She even knows how much is in the goddamned account. *And* someone said that now she's writing stories for the damned *Washington Post*. She knows about Victor's brother, too. How do the two of you even find time for sex?"

"She knows about the money in the charity account?" I said.

"That's what I was coming down here for," he said and a wide smile spread across his face. "Taylor finally came clean, Jack, admitted everything—the money, the kidnapping, the accident."

"How'd you guys pull that off?"

Perkins spread his hands before him. "He ran to Miller, white as a ghost, said he got a phone call from someone Victor sent to his hospital room. Said it was dark and he couldn't really see him, but that the guy held a knife to his throat in there. He says now the guy has threatened to kill him and his family."

"But Emilio had already come to me," I said, "about the money."

He was nodding, as I pieced things together.

"Right," he said. "So, effectively, it was too late to threaten Taylor. The government will probably get the money."

"You trace that call Taylor says he got?"

"Tried. Nothing looks unusual. Phone in his room was ringing off the hook after they got Catherine back. A couple calls came from the lobby, but they ordered some take-out food and delivery guys always call from the lobby when they arrive."

"Needle in the haystack?" I said.

He shrugged and exhaled slowly. "We looked. Everything is accounted for."

"What did Brian confess to?"

"Taylor says Victor originally approached him with a legitimate donation. Then Victor came back with a deal and a threat: Victor paid him two million bucks to run sixteen mil through the Tour's Charities Office and leave it in a dummy charity to be picked up. If Taylor said no, they'd take his daughter. He took the two million. When he didn't move the rest of the money, they took Catherine."

"Who's the guy with the knife?"

Perkins shrugged. "Silco won't cooperate. Isn't saying a thing."

"The brother?"

"Goddamned if I know. Anyway, Taylor said he got cold feet and didn't move the money, thought he might get caught."

"And now he did."

"Yeah," he said. "Taylor's got three accountants and Emilio overseeing them. Said he was nervous about getting caught. He was trying to come up with a safe move, so the transaction wouldn't come back to him."

I shook my head. "Tough to do when it's part of an account you won't let Emilio or his staff see."

"He shot himself in the foot with that move," he said. "Being secretive breeds suspicion."

"He was in a no-win situation."

"Two million doesn't sound like no-win to me."

"A guy shows up with a legitimate donation to a civic project that's the crowning achievement to your career? Of course you welcome the original donation. Then he returns with a deal that, if you turn it down, he'll take your child?"

"Got to have balls," Perkins said.

"Easy for you to say," I said. "You've seen Taylor. All he does is cry. No wonder he was too nervous to move the money."

"I don't feel bad for the guy," he said. "He broke the law. He'll have to face up to it."

"Which is what?"

"He wants immunity for testifying against Victor. Probably get off with no jail time."

"They want Victor," I said.

"He's the guy with the answers."

I shook my head. "What about Sharon Taylor?" I said. "Where's the murder stand in all this?"

"No one knows, but you've got to figure Brian wouldn't come clean, even if he did it. His own brother's wife? He wouldn't admit to that."

"Good point," I said. "But he was in El Paso getting Catherine when she died. You think he had her killed?"

He shrugged. "Miller doesn't seem to think so. With Victor not turning on his brother, it makes the brother number one for everything—including world hunger—on my list. We can talk about that when we get downstairs."

"I need to mention something."

He heard tension in my voice and sat up straight again, looking at me, his gaze weighty and serious.

"Nash's run-in with Sharon Taylor," I said. "Like I told you before, it was nothing serious, but I know you guys are looking into her death. When and if this ever went to trial . . ."

He made a dismissive gesture with one hand. "I've thought about that already. I'll let Miller know. Someone will ask Nash a few routine questions, but he's not our guy. He was with me, lifting weights, at the time of the murder."

"That's right," I said and nodded.

"Jack, the pregnancy is heavy. What are you two going to do about the baby?"

"I'm going to start by talking to Lisa," I said. "Something I haven't done enough of lately."

. . .

The inside of the suite didn't help clear my head. The place reminded me of Lisa, of the living rooms in suites we usually shared. The carpet was the same off-white color as the carpet Perkins and I had in our room, except obviously much newer; it was brighter and thicker. There were glass end tables, a white bar matched the carpet, and a loveseat and sofa set. Several portable tables had been set up in various spots. The room smelled of old coffee and cigarettes. The sliding-glass door was open to the balcony and, beneath the outside light, I saw a smattering of cigarette butts. There were notepads, paper coffee cups, and pens strewn throughout.

I was there to make an official statement. Miller had been waiting for us. He shook my hand when I entered. Perkins had said Miller and the feds wanted details of my original meeting with Brian Taylor—when Victor Silco had first appeared—of the trip to the Florida hospital, of the recent phone call begging me and Perkins off, and of my talk with Emilio.

Silco and Brian Taylor were seated on the sofa, across from two guys wearing suits and sitting on folding chairs. Paper coffee cups sat before each of them, neither man speaking. Silco shifted in his seat when his eyes met mine.

Miller introduced me to an FBI agent named MacDonald, who was maybe my height, but thinner, and wore a navy blue suit. He had neatly trimmed brown hair and a diamond stud in his left ear. At the table next to MacDonald, a guy had a laptop open and was doing something on the computer. Emilio was there, next to the guy, talking in an excited voice, pointing at the screen. He looked over and waved.

I saw Brian Taylor look at Emilio from across the room. The look was one of disgust—he had hired this kid, after all; now the kid was working with the feds to nab him. Taylor looked terrible, sitting low on the sofa, his blond mane mussed, white dress shirt wrinkled, and his maroon silk tie flying at half-mast. He no longer looked like the Tour's Chosen One. Now he looked exhausted. He also looked lost, confused, aimless, like things were coming at him at a pace with which he could not keep up.

MacDonald walked me over to Taylor and Silco. When he moved, there was no extra motion, graceful, yet direct. We stood in front of them. No one spoke. I hoped he wasn't going to ask me questions in front of the two of them. I had expected to write the statement, alone, left to ponder and recall details. As we stood before them, I wondered what Miller thought of the FBI involvement. I also wondered who was in control of things now. Regardless, neither Miller nor MacDonald seemed hostile.

"We're going to start back in January, at square one," MacDonald said, still looking at Taylor and Silco. "Dr. Silco, maybe Jack will be able to add something for us, since you don't feel like cooperating."

Silco just looked at him.

"As I've said all along, Dr. Silco, you have been charged but are free to acquire an attorney and review your options—maybe post bail, possibly even leave here."

"He won't leave?" I said.

"Strange, isn't it," MacDonald said. "You'd think he knew something we didn't. Like who killed Sharon Taylor and where that person is. Even what the killer's agenda is."

Taylor looked at Silco, then at MacDonald. Then he stared at the floor, as if waiting to be lashed.

"How's it going, Brian?" I said.

He looked up, his head moving slowly. "'How's it going?'" His head shook back and forth. "I've lost everything—my family, my job, my reputation."

I couldn't bring myself to feel sorry for him.

"But," MacDonald said, "you've been very cooperative. That'll count for something. Dr. Silco, on the other hand, seems to have forgotten how to communicate in English, ever since we asked about his brother and where he acquired some twenty-four million bucks on a research fellow's salary."

"What does Sharon's death have to do with all this?" I said.

MacDonald shot me a look, the expression telling me I was the golfer; he was the FBI agent, so he'd do the asking.

Miller came over and looked at Taylor. "Brian, Dr. Silco, we've got some food coming. Why don't you wait in the bedroom while we talk to Jack?"

Two other suits led them out. Miller pointed to the sofa and I sat. MacDonald sat beside me, where Taylor had just been.

"You're winning the tournament," Miller said. "Congratulations."

I had all but forgotten. I managed to nod modestly. Talking golf, however, was not going to move this along. It was 9:30 P.M.

"Chief Miller has informed me of your status in this case, so I will update you, hoping you may be able to add something."

I waited.

"Taylor turned on Silco today," MacDonald said. He spoke like he walked—no wasted time. The golf conversation was over. "Taylor is terrified, says someone—not Victor—is demanding the money be moved to the dummy account. Says the guy making the calls is threatening his family. Said he had an accent similar to Silco's. What did Brian tell you when he called?"

I told him.

"Taylor says someone came to his hospital room, held a knife to his throat," MacDonald said. He was sitting with his forearms resting on his thighs. "Taylor mention any of that?"

"No."

"Any idea who that might have been?"

"Excuse me?" I said.

MacDonald shrugged politely, as if it had been something he'd had to ask. "You were in the hospital room the same day it happened. See anything or anyone?"

"No."

"When you were in Florida, you see any photos on Dr. Silco's desk that you can recall?" MacDonald said.

"No," I said. "I don't think he had any pictures out. You think the money belongs—belonged—to Victor's brother, huh?"

Miller grinned. MacDonald just looked at me for a time. Then he slid a pad and pen to me and pointed. I knew MacDonald had tolerated my final question. I flashed Perkins a grin that said I had enjoyed bugging the feds, then went to one of the folding tables and proceeded to write.

. . .

Absurd. When Perkins told me, it was the only word that came to mind. I had passed in my report, like a timely school kid, and was on my way out of the suite when Perkins approached with an expression that fell somewhere between disgust and humor.

"We've got a houseguest," he said.

I paused in front of the door.

"Taylor is staying with us," Perkins said. "Says he needs protection. MacDonald and Miller spoke to the Tour security guy, Schilling. Although, the Tour fired Taylor, Schilling said they will keep me on a little longer to watch Brian for the next few days."

"Bodyguard?" I said. "Isn't that beneath you?"

"Hell," he said, "I didn't exactly find the girl, which they hired me to do. Someone dumped her at a hospital. Christ, working school crossings might not be beneath me, right now."

"I can't make fun of you if you're being self-effacing."

"Exactly," he said. "But it's the truth. I was hired to find the girl and didn't. I'll stick around and do what they want. If it's bodyguard stuff, I'll do it."

"For what it's worth, they must've had Catherine hidden pretty damned well."

"Do I try to make you feel better after you shoot seventy-six?" he said.

"Never."

"There's a reason. Just let it go. This is a fresh start. It *will* go better."

"You think he's in danger?" I said.

"Damned if I know, but someone killed Sharon Taylor. Could be a connection to this. Miller talked to her husband for a long time. Pete told Miller she wasn't always faithful. That could mean a lot of things."

"Like she got mixed up with the wrong guy?"

He nodded. I saw Brian Taylor approaching over Perkins's shoulder. Taylor looked no better. The front right side of his shirt was not tucked in. He did, however, manage a smile. He pulled a black rolling suitcase.

Completely absurd. We had been trying to help this guy for months. He had fought us, confused us, and insulted us the entire time. Now he smiled, wanting our help. Perkins saw this as a chance for redemption. I, on the other hand, wasn't looking forward to having Taylor crying in our hotel room; I had my own concerns: Lisa, a baby, the Buick Classic.

My expression must have relayed my thoughts because Taylor said, "Thanks very much, Jack. I have nowhere else to go."

"Let's get going," Perkins said and led the way.

The newspaper's headline made his hands tremble. Nik moved quickly to the television. He scanned several channels. Then he saw her face—the pretty brunette, her name beneath that tanned smooth face: Lisa Trembley. He sat on the edge of his hotel bed and listened as she explained what PGA Tour official Brian Taylor and University of Miami professor Dr. Victor Silco had attempted. He listened with dread, the sensation so overwhelming, so completely overpowering, her words seemed to reverberate in the room, echoing in his head as if forcing him to listen twice.

Then, uncontrollably, he laughed—it was the only thing he could do.

As if some internal switch had been thrown, he grabbed the digital clock off the nightstand, yanking the cord from the wall, and threw it—with every ounce of his being—against the wall over the television. It exploded, bursting into plastic fragments, and littered the carpet below.

Her final sentence rocked him into a cold, deadpanned glare.

"The money is being held and will be seized by the U.S. government if Silco is convicted. Also, *CBS Sports* has learned from a high-ranking law official wishing anonymity that Taylor is seeking immunity to testify against Silco."

Nik sat staring. The television remained on, although he heard nothing. He felt as though he were watching himself from outside his body, a bystander observing his movements, as he fell backward and lay on the bed, staring at the ceiling.

The transaction had not been made.

Would never be made.

He knew that now. He felt as if the air had left his body. He sat up quickly, gasping for breath. His throat constricted; nausea overtook him. He stood and ran to the bathroom and vomited. He stayed in the bathroom a long time.

Only an hour earlier, he had awoken, showered, and dressed in a conservative business suit, and called down for bran cereal, orange juice, and the paper. He had planned to revisit Brian Taylor, to seek him when he was alone, and watch him make the transaction, then end their association forever.

Nik no longer had the little girl. That had been a major blow; however, he had thought it hadn't been insurmountable. Taylor had obviously confessed the details of the money—where it had been hidden; where it was to go—when he had handed over Victor. *That* was insurmountable.

Victor. Taylor had given the authorities Victor. Would Victor in turn give them Nik? Victor had not even called the Miami house. Surely he knew Nik would not be there, yet he could have left a message, some coded warning, some signal informing Nik that Victor was being taken in, questioned at first, and surely would be charged. Instead, Nik had received nothing.

Why no warning? Was Victor keeping Nik in his back pocket in case the need for self-preservation arose? Surely that time was now upon Victor. Or worse, had his brother Cain instantly offered Nik when he learned Brian Taylor had turned on him? If that was the case, Nik could never return to his Miami house. The authorities would be waiting.

His cheek resting against the cold porcelain of the toilet rim, images of their childhood flashed before his mind's eye, as if pictures from a slow movie reel: Victor and Nik as children—wearing torn brown trousers, tattered shoes, soiled button-down shirts—playing in the fields around their farm. He had always been the leader in their games. He was the oldest. He remembered Victor had once been afraid of the chickens, how he would enter the coop as if walking on a bed of nails. Nik had shown there was nothing to fear, leading the way, tossing seeds underhand, scattering them across the floor. Then he had stood back and watched as Victor had gained confidence and slowly approached the birds.

He recalled their mother's funeral, how she looked in the casket, young Victor tugging on his sleeve, sniffling, then finally bursting into tears. He remembered holding Victor close, telling him things would be fine, that he would see to it. Then he had, sending Victor to the university in the United States. He would never forget the day when he had sent Victor toward his future, a better future, in the United States.

The look of gratitude had been so sincere that day. Where had that gratitude gone? Now Victor had come to this very hotel in suburban New York and spoken to authorities. What had he said?

The previous evening, Nik had ordered room service and a bottle of $100 champagne. The busboy who had brought it had given Nik the respect he deserved, the respect he had *earned.* The kid had called him *Mr.* Philco, the name Nik had registered under. When Nik tipped the kid $50, he had seen the appreciative gaze, the awe that money provided. Victor had once looked at him that way. Brian Taylor should have looked at him that way, too. After all, he paid Taylor handsomely and had trusted Taylor to follow through on his word. A man is only as strong as his word. Taylor's word had proven pathetically weak.

Nik climbed to his feet and stood looking at himself in the mirror. There was a spot of vomit on his shirt collar. His face looked pale, blotchy. His breath tasted rancid, acidic. He did not like the face that peered back at him. It was a desperate, urgent face. One that now craved the look the busboy had given him, the look Katrina's face held when he had first met her, the look that even Oleg, when offered the job, had sported. Looks of admiration, all. Of respect. The money that would have forever brought all of that was now gone.

Nik moved quickly to the bedroom, pulling the knot from his tie as he moved, unbuttoning his shirt. He flung open the drawer and pulled out blue jeans and a white T-shirt. Beneath the layer of clothing lay a Smith & Wessen nine millimeter. He checked the load: eight rounds, plus one in the chamber.

There was only one thing left to do.

It had all slipped away: the baby, the money, and now, he knew full well—due to the publicity and Brian Taylor's potential immunity—the life he had wanted was gone as well. With that life, his last possession had also been lost: his dream, the dream for which he had taken so many risks, done so many things that would have terrified most others, the dream that had carried him from his former land to Miami.

There would be no money to buy into the Canadian restaurant chain, no money to pay the contractor for the beachfront house. It was gone. With it, Nik felt himself drifting away, too. Shriveling, shrinking in upon himself, drying up, cracking. More than anything, he felt himself cracking, as if he were screaming, mouth agape, veins protruding on his forehead, his pulse racing along his throat.

But no words came.

Then he was sitting on the bed. The clock told him more than an hour had passed, but he couldn't remember it. It didn't matter now anyway. Time didn't matter. It would all be over soon.

There was just one thing left to do. He could not get close to Victor without himself being apprehended. That wasn't how this would end. He had come too close to have this end on someone else's terms. He could accept never being able to ask Victor just what he had told the men in that room, what he had been asked, if he had admitted whose money it was, or that Sharon Taylor had originally mentioned the Russian golf plan, which, doubtless, would point authorities at Nik for her murder. He had done right by Victor. If his brother had not done the same, so be it.

Which left only Brian Taylor, the man responsible for all this—for the loss of the money, for the death of Sharon Taylor, for what would certainly be the downfall of Victor's academic career, and for what Nik was about to do.

Thankfully, Brian Taylor had gone back to our room and went directly to sleep—on a cot Perkins had set up for him in the corner of the room. I had not had time to see Lisa. I knew her schedule. She had run off to the course to prepare before I'd awoken. She had worked through lunch, filing updates to the story she'd broken earlier that morning. It had been a tell-all, detailing the money laundering and saying authorities were looking for Silco's brother for questioning.

It was now 2:22 P.M. on Friday. Nash and I were on the first tee, again with Grant Ashley and Padre Tarbuck. The field would be cut after this—the second—round, the top seventy players (and ties) staying to play for the purse on the weekend. Mickelson had played early and shot a sixty-four and was now alone atop the leader board at 129, thirteen strokes under par. Several others had made moves, while rookie Mike Miller had faltered, shooting seventy-six. I stood on the first tee—at six under par—now in third place, anxious to regain my position as a tournament leader. Doing so would mean birdies. Which would mean stiff approach shots. And solid putts. And straight tee shots. And accurate positional shots.

I sighed. That was no way to think. You had to let the game come to you. Forcing things never did any good. The closest I had come to winning had been a playoff loss. During that week, I had shot rounds of sixty-seven, sixty-seven, sixty-nine, and sixty-eight—four consecutive rounds in the sixties. Given Mickelson's start, I knew similar play might be required. To do so, however, I would just go play and see what happened.

The second hole at the Westchester Country Club—a par-four, 384 yards—averages a little over four strokes, but can be had. Although the green is heavily guarded by bunkers and the standard play is to hit a "positional" tee shot, I had parred the first hole and, standing on the second tee, selected my driver. Padre glanced at me out of the corner of his eye, but said nothing as he pulled a four-iron.

I had retained honors and brought the club back slow and low, making a wide shoulder turn. I stopped near parallel at the top, then exploded like a tightly wound coil, springing down and through the ball. The swing was hard—maybe 90 percent full throttle—yet balanced, and I held the follow-through. The ball stopped seventy-five yards from the front of the green.

Grant shook his head. "Ate your Wheaties this morning, huh?"

Padre said nothing. I knew he had long pulled for me to break through and win. In retrospect, I believe he was letting me play, keeping quiet, hoping I'd find a comfort zone, enter it, and stay there for the round. Each of my playing partners hit conservative tee shots into the landing area, near the 150-yard marker.

Thus, I was last to hit my approach shot. Typically, I tried to leave myself a full sand wedge to the green. This time, though, I was doing things differently. It was not something easily explained. I had not *thought* about what club to select at all; rather, I had *felt* driver was the club to hit. Instinct. When you have played well enough to last a decade on tour, but have never won, you have played yourself into contention many times. I had spent the winter considering why my previous season's final round scoring average (73.2) had paled compared to my Friday scores (69.72).

I was not the noted sports psychologist Dr. Bob Rotella. The only thing I had come up with was that by Friday—the second round—I had either played myself out of the tournament and, thus, had nothing to lose, or was on the cut line with my back to the wall, fighting to play the weekend. That was *desperation* not *pressure*. The two are very different: Pressure is playing the back nine Sunday with a one-stroke lead. To hold your lead means exemption, financial security, and a PGA Tour win under your belt when you entered the locker room.

More than anything, that was what I wanted—to be considered, among my peers, one who had faced the pressure of having the best players in the world gunning for you, looked them in the eye, stared them down, and won. Therefore, I had vowed that if and when I got into contention this year, I would not think. I would trust my swing and react instinctively to what the course gave me. Driver felt right; and that club selection had been effective.

Now I stood behind the ball, sixty-degree wedge in hand, and took two practice swings, my eyes darting from my ball to the pin as I tried to feel how far to hit the shot. When I was ready—when the tension had left my shoulders, when my grip was relaxed—I moved to the ball and stood over it, hearing only silence. I opened my stance, then brought the club back short of parallel, then down across my body, an outside-to-in motion like I would use for a bunker shot, holding my right hand open through impact, not allowing my wrist to turn over throughout the swing. The result was a medium-sized divot and a lot of spin. The ball carried to the pin, hit, and backed up nearly six feet. I was inside both Padre and Grant and would be last to putt.

On the green, I had no one to learn the break from—Grant was putting from left of the hole; Padre was putting across the green—so I read my putt, then visualized the ball following the line, and dropping, as I waited for the others. Neither made his birdie attempt, although each left only a tap-in for par. When my turn came, I replaced my ball, positioning the MAXFLI logo so that it made a vertical line, stood, and leaned over the putt. Then I wiped my mind clean—a gray, empty void of tranquil nothingness—and stroked the ball.

The Maxfli line blurred into a tight spiral, never wavering, until the ball hit the bottom of the cup. A birdie. My tee-shot decision had paid off.

. . .

The sixteenth hole is, statistically, the most difficult par-three on the course. It's a downhill 204-yard tee shot into a narrow green the size of a postage stamp. I stood on the tee with honors—and was seven strokes under par for the day, thirteen under for the tourney. "In the zone" didn't do justice to my state. I had fallen into a place where golf gods, or fate, or my own swing had mistaken me for Jack Nicklaus.

I had made no bogeys on the front and gone out in thirty-one, five under par. I was two under on the back and trying to stay in the moment; however, I had looked ahead enough to realize that if I could par in, I'd record a sixty-four. Most importantly, I was shooting the lights out with my putter. Everything had fallen. Especially the must-make putts. I made a twenty-five-footer to save par after an approach shot from the woods on thirteen and had hit a fifteen-footer to get up and down from a bunker on fourteen. I was in sole possession of first place, so the sixteenth green didn't look all that small on this day.

I had a five-iron. There was no breeze. In fact, the heat had been brutally bad, but I was so focused I had not noticed. In years past, I routinely hit four-iron here, but was jacked with adrenaline and knew it would add one club to whatever I selected.

When I brought the club back, there was no sound, no thoughts, as if I had reached some heightened state of consciousness. Regardless, I did not analyze any of it until much later. It would have been greedy to do so while in the moment. If the golf gods were in fact smiling on me this week, I would simply ride it out.

I held the follow-through, staring the ball down. It landed in the center of the green, bounced once, and rolled forward, stopping twelve feet to the right of the pin; I would have a sidehill putt for birdie.

Grant was not going to make the cut. He shot seventy-six the day before and the wheels had completely fallen off this day. He would later finish with an eighty-one, and his tee shot on sixteen buried in a green-side bunker. Padre shot even par Thursday and was on his way to a sixty-nine. His tee shot on the sixteenth landed in the center of the green, inside my ball.

After Grant blasted to within a foot, then putted out, I was up.

I judged the break to be two feet, left-to-right, picking up speed near the hole. It wasn't a putt to get cute with. I was leading the tourney and on a roll. A two-putt par would keep my momentum going. I imagined a two-foot circle around the hole—*leave the ball anywhere inside that circle.* I hit the ball off the toe of the putter—to deaden the strike—and it rolled high above the hole, the Maxfli label blurring once again. When the ball was six feet from the cup, I was certain I had played too much break—a common occurrence on the sixteenth green.

Then it started to turn. At two feet away, it darted to my right, dropping, center cut.

Nash was giggling. "Like watching Jordan go off for fifty."

"Not quite," I said. "Seeing a guy shoot a fifty-nine would be like that."

"Man, this is your day, Jack. That ball didn't go in, it would still be rolling."

Nash was right. I had hit it too hard. Probably too hard to even take the break, yet somehow it had.

I was fourteen under par with two holes left to play on Friday.

. . .

We were at the seventeenth, the hole on which I had constantly struggled. On this day, times past were not on my mind. Rather, I hit my driver 307 yards down the center of the fairway, leaving a full sand wedge, uphill, to the green. Grant hit driver, too. It was his best drive of the afternoon and had left him ten yards behind my ball. Padre, as usual, was thinking his way around the course. He had hit three-wood, then fired a nine-iron to ten feet from the cup.

Grant hit next. I had to turn away. He dumped the shot into the fifteen-foot-deep bunker guarding the front of the green. It wasn't something you want to watch before attempting a similar shot. He cursed and slammed his pitching wedge into his bag.

I went through my preswing routine, then squared my feet and shoulders to the pin, which was tucked only four paces beyond the craterlike sand trap that had swallowed Grant's ball. I made a simple, controlled, swing with my sand wedge, finishing with my right arm held firmly across my body—an abbreviated follow-through. I saw the ball fly over the trap and bounce once. From my vantage point, that was all I could see. When the gallery went crazy, I knew it was close.

Close turned out to be three feet and I made the birdie putt.

I parred the eighteenth, ending with a sixty-two, the best round of my career, totaling fifteen under for the first thirty-six holes and a two-stroke lead heading into the weekend.

. . .

By the time I got out of the media tent, it was close to 7 P.M. I wasn't accustomed to being interviewed extensively after my rounds, although I wasn't complaining. A reporter had mentioned that Bob Gilder had gone fifteen under for thirty-six holes in 1982 and that I had tied that record score. *How does that make you feel?* he asked. How did he think it made me feel? In any case, my play appeared to be the story—but not for what I thought was the right reason.

I sat on the stage in a high-backed leather chair and fielded questions about my round—in contrast to my season. It got annoying—*Where did these two rounds come from?* My ability level, I felt like saying. *Was there any indication this play was about to surface?* I work my ass off; why wouldn't it surface? I wanted to say, but didn't. My time with Lisa had taught me a lot about the job of the media.

I patiently answered questions and tried to understand how the reporters could be surprised by my near record-setting performance.

I was hungry and exhausted and wanted only room service by the time I finally arrived back at the hotel. More than that, I wanted to talk to Lisa. The first thing I did was go up to her suite.

The elevator doors opened and I stepped into the corridor. A man with a pale complexion stood in the hall wearing jeans and a leather jacket. A line of perspiration ran across his forehead. When he saw me, he moved past, several doors down from Lisa's room, to the ice machine.

I heard no rumble or clang. He wasn't getting ice. In fact, he had no bucket. Something was wrong. I walked past Lisa's room to the ice machine myself.

He was leaning against the wall next to the machine. He looked dazed like he was on something. I didn't say anything. I could tell he was upset. He didn't speak, yet his mouth moved as if mouthing words to an invisible bystander. I smelled the salty scent of perspiration. Suddenly, he pushed himself off the wall and moved languidly away, down the corridor, rounding the corner, moving out of sight.

Although I had never seen him before, I recognized him. It had to be Victor Silco's brother, Nikoli Silcandrov. The facial resemblance was uncanny. Everyone in the world was looking for him and he was here, moving among us.

And he had been in the hallway outside Lisa's room.

. . .

Lisa sounded annoyed when we tracked her down on her cell phone in the media center. I hadn't seen her during my interview session. Now she sounded as if we had disturbed her in the middle of a sit-down with Arnold Palmer.

People moved in and out of the hotel lobby as Miller, Perkins, and I stood at the front desk like three guys leaning on a bar. Brian Taylor sat near us on a sofa. Perkins did not face the desk; rather, he leaned back against it. He had on blue jeans and Nikes and his huge arms, hidden beneath a windbreaker zipped to his chin, were crossed in front of his chest. On his face, he wore a scowl, glancing at all who entered or left the hotel; he was still Taylor's personal watchdog. His irritable expression made most people quicken their pace. I didn't know if he was doing that intentionally; it was, however, effective in keeping people away.

I had the phone and told Lisa who and what I had encountered in the hallway outside her room.

"When are you coming back here?" I said.

"We'll send a car for her," Miller said.

I handed him the phone. They worked out the details. Miller argued with Lisa about having a uniform stay outside her room for the night and tail her the next day. It took several minutes, but he didn't back off. I was glad. When he hung up, he looked at me.

"That's settled," he said. "Let's get down to business. Tell me what he looked like and what he did."

I told him. Miller sent for a sketch artist.

"So, Nikoli is here," Perkins said.

The three of us sat near Brian Taylor. Perkins took the opposite end of the sofa on which Taylor was seated. He readjusted his gun, which he wore in a small leather holster clipped to his belt, behind his right hip. Miller and I sat in a pair of matching leather chairs.

"And Sharon Taylor is dead," Perkins said, finishing his thought.

"While Victor is sitting in the local police station," Miller said, "having delayed hiring an attorney, who could help him fight the risk-of-flight tag and would probably try to get bail set for the laundering charge. Also, judging from his recent financial moves, he should be able to afford almost any bail."

We were quiet.

Then Miller turned to Brian Taylor. "How long has Victor's brother been in town?"

Brian flinched. He had been staring at the floor and nearly jumped at Miller's question.

"I—I don't know."

"Bullshit."

"Honest," Taylor said. "I've told you everything else. I'm not lying. Christ, I want him caught, too. I'm scared shitless."

He was. You could see it in his eyes. He was still dressing preppy—khaki pants, penny loafers, a white golf shirt that read PGA TOUR on the left breast. None of it helped his appearance. He looked pale. His eyes were sunken. He looked thinner. His shoulders were hunched, as if he were constantly tense. He looked like a guy who *needed* a bodyguard.

"Everyone is looking for Victor's brother and he's here," Miller said.

"And he's desperate or crazy," I said.

Miller and Perkins looked at me.

"He was talking to himself, muttering, sweating."

Miller and Perkins looked at each other. Taylor stared at Miller like a little boy desperate to follow the conversation.

"Did he appear angry?" Miller said.

"Yeah," I said. "He was in his own world. If I pushed him, I knew he'd snap."

"How could you tell?" Miller said.

"I just knew. The way he looked at me." I thought of my time in Nash's Boston neighborhood. "Like those gang kids you see, the ones who don't give a shit what happens. He had that look."

"He's dangerous," Miller said. "I'm going to arrange a room-by-room sweep of the hotel. You two take Brian back to your room. I'll send the sketch artist up and stop in later."

"You think he's still here?" I said.

Miller shrugged. "If so, we'll get him."

The elevator doors parted. Perkins stepped out first. Our room was at the end of the hall. Brian Taylor followed Perkins. It had been a long day and I had been tired when I'd left the pressroom over an hour and a half ago. It was almost quarter to nine. I still had not eaten dinner.

I was the last one off the elevator, my head down, thinking about Lisa, about her tone when I'd reached her on her cell phone. She had sounded put out by my call, too busy to talk. Maybe I was simply reading into it. Maybe I should adopt the same strategy—my let-the-game-come-to-me approach, which I had used for the second round.

I took only three steps before walking into Brian Taylor's back. He had stopped short. Perkins was to Taylor's right.

"Oh, God," Brian said. His voice was a whisper, the words stifled, as if constricted by his throat.

"Get back on the elevator," Perkins said, his voice even and calm.

Brian started backing up, pushing me back as he went.

I looked up, peering over Taylor's shoulder. Silco's brother was there in front of us, maybe ten yards away, a flat, silver gun—a nine millimeter—drawn. His mouth hung partly open, he was still sweating, and his eyes darted from Perkins to Taylor.

The elevator doors whirred shut. I heard cables jangling as it departed.

I turned back to Silcandrov. To the right, Perkins had his gun drawn now.

Silcandrov's mouth moved slowly. I heard no words; he might have been talking to himself again. Maybe he was whispering. His eyes left Brian Taylor, refocusing on Perkins. Then his mouth closed slowly. His gaze set heavily on Perkins, he made a loud sigh, then an exaggerated shrug. The expression and the movements are something I have never been able to forget—we had watched him reach a decision, a conclusion of sorts that he would force us to help him play out.

Finally, he grinned, a wide ear-to-ear grin, staring straight at Perkins.

Perkins's voice was steady, "Put the gun down, Nikoli."

Silcandrov seemed surprised he had known his name. His eyes darted to Taylor, then back to Perkins.

"Move back to the elevator," Perkins said to Taylor and me.

Silcandrov made a tiny head shake, as if to himself.

Brian retreated, backing into me. It was not to be.

There was a loud blast, then several more in quick succession. Taylor seemed to leap backward, hitting me, knocking me to the floor. As I went down, I saw Perkins's pistol leap continually in short bursts. From the floor, I saw Silcandrov knocked backward with each shot like a leaf pausing between gusts, before he finally toppled and lay motionless.

The entire sequence had probably taken fifteen seconds. However, in the slow motion that crisis brings, the details my mind captured played out in vivid clarity at a much slower rate.

As I lay on my back, Brian Taylor partially covering my body, the sound of the gunshots in the enclosed area reverberated for lingering seconds. Afterward, the air was dense and peppered with the heavy scent that follows gunfire.

I lay still. I had no gun. If Silcandrov was alive, I didn't know what I would do.

Brian Taylor began to moan.

To my right, Perkins stood staring at Nikoli. His gun still on Silcandrov, he moved slowly toward him, kicked away the gun that had fallen near Nikoli's motionless hand. Then he backed up, bent, and vomited.

I slid out from beneath Taylor and climbed to my feet. Taylor had been shot and lay back on the floor, a pool of blood forming beneath and beside him.

Perkins wiped the long stream of drool from his chin. "Jack?"

"I'm not hit," I said.

"Brian?" he said.

"He looks bad," I said.

Voices and the clacking echo of footsteps sounded from the cement stairwell. The door burst open. Miller ran in with several uniformed and plain-clothed officers. MacDonald was there, too.

Perkins tore off the windbreaker. I saw the navy blue vest. It looked like a cross between a Superman costume and a water-ski life preserver. There were two Velcro straps securing it and three rows of some sort of thick padding. Perkins fumbled with the Velcro, released the vest, and pulled it off.

"Makes me sick," he said. "It was a murder-suicide attempt and I was the tool."

"Had no choice," I said.

"I'd heard about it—a guy forcing a cop to shoot him. Makes me sick."

"You had to," I said. "Let's hope Brian pulls through."

Nikoli Silcandrov was dead. I could see that from Perkins's side, yet I moved closer. Brian Taylor's blood was on my shirt. Miller approached me and said something I didn't hear as I continued toward Silcandrov. People raced around me. I was a zombie crossing a busy intersection. No one grabbed me, or if they did, I did not notice.

I stood over Silcandrov, looking down. He had entered our lives seven months earlier, although I had only seen him two times, both within the last hour. Yet, the look on his face, before the shooting had begun—that stare, which he had given Perkins—suggested he had in fact selected Perkins to assist him in this end. I found it all profoundly disturbing and knew why Perkins had vomited. I had been forced to kill two men a year earlier, not in this fashion; it had been self-defense. This had been a suicide in which Silcandrov had recruited Perkins to assist him.

As I stood over the corpse of Nikoli Silcandrov, whose life it seemed was still seeping out of him, I felt numb. Yet I could not stop staring at the bizarre grin that his face held, the crooked smirk of one certain he knows more than the rest of us.

37

I was seated in MacDonald's FBI suite with Perkins, Miller, a young guy appointed to serve as Victor Silco's attorney, MacDonald, and a few other guys who shared what could have passed for a familial resemblance to him. MacDonald hadn't wanted me there; however, Miller had told him I had been "recruited and flown all over the goddamned country trying to help with this case, and damned near shot." So MacDonald gave in, but told me to keep my mouth shut; that he'd do the talking. That was fine with me. I was too tired to talk anyway.

The suite no longer hopped with the intensity of a subway station at 5 P.M. In fact, I thought it had the emotional energy of a comedown; *it* was over. Now, they had brought Victor Silco in to see what exactly *it* had been.

Silco sat across from us in an uncomfortable folding metal

chair. He wore dress pants and a white shirt with no tie. The collar of the shirt was not buttoned down. His pale face looked weary. I thought there was a little relief in his expression, too.

"You identified the deceased as your brother," MacDonald said. He wore his uniform navy-blue suit and sat back in the sofa, crossing his legs casually. This might have been a dinner party.

"Yes," Victor said, taking no cue from MacDonald; he sat rigidly erect.

"Let's start from the beginning," MacDonald said.

Victor looked at him. I saw his jawbone flex.

MacDonald picked up on the tension, too.

"You said you would cooperate," MacDonald said, "that you didn't even need an attorney, because your brother forced you to participate."

"That is true," Victor said and slouched, trying to sound confident, relaying facts.

I didn't know if MacDonald was buying it. Perkins sat staring at Victor. He rubbed his midsection absently. Perkins had unloaded his nine millimeter into Nikoli Silcandrov, who had fired once—hitting Brian Taylor—before Perkins's rapid shots had sent him into a black vortex. Brian had been rushed to the hospital; I had received no word as to his condition.

Victor Silco sighed heavily. "Are you familiar with beryllium?"

"What?" Miller said.

"I am," MacDonald said.

"My brother made one large sale to some North Koreans. He met Sharon Taylor who told him about Brian's idea. With that money, he came to me and asked me to take it to Brian. Brian told you about the two separate amounts, correct?"

"Yeah," MacDonald said. "The legitimate donation and the second amount to be laundered. Why you? Why didn't your brother do it himself?"

"He paid for my education, sent me to this country years before himself. I owed him. He made that clear."

"You had nuclear connections?" MacDonald said.

"The conference in Korea," I said, blurting it out like a kid finally able to answer a question.

My outburst could not have offended MacDonald more if I had held up a nude photo of Mother Theresa.

Victor sat staring at me. He glanced once at his attorney, then back to me, trying to figure out how I knew about the conference.

Miller told MacDonald about the helpful physics chair at the University of Miami.

"So that was where he finalized the deal?" MacDonald said to Victor.

"I don't know, maybe the North Koreans came to Seoul to meet him. He came to me with two plane tickets. I had to go. I attended the conference. I didn't see him once we got there."

The room fell silent. I was trying to read MacDonald's face. Did he believe Victor? If I went to Vegas, I'd take MacDonald with me. He sat stoically, absolutely still, and appeared to be processing it all. Perkins looked ready to spit. Miller sat grinning, shaking his head.

"What was your cut of that sixteen million dollars?" MacDonald said.

"Nothing," Victor said.

"You participated in a felony only to repay your brother for an education?"

"I have stayed in jail for a reason," Victor said. His face was sullen now. "My brother is—was—very dangerous. His *asking* for help was much more than asking."

"Did he kill Sharon Taylor?"

"I am almost certain of it. She knew of the plan. Brian knew of the plan. I knew of the plan."

"Two down," MacDonald said. "Good reason to sit in jail."

Victor said nothing. He didn't have to. We had all seen what his brother was capable of. Jail was a very smart move on Victor's part.

"How is Brian?" Victor said.

MacDonald shook his head. "Didn't make it. Died on the way to the hospital."

I felt a twinge in my chest.

"What I've told you is all I know," Victor said. "I will put it all in writing and fill in any details, if I can. I do not want to go to prison."

"Then you'd better hope you have a good attorney," MacDonald said and, for the first time, he showed emotion—it was a broad smile. "But we do appreciate your honesty."

38

Saturday had proved to be my one bad round, which probably could have been expected, given Friday night's events. The bad round, though, produced only a two-over-par seventy-three. If the breaking stories of the golf world—the weekly tournament, the money laundering scandal, and the shooting—were keeping Lisa busy, imagine being at the center of all three. The media crush was unyielding; I had taken my phone off the hook.

Heading into Sunday, I was tied with Phil Mickelson for the lead, at thirteen under par, and had been a prominent player not only in the shootout but also the events that had lead to it—meaning I had inside knowledge, which, it seemed, every journalist in North America sought. Although Lisa had no problem interviewing me regarding standard golf issues, the Brian Taylor mess was different, a criminal case, headed to trial. She saw dealing with me regarding such a serious matter to be a conflict of interest and acquired her information from others, namely Perkins, who, as the shooter, was an even better source anyway. Of course, Lisa being the only reporter Perkins would agree even to look at made it all the more a coup for her. We had seen each other briefly after the shooting, just long enough for Lisa to check me for bullet holes and to tell me she loved me. I had said the same. We had promised to meet Sunday night and spend the evening discussing the recent events of our relationship, which seemed to dwarf the other situations.

But that was neither here nor there. Now Nash and I stood at the sixth hole on Sunday morning, one stroke back—and lucky to be that close.

It was nearing ninety degrees with 95 percent humidity. My shirt was already sweat-soaked and my khakis stuck to my legs. While I had scrambled all day to remain even, Mickleson had fired at the flags and missed four birdie putts. His long, flowing forward-pressed stroke had made him one of the world's premiere putters. I knew it was only a matter of time before he started depositing those birdie attempts.

The par-three, 133-yard sixth hole is played by the Tour pros as the third easiest at Westchester. Three large bunkers await errant tee shots. However, anytime you put a nine-iron or a pitching wedge in the hands of Tour pros, they will eat the hole up. Thus, I knew this was a must-have birdie. The third-place player was four strokes behind my thirteen-under score. At this point, Mickleson and I were, in effect, playing head-to-head. With that mindset: He had putted for birdie each of the first five holes—and had missed four of five. He should be up five strokes. If I could make birdie here, it could prove a demoralizing blow—he had been given the opportunity to blow the tournament open, and had not done so. I had weathered the storm and then—assuming I made two here—had struck back to tie.

The pin was tucked in the back left portion of the green, which was shaped like a reversed C. The hole had been cut six paces from the left trap. One would have to carry the gap in the C to get the ball close to the hole. I had scrambled all day—and had one-putted five consecutive holes. I was ready to gamble here. I had nothing to lose; I was the underdog. Mickelson had to be feeling the opposite.

I knew his reputation for aggressive play. He had honors and pulled what looked like a wedge. I saw him take dead aim and knew he was living up to his reputation. He was gunning for the flag.

The swing was his first bad one, a push into the left trap. It would be a tough up-and-down.

"Here we are," I whispered to Nash. "This is what it's all about."

"You told me you weren't thinking," Nash said. "Don't start now."

It made me smile. "You know, you're becoming a hell of a caddy."

Silver and Perkins stood in the first row of spectators behind the tee box.

"Here we go, Jack," Silver said.

I pulled the same club Mickelson had hit and teed my ball. Then I took my two practice swings. I could feel the adrenaline and felt like I could lift a car off someone, so I readjusted my tee, setting the ball slightly higher than usual to hit it higher to counter the adrenaline rush.

Immediately upon the strike, I stared the ball down. Everything was silent for what seemed three beats. The ball carried the trap, hit six or so feet from the pin, bounced once, then checked, stopping four feet from the hole. Nash tapped my fist with his.

Behind us, the gallery roared. I saw Silver hug Perkins. Perkins scowled and pushed him away.

Phil Mickelson was a gracious, polite competitor, but obviously knew the situation (he had doubtless been here more often than I) and kept to himself. We walked down the fairway in silence.

I knew he was in trouble when we got within fifty yards of his ball. He had a fried-egg lie; only half the ball was showing. It lay close to the edge of the bunker. He'd have to get it up high very quickly. However, he possessed one of the world's two or three best short games. Indeed, maybe *the* best. If anyone could save par from this lie, he could.

I put his predicament out of my head. I would count on him making par. Thus, I had to make my putt. Four feet, uphill. It looked straight. That was all I would think about. I wouldn't overread it. Just make a good stroke. I went to the edge of the green and stood next to Nash.

"You going to look it over?" he said.

"I did."

"Don't you usually. . . ?" He let the words fade and we watched Phil.

He hit a shot that, given the circumstances, was about as good as one could produce. It flew to the pin, hit next to it, and ran just off the back of the green, settling in the long rough. He'd be chipping to save par. We were looking at—at least—a two-stroke swing, if I could make birdie.

He was still away and selected what looked like an eight-iron, choked down on it, and punched a little runner onto the green—and damned near holed it to save par. It stopped four inches wide of the hole.

"Great shot," I said.

He thanked me.

Then it was back to business. I made two practice strokes to get a feel for the speed. The humidity was oppressive; my hands were wet. The rubber grip felt slick. I wiped my hands on my pants. I managed to clear my head as I leaned over the putt—hands soft, mind blank. Then I struck the putt. The ball never wavered and the roll made me look more confident than I was.

It dropped, dead center. I was leading by one stroke.

After nine holes, I was still leading by one at fourteen under par.

. . .

Westchester's tenth hole offers a choice: driver or iron. It is a par-four, yet only 314 yards. On a very good day, both Mickelson and I could reach it, but given that we remained in a two-man race, his decision would depend upon the results of my tee shot. The tees were in the back. There are trees on both sides and fairway bunkers with which to deal. Also, there were bunkers greenside. I pulled a three-iron. I was leading and would let Phil come after me.

My three-iron landed on the left side of the fairway and cut back to the center, leaving maybe 120 yards. Nash had the pin sheet and we would figure out the exact distance once we were in the fairway.

Next, Phil did what I expected: He took the driver from his bag. He stepped back and took four or five practice swings—

not stopping between them; rather, making long, loose, back-and-forth, rhythmic motions, as he got focused to hit what might be the round's make-or-break shot. He addressed the ball and there was dead silence. Then he brought the graphite shaft of the Titleist driver back smoothly and, finally, exploded down, catching the ball flush. I saw him stare it down and knew he liked it.

As he should. The ball found its way onto the fairway, then rolled between the front traps, up an incline, onto the green. It had been a hell of a shot—mammoth. With the tees back and considering the pressure, it had been more than long. It had been outstanding. I told Phil as much. He smiled and nodded in acknowledgment. We both knew he was attempting to steal the momentum.

At my ball, Nash and I reviewed the pin sheet and calculated my shot: a hundred yards to the front, 115 to the pin. A smooth, well-controlled pitching wedge would be the club to carry the ball to the hole. Only moments earlier, I had been the underdog, leading one of the world's top players by a stroke. Now, I had to hit a very good approach shot just to stay even. Mickelson's shot had produced a dramatic shift in my psyche, which was probably what he had intended.

I went through my preshot routine, then aligned my feet and shoulders to the target, and swung the club. I knew I had come over the top of it immediately. It was ugly and got uglier in a hurry—plugging in the front right bunker. It had been a cardinal sin, maybe worse than three-putting—*never miss a green when you've got a wedge in your hands.*

The bunker was deep, which only added to my problems. I closed the face of my sand wedge and swung hard, leaving the club face buried in the sand. The ball popped up and landed on the green, but remained a long way from the hole.

Mickelson was thirty feet from the hole, putting for eagle. The putt would not be a simple one, but he could three-putt—which wasn't likely—and still make par. I, on the other hand, was putting from twenty-five feet to save par. The gallery was rumbling. People could sense the importance of this hole, of the two tee shots, which had suggested two distinct approaches. As I watched Mickelson roll his ball toward the hole, I was second-guessing my decision to hit three-iron. I had played the game long enough to know rethinking my shot after the fact was the wrong thing to do, that it was counterproductive. Yet there it was: Mickelson's ball was inching its way toward the hole for eagle and I would have my hands full saving par. When his ball dropped, the gallery went nuts. Behind me, I heard David Feherty, the CBS on-course commentator, say in his Irish accent, "Ladies and gents, what you've just witnessed is one of the gutsiest plays I've seen in more than twenty years in this game."

I agreed. I had seen and played enough golf to appreciate what Mickelson had just done, although I wasn't ready to throw in the towel and accept a three-shot swing. I was grinding over this putt, taking practice stroke after practice stroke. The putt would travel up the green, I believed into the grain and, thus, be slow. It would take a firm stroke to get the ball to the hole.

Except, the ball did not react as if hit into the grain; rather, it darted six feet by the hole. Whether it was the situation or simply a bad read, I cannot say for sure. However, I had played this course for a decade. A bad read seems unlikely.

It didn't matter. What did matter was getting down in five—saving bogey from six feet, which would leave me trailing Phil by two.

Six feet. Not even as long as I am tall. Yet it was much farther. Continents seemed to separate the ball from the hole. I tried to slow my breathing. I heard people moving, creaking of lawn chairs, whispered voices, even shoes in the distance pounding down the paved cart path. Yet, I brought the putter back very slowly and followed through on line. The ball caught the left edge and tumbled in. I made a short fist pump, celebrating something no one else probably understood: The wheels had begun to fall off; however, I had prevented disaster. I had *willed* that ball into the hole.

. . .

I had not been able to get anything going for the next six holes. We came to the seventeenth, my nemesis, exactly as we had walked off the tenth—with Mickelson holding a two-shot lead.

"I've birdied this hole this week," I said to Nash.

"Do it again," he said simply.

On the 374-yard, par-four, I hit driver into the heart of the fairway, leaving only 130 yards to the hole. The pin sheet told me the hole was cut in the center-back portion. The rough slopes away on a steep decline behind the green. The pin placement was meant to test one's resolve—would you go for it, with the chance of being long and running down the back slope?

"Smoked it," Phil said to me and smiled.

"Yeah," I said. "Thanks."

He looked down the fairway for several seconds, then he returned to his bag and switched clubs. It occurred to me what he had just done: He had been about to hit his three-wood, which would have been the safe play. After seeing my shot, though, he was going for it—again taking a risk. He brought the club back slowly, but I could tell he had gotten quick on the way down.

The result was that his hands had been in front of the club face at impact, snapping the ball right, which for him—being left-handed—was a pull hook.

From where I stood, I could see that the ball had come to rest near a pine that looked as if it might constrict his swing.

Nash and I walked down the fairway and stopped maybe thirty feet from Phil's ball. It lay beneath the tree, under a canopy of low-hanging branches. Being left-handed would be a major advantage for him here. A right-handed golfer would be forced to stand with his back against the tree. Still, he had a very limited shot. He punched out, leaving himself 140 yards to the hole. He was still away.

The gallery had sensed the momentum shift. Those that were rooting for Phil began to cheer encouragement. Had we not been in a head-to-head situation, I, too, might have said something positive. Instead, I remained silent and watched the events unfold.

And unfold, they did. Mickelson's third shot was long. He had taken only a nine-iron but blew it over the green, into the thick rough that sloped away from the putting surface. We couldn't see his ball from our locale, but even with his short game, he would struggle to get up and down to save bogey from there.

I was next. It is what we play for. The opportunity to contend; you have only yourself to rely on, your abilities, the skills you've spent countless hours honing. I had been given the chance to make a two-shot swing in my favor here. I pulled the pitching wedge from my bag and went through my preswing routine. Next, I moved quickly to the ball, set myself, and swung—hard. It was a full, aggressive swing. The opportunity to gain ground lay before me. I was going for it. The ball cut a line through the porcelain blue sky and landed at the back of the green and sat. I was putting for birdie.

Phil chipped his par attempt to within three feet, a distance from which he had, at times, struggled. He marked his ball and waited for me. My ball lay eight feet to the right of the hole. It was straight. I took several practice strokes to get a feel for the distance, then I stroked the ball.

There are times in this game when you hit a shot so purely, strike the ball so well, that you know the results will be excellent before the ball has landed, or stopped rolling. The putt fell. I had made three. Mickelson took several long seconds to line up his three-footer, but eventually sunk the putt.

. . .

The eighteenth. All even. I had gooseflesh. I couldn't remember the last time I'd been in this position. I had been in contention on Sunday several times, but never tied heading to the eighteenth hole. I was not nervous. Given my world ranking compared to Mickelson's, in hindsight, maybe I should have been. I, however, had nothing to lose. As I fired my tee shot at the 526-yard, par-five finishing hole, I actually believed I would win. I hit a long draw into the center of the fairway. I could go for the green in two.

Phil's ball landed just short of mine, which gave me a slight advantage. I could see what he would do, then make my club selection, possibly laying up, if he did so.

He quickly took that option out of the equation. He pulled the three-wood. Then he hit a laser that landed on the front of the green and scooted to the back portion, rolling just onto the fringe. The gallery went wild. The fans knew the difficulty of the shot and appreciated the result. I waited longer than I wanted to for the fans to stop cheering.

I hit the same club as Mickelson and got nearly the same result, my ball rolling to the second tier of the green, leaving maybe twenty-five feet. He would have a flat putt; mine would be up and over one tier, thus, breaking.

I was away. There was no question his putt was the easier of the two. Mine would break, I estimated, two feet, left to right. I had to roll it up a level, to the third tier. At least I knew I could be aggressive and hit it firmly. As I crouched behind the ball to read the green, I knew it would be a moment—win or lose—that I would never forget. My chest seemed to throb, as if my heart were going to beat through the skin. My hands were damp. I wiped them on a towel Nash had over the bag. I yawned, as Lee Trevino said he did, to get extra oxygen.

Then it was time to hit the putt. I knew I'd be anxious to see the result, so I crouched over the ball, slightly lower than usual, in hopes that I wouldn't look up too soon and pull it. I did not. I stayed down on the ball until well after impact.

I looked up only to see the ball miss on the high side, by more than a foot. I had overread the break and had two feet left.

I marked my ball and watched. It was all I could do.

Mickelson took enough time to let me know he was really thinking about the putt. I wondered what that meant. Was he nervous?

When he stroked the ball into the cup, something in my stomach moved. As the ball fell over the edge, the gallery, like a balloon bursting, broke the silence.

I made my two-footer. It was no consolation. I had played someone head-to-head, shot for shot, and been beaten. He had hit that one drive on the tenth hole that had really separated us. He had taken the risk and walked away the Buick Classic champion. I had not taken that risk and left with the largest check of my career—but had walked away knowing it was second-place money.

Sunday night at 8:30, I stood at the door of Lisa's suite, holding a pizza box. The door opened and Lisa, still dressed for work in cropped sky-blue pants with a palm-tree print and an apple-green linen jacket, smiled. Her feet were bare, the only hint that she had settled in for the night. Past her shoulder, the suite was brightly lit. I saw a black laptop open on the coffee table.

She nodded at the pizza box. Her smile ran to a grin. "Don't you deserve a steak after the way you played?"

"I lost."

"So did a hundred fifty-five other players, Jack. *You* lost on the eighteenth hole."

I sighed. "Thanks. I should have hit driver on the tenth."

"That's crazy," she said. "He hit a lucky shot. Come here."

She took the box from me, set it on the floor, then hugged me. I wrapped my arms around her. We stayed like that for a long time. Finally, she pulled away, then moved her hands up to my face, and kissed me. When we broke, she was crying. Not full out, but tears rolled down her cheeks.

"I heard those gunshots," she said, "and I started running toward the sound. Then someone said it had been you—that you had been there."

"But I was fine—thanks to Perkins."

"When I went to find you, I couldn't—and the details were sketchy."

She stepped back and her arms fell rigidly to her sides as if she were trying to find a place for them. I took her hands in mine.

"I was told three people had been shot," she said. "They said there had been only four people there—"

I cut her off by leaning in and gently kissing her forehead. Her vulnerability was something I did not get to see often. It was wonderful, although I could tell the experience had been painful. I stopped her from continuing to relive it.

"Let's go inside," I said and bent to get the pizza.

The inside of the suite made me feel like I was Oscar to her Felix. The place was spotless. There were no empty paper coffee cups on the tables, no books on the floor, no golf balls and putters and overturned glasses on the carpet. Without me, the place remained immaculate.

We sat on the loveseat in front of the coffee table. Lisa reached forward and closed the laptop.

"As you know, I filed stories about the shooting," she said. "So I know what happened, but at the time, I was just so scared, and then. . ."

She turned to me and looked straight into my eyes.

". . . when you didn't come to see me right away, afterward, I was very angry, Jack."

She wasn't crying now. It wasn't a look of anger, more like concern. She wanted me to explain, maybe justify, my actions.

"I was with Perkins and the others. They wanted to know what happened. I had to be there. Then they brought in Silco and that took a while."

She nodded and looked down.

"I haven't been the easiest person to deal with lately," she said and gave a smile. "My hormones are out of whack, but I've come to a lot of decisions about my life, my future."

I sat quietly, letting her have the floor. The inflection of her voice suggested this weighed heavily on her. Which meant that what she was about to say would weigh equally heavily on us.

"When I heard the shots, I wasn't only frightened for you and me," she said. "I hope you know that."

"I do. It's why I'm here. That's what I want to discuss."

We were quiet for a while, each thinking.

"Poor Brian Taylor," she said.

"Poor Catherine Taylor," I said.

She looked at me. Then, slowly, she nodded, understanding what I meant.

"A little girl will grow up without a father. That's what I've been thinking about, Lisa."

"I needed to be alone to think about you," she said. "We've known each other two years, but I didn't know what you would want. I have never, for one moment, considered not having the baby, Jack."

The air conditioner hummed lightly.

"I was shocked when you first told me," I said.

"I know you don't want to get married," she said. "We've been through that."

I shook my head back and forth. "Things happen for a reason, Lisa. I've done a lot of thinking, mostly about things I already knew. . . ." I paused and looked at her.

She waited for me to finish.

The curtains had not been drawn. She had had other things on her mind. Outside, beyond the sliding-glass doors leading to the veranda, the moon was already full in the distance amid the day's last light. I didn't know if I could explain it any more—or any better—than that. So I let it go. Instead, I took Lisa's hand.

When I got down on one knee, she began to cry.

In October, the only ones still playing golf were the players I aspired to be. I had plenty of time to finish the Philip Levine book. On this day, neither Levine nor golf was on my mind. Perkins, wife Linda, son Jackie, Lisa, and myself, were seated on metal bleachers at D. Forbes Will Field in Milton, Massachusetts, where the leaves were vivid reds and oranges and yellows. Lisa wore a dark wool turtleneck sweater with white snowmen on it, white corduroy pants, and hiking boots. She sat on the bleacher below me on a blanket and leaned back, between my knees. I had my hands on her belly, which had grown, but only slightly.

Nash was the star this day. It was Parent's Weekend at Curry College. He had rushed for 137 yards at the half. Curry was losing 14–7; Nash had Curry's only touchdown. More importantly, however, he had a 2.5 midterm GPA. Maybe even more important—considering the Sharon Taylor near-fiasco—a young coed named Michelle was seated with us, wearing Nash's football jacket.

As the second half began, Lisa was talking to Linda and held out the engagement ring I had bought with some of my Buick Classic money. Linda was what I had long believed stabilized Perkins. She had taught second grade for years before Jackie had been born. Now she was a stay-at-home mom. She had arrived with baby gifts for Lisa.

Perkins and I were riveted by the action. During the third quarter, Nash took a handoff, hit a hole in the line at full speed, and met a linebacker head-on. He knocked the would-be tackler several feet backward and dragged the next tackler five yards, before finally going down.

"Never seen a golfer do something like that," Perkins said.

"We play a civilized sport," I said, although I had just sat down after yelling like a bloodthirsty Cleveland Browns fan.

"Civilized or sissy?" he said.

Nash scored on the next play, a twenty-three–yard dash down the sideline.

Late in the fourth quarter, Lisa called Perkins by his first name. He turned from our second argument about golf being more challenging than football.

"I'd like to thank you for saving the man I love," she said.

"I had to think long and hard about it," he said.

"Well, I know you love him like a brother," Lisa said. "Although it's early, we're fairly certain we're having a girl."

"We'd like you to be the godfather," I said.

He reached over and extended his hand. "Honored."

I shook it. Lisa gave him a kiss on the cheek. Then she said, "Given that your first name denotes either sex, we also plan to name her after you."

"I never liked my first name," he said.

"Even better," I said. "Now you can hear it over and over."

With thirty seconds left on the clock, Curry scored on a passing play to make it 21–20. Earlier, they had missed an extra-point attempt. They weren't going for the tie; they were attempting a two-point conversion for the win. The coach left Nash on the field. He had carried the ball thirty-five times and gained more than 200 yards—breaking Dave Christopher's single-game mark which, according to the program, was set in 1978.

Everyone in the stadium assumed he was getting the football. Including the defense. Nash took the handoff and hit the line hard, but there was nowhere to go. Curry lost the game.

Nash didn't hang his head, though he looked dejected. I watched him, in line, shaking hands with opposing players, his purple, silver, and black uniform covered in dirt. There were bloodstains on his pants. He had given it everything he'd had; yet he'd come up short.

I couldn't help but think back to the Buick Classic, to my final eighteen holes. Since my season had ended, I had read the title poem from Levine's *The Simple Truth* over and over, and the words came back with vivid clarity:

> Some things
> you know all your life. . .
> it stays in the back of your throat like a truth
> you never uttered because the time was always wrong,
> it stays there for the rest of your life, unspoken,
> made of that dirt we call earth, the metal we call salt,
> in a form we have no words for, and you live on it.

I looked at Lisa, my hand resting gently on her belly, touching our daughter. Then I looked from Nash to Perkins to Linda to Jackie. I had beat myself up for a long time over the Buick Classic, for the loss. I looked from face to face, before my vision settled back on Lisa. I pulled her close, smelling the strawberry scent of her hair, feeling the warmth of her. Then, beneath my hand—for one irrational yet wonderful moment—I truly believed I felt my daughter kick. In that single, shining moment, I knew what it had all been for—I knew *the simple truth.*